Her L

Julia Stone has a background in business psychology and has previously worked as a director/partner in two management consultancies. She is also a registered psychotherapist and chartered coaching psychologist. Following cancer treatment, she decided to take a break from the business world and direct her energies towards her creative side, studying art and ceramics, then film script and novel writing. She now runs her own coaching and therapy business part-time, where she helps other creative people work on the emotional challenges and limiting beliefs that are getting in the way of their writing or artistic ambitions. She lives on a small holding in Suffolk with her partner and varying numbers of ducks, muntjac and rabbits.

Twitter – @JuliaStoneWriter

Her Little Secret

Julia Stone

First published in Great Britain in 2021 by Orion Dash,
an imprint of The Orion Publishing Group Ltd.,
Carmelite House, 50 Victoria Embankment
London EC4Y 0DZ

An Hachette UK Company

1 3 5 7 9 10 8 6 4 2

A CIP catalogue record for this book is
available from the British Library.

ISBN (Paperback) 978 1 3987 0903 4
ISBN (eBook) 978 1 3987 0779 5

Typeset at The Spartan Press Ltd,
Lymington, Hants

Printed and bound in Great Britain by Clays Ltd,
Elcograf S.p.A.

www.orionbooks.co.uk

For Mum and Dad

Chapter One

Downstairs the phone rings and I curse. I'm having a lie-in with Davy – my on/off ex – and it's snug here. Davy cuddles closer, flings his arm across my waist, a 'don't go' gesture.

'I've got to get it. Could be Clare,' I say, throwing back the duvet and wriggling loose. He tugs the covers back around him, capturing the escaping warmth as I grab my dressing gown then rush for the stairs.

The answerphone clicks on as I reach the bottom step, buying me a second or so to catch my breath. His voice echoes around my small hallway. A deep dark-brown, educated timbre. Gravitas, but ill at ease.

'Hallo? I … I wanted to speak to Cristina Hughes …'

The flattened tone suggests depression. My bathrobe flaps about me as I hurry to grab the receiver before he rings off, concerned he'll disappear without leaving contact details. I know how hard it is to psych yourself up to contact a therapist – preparing what to say, picking a time when you feel ready to make the commitment to talk about your problems. It's not easy; if you don't actually get to speak to them in person, the emotional crash can be too much.

'Hallo, Cristina Hughes speaking.' The hall clock says ten. We'd had a late night. 'Good morning.'

There's a pause as the man registers he's no longer talking to a machine.

'Hi. How can I help you?' I prompt.

'My name is Leon. Leon Jacobs. I wondered if I might make an appointment to see you?' He speaks slowly as if each word requires careful thought.

'Of course. Can I just take some details?'

'I lost my partner ... It's been very difficult ... I feel I've lost everything.'

I close my eyes, take a deep breath. *Bereavement.*

'I'm sorry to hear that.'

'It's been hard since she died,' Leon Jacobs continues. 'I keep thinking about her ... Can't concentrate on anything else ... And there's no one I can talk to ...'

It's often like this; like a valve opens in these initial calls, the relief of being able to speak to someone they believe will understand leads to everything pouring out. The trust moves me every time, drawing me into their life from the start.

Behind me I hear Davy coming downstairs. He pauses beside me mouthing, 'Tea?' and I shoo him away, trying to focus on Leon Jacobs, all the while aware of the soft pad of Davy's bare feet on the tiles as he heads to the kitchen.

'It must be hard for you, especially if you have no one to talk to. How long were you married?'

'We weren't married. At least not to each other.'

Illicit lovers then. An affair.

'Sorry, of course you said "partner".'

Five minutes later, contact details exchanged and appointment booked, I hang up. It seems he got my number from a find-a-therapist website, had seen that I'd just started taking on clients again. He's read my blog – my first posting, at the end of my year-long sabbatical, after Dad died.

Dealing with Grief.

Even after all these years as a therapist, it can still take conscious effort for me to push my own emotions and memories to one side; to stay in the room, listening, rather than off in my own head. It's a skill, *Epoché*. It means suspension of judgement, not reacting automatically to things the client says.

Bereavement.

An affair.

He's triggered a lot in that first phone call.

The smell of burnt toast wafts from the kitchen. Davy hasn't got the hang of my new toaster yet. He's scraping the singed bits over the bin, a light dusting of black crumbs cover the surrounding floorboards and his trainers.

'Work,' I say.

'Yeah, you was doing The Voice.' He claims I adopt a 'posh voice' when I speak with clients. 'Tea's there.' He gesticulates with his elbow, intent on the task of salvaging his breakfast. Two mugs stand on the draining board, the teabags no doubt stewing in the depths of the tepid milky brew.

'You got any jam?' he asks, plonking the toast on a side plate, satisfied with his efforts.

'Marmalade. But it's the chunky-cut stuff with peel.'

He turns up his nose, gives a resigned shrug. 'It'll do. I'll dig the bits out.'

Had the previous night been planned I would've made sure I stocked up on Davy's breakfast requirements: white bread, salted butter, strawberry jam, builder's tea. But it had been a bit of an impromptu evening. Hard to believe it's been over twenty years since we divorced but some things don't change. We're still great friends and – as long as neither of us is in a relationship with someone else – we fall back on each other for affectionate, uncomplicated sex now and then. It's cosy rather than passionate; neither of us having to hold in our stomachs or worry about our stretch marks.

Davy plasters his toast with butter while I eat my yogurt staring out the window at the back garden. For months I've been planning to requisition the summerhouse from its role of shed/dumping ground and turn it into a garden office where I can meet my clients. Of course, I've never got round to doing it, blaming the cold weather, the price of paint, my morose winter lethargy. Until my sabbatical I always used the front room to see clients, which meant keeping the decor bland and having to tidy up before each person came. It would be nice to spoil myself with a designated professional space. With Leon Jacobs' appointment in the diary for the following week, a new office could be the thing I need to gear me up for a fresh start.

'You busy today?' I ask Davy. 'If not, I could do with a hand.'

By lunchtime we're well under way with project refurb. Davy is like one of those wind-up toys: once the key is turned and he's set in the right direction, he's off. We've always made a good team on practical projects: Davy's good humour balancing my indecisive faffing; both of us willing to turn our hand to hard work, neither of us too perfectionist in the execution.

I step back from the oblongs of colour I've painted on the wall. It's taken a while but I've got it down to three: Tranquil Garden (the traditional shade of green found in 1970s schools and old lunatic asylums); Pink Clouds (psychologically calming according to research experiments in prisons, but a bit teenage bedroom); and Fresh Cream (the bland neutral of magnolia).

'Well, which do you think?'

Davy's been puffing his cheeks beside me as I vacillate. Home decor's not his thing.

'One wall of each.' He scratches his head like Stan Laurel, although his build has become more Oliver Hardy over the years. 'What's it meant to look like? You're the shrink.'

'I've told you – I'm a therapist, not a psychiatrist.' I thump the lid down on the paint pot, hard enough that it hurts my hand. 'You have to do a degree and years of training to be a psychiatrist.' I rub the heel of my hand, circling my wrist to ease the throbbing.

'It don't really matter what it's called – you still help people sort themselves out. That's why they come to see you. 'Cause you understand how to fix them, not 'cause of some fancy title.' He stretches his arms above his head, arching his back, his T-shirt pulling up showing his hairy belly. 'I'm starved,' he says, patting the exposed flesh.

'I've got some cake in the bread bin. Madeira. The one with icing.' I'm keen to make amends for snapping at him.

'You know the way to a man's heart. I'll get the kettle on while you make up your mind.'

By the time he returns from the house with the mugs of tea, I've painted the first coat of magnolia over all the samples. Better safe than sorry.

The night before Leon Jacobs' appointment, my stomach's dancing. It's a familiar feeling with a direct line back to the first time I ever performed on stage: only 'Third Shepherd' in the school nativity, but I thought I'd physically burst with the combined excitement of having Dad and Mum in the audience and the anxiety of wanting to do my best.

Tonight I'm not approaching bursting point, but I still can't resist a final inspection of my new office, even though I know it's ready and there's no more to do.

There's a tingle of pleasure as I unlock the door and take stock. I run my finger along the spines of the textbooks on the shelf above the two-drawer filing cabinet in the corner. ACT, CBT, NLP, TA: so many acronyms but their familiarity is reassuring – I *know* these things. I straighten the coasters on the coffee table, ready for the jug of water and glasses I'll bring from the kitchen first thing in the morning. Make sure the obligatory box of tissues is discreet but within reach.

It's perfect. It says *Professional*.

Back in the house, the final step in my preparation is to select my outfit. Not that there's much to decide. From the start I've modelled my style as a therapist on Clare, originally my tutor and now my supervisor. We meet once a month to discuss my cases and even now she always wears the same 'uniform': dark top and trousers; low-key, unmemorable jewellery. Our aim as therapists is to blend into the background, to be slightly anonymous, 'not to get in the way of the process'. For Clare it seems natural. For me it's all part of the role, as essential for me to become The Therapist as the tools of any method actor.

I lay the chosen outfit on the back of the armchair in my bedroom, place my watch on top. The wind-up Timex Dad gave me when I started secondary school at Wellington Drive; the first occasion I'd ever needed to find my way anywhere on time.

A deep breath.

I'm ready. *The therapist will see you now.*

Waiting for Leon to arrive the next morning, I've little idea what to expect. Unlike prospective employers, it would be frowned on for a therapist to search social media for background information, check out websites, or scour LinkedIn CVs, even if we might be tempted. All we have to work with is what the client chooses to share with us. At this moment

I only know the little Leon has told me on the phone. Bereavement; an affair.

He rings the doorbell a few minutes early, catching me out. I'm still in the downstairs loo, checking my unruly hair, which I've pulled into a tight chignon, spraying it into an immobile helmet so it doesn't flop in my eyes at the wrong moment. The lipstick I applied five minutes ago now feels too loud so I hastily rub it off with a tissue, check my teeth in the mirror. *Smile.*

As I open the door he extends his hand and I have to juggle my leather-bound folder to the other arm in order to respond.

'Leon Jacobs.' A firm professional handshake. Around fifty, he's a very good-looking man in a boyish kind of way, more Tom Cruise than Bruce Willis. But taller than Cruise, an inch or so off six foot I guess. Fashionable short beard, full head of dark hair. Smart grey suit and open-necked shirt, as if he's on the way to or from work.

'Hi. I'm Cristina.'

He nods. His smile is tight-lipped, like his body language. Controlled and contained, with that confident air typically instilled by a boarding school upbringing.

I lead the way around the side of the house and across the lawn to the paint-fresh summerhouse. Mercifully the walk is short enough that there's not much need for small talk and my enquiry about how easy he found parking proves sufficient.

Once seated on the suede-effect IKEA sofa he looks around slowly, taking in every inch. And following his gaze, I feel exposed, my pride in this room snatched away, worrying that he sees it for what it is – a jazzed-up garden shed. It feels like I've gone to too much effort. It all seems too staged, like a film set.

Focus. This is not the moment for doubts. With Leon, my first new client, sitting before me, I have to assume my role.

I start with my introduction, a well-rehearsed spiel after fifteen years: from the logistics of session length and fee structure, to reassurances about my professionalism – my monthly supervision with another qualified therapist, details of my registering body should he have a complaint, respect for confidentiality.

'Any notes I take are merely an aide-memoire. No one will see your file but me.' I pass him a copy of the 'working contract' To sign, seeking his agreement to the process I've outlined.

Leon pulls a fancy pen from his inside pocket as I continue, 'Boundaries are very important in our work together.' I lean forward and tap on the document to show him the paragraph. 'As it says in the contract, to maintain your privacy I will only contact you if we've agreed it in advance. If I bump into you outside the therapy room I won't acknowledge you unless you speak to me first. And if you're on social media I can't accept friendship requests.'

He looks up, raises his eyebrows. 'Seems very formal.'

'I prefer to think of it as respectful of your privacy. You might be with someone who doesn't know you're seeing a therapist and it could put you on the spot if you had to introduce me.'

'Ah yes.' He passes the form back. A neat, cramped signature, unusual for someone left-handed. He's added the date even though he's not been asked. 'As you can tell, I've not had therapy before. It's a new and somewhat unnerving experience.'

'Unnerving?'

'Exposing my vulnerable underbelly. I'm not used to talking about myself. Not one for emotional unloading.'

'We'll go at your pace. There is no need to discuss anything that makes you uncomfortable if you aren't ready.'

'I feel in safe hands. You clearly get results. The testimonials on your website are very impressive.'

Ah my website, barely touched in years; my bereavement blog, ironically, the only sign of recent life.

He continues: 'Integrative psychotherapy. An interesting holistic approach. I did some research to make sure I understood what I was getting into. Tailoring the therapy to the client. It makes perfect sense.'

Validation. I breathe a sigh of relief.

'Thank you.' I look at my watch, not really registering the time; a subconscious signal to both of us, the starter's gun. 'It would be good if you could tell me a bit about yourself. Could we start with your family background?'

He tells me he has a brother and two nephews he never sees. An elderly father who lives abroad. Mother died when he was in his twenties. I was right about the boarding school: he was sent away at seven years old. His delivery is emotionless, even when he mentions losing his mother.

'As a family we were never close,' he says, looking down at his lap.

'How do you feel about that?'

'Hunter S Thompson said, "You can't miss what you never had..." That said, I'm conscious that I'm quite alone in the world. Even more so at a time like this.'

'Do you have friends you can talk to?'

He shakes his head. 'No. I live alone and I'm not really a social animal. That's why I wanted to come to see you. Your description of bereavement... it just summed up what I've been feeling.'

He is lost, completely alone. 'If you feel ready, can you tell me what happened, how you came to be bereaved?'

A lengthy silence follows, his gaze now fixed on the ceiling. When he starts speaking he keeps his eyes averted.

Her name was Michelle.

She was a mature student on a course he runs at the college where he is head of department. A secret affair.

He hadn't spoken to her for a fortnight; she hadn't come to her classes. While concerned, he didn't want to keep ringing her mobile, wary of her husband.

'It was a Tuesday,' he says. 'I was setting up for a lesson. A couple of students had arrived early. One of them wanted to ask me about his idea for his final project. Just a normal day.'

That's how it always happens. On a normal day. In the real world there are no thunderclaps, biblical plagues or music that heralds doom.

'One of the school administrators interrupted us. I could tell from her face it was urgent. Her job is pastoral care for students and I thought one of them must have been taken ill or had an accident on site. I never thought...'

He never thought it would be Michelle.

'The administrator had phoned Michelle's home to find out why she hadn't been in class for two weeks.' He pauses and the seconds tick past but I hold the space, allow him time. 'There had been a car accident the week before.'

He hadn't known for days, carried on with his everyday life: going to the supermarket, paying his bills, doing the washing up; all the while not knowing that she lay in hospital in an induced coma. To add to his trauma, he was unable to visit her for fear of meeting her husband and family. Even in the guise of her tutor from college he was worried he'd show emotion, give away the connection between them.

He didn't attend the funeral.

I make a note on my pad: *No closure rituals. Danger of complex grief?*

'Have you told anyone this before?'

'No. There is no one I could tell.'

'How do you feel, describing what happened?'

'I really don't know. How do I sound?'

'Unemotional. Like it's someone else's story. Like you're not allowing yourself to feel anything.'

'I don't know how I should I feel.' His flattened tone and shrunken posture convey everything he's unable to say. 'I don't think I have the words.'

'Tell me the first things that come to mind.'

His eyes flick from me to the floor and he sits very still for several seconds.

'Desperate for answers. Helpless. Annoyed with her for having such a stupid damn accident, for not being here with me ... Wanting to talk to her, just to have one last conversation.'

'What would you want to say to her if you could have that conversation?'

'I don't know ... I'd just want to sit with her, be there for her ... Tell her that she can't leave me alone like this, that I need her ... We belong together ...'

His voice is quiet, but tinged with anger: blaming her, blaming fate. In textbooks this is the second stage of grief: denial – anger, followed neatly by bargaining – depression – acceptance ... But in reality it's not a formulaic five-phase process; for some there are loops, for others leaps, while many are unable to move through at all.

He sighs deeply, bringing me back to the room. 'I'd tell her I need her. That this doesn't change anything. I'll always love her.'

I leave a space for him to continue but he doesn't say more.

'How would Michelle have known that you loved her?'

He shrugs. 'How does anyone know? Words, gestures, the things I did for her, the tokens of affection.' It's a superficial answer.

'Where do you *feel* your love for her?'

He places his hand on his chest, over his heart, and breathes in deeply, screwing his eyes tight shut. It's a while before his pallor returns to normal. 'She was everything I ever wanted. From the moment I first saw her I wanted to get to know her ...'

He opens his eyes, rubbing at them as if he's tearing up, then clears his throat. But, even so, when he speaks his voice is choked. 'It was at a charity dinner. I can see her now – her emerald green gown, her perfect skin, the way she moved ... So elegant. So beautiful. She was helping with the gift auction and I placed the highest bid for an appalling painting, just so I could speak to her.' He lowers his head and it's some moments before he speaks again. 'And now, she's gone, but I still have the wretched thing ...'

Having escorted him out at the end of the session, I sit down heavily on the sofa he's just vacated. I'm exhausted. Juggling so many emotions – his, my own. Trying to wrestle away my judgements and stay focused.

What do I feel about him? Certainly he's a charming and good-looking man and I can see why Michelle could fall for someone like that. But she was married. And he knew that. Yes, I can see he's grieving, feel his pain, but a thought arises that I feel guilty for: it's so much worse for her husband.

There's a tension in my temple saying something doesn't sit well with me and I know what's causing it. Clare would call it counter-transference. This feeling is not really about Leon, but what he represents to me. The deceit of an affair, the lies and secrecy of my own mother and her lover. The selfish destroying of love and families. Had I hidden this gut reaction? Had I appeared the professional I work hard to be?

Looking across the room to my empty chair, I try to see myself through his eyes. Arrayed on the wall, my certificates proclaim my capability. It's the first time I've seen them from this angle. Hung by Davy, none of them are aligned. He's not measured the space and this year's *Psychotherapy Practising Certificate* is crammed against the window, like an afterthought.

Chapter Two

The next evening Davy comes over and we cosy up on the sofa to share a few beers and watch something unchallenging on TV.

I tip Davy's favourite smoky bacon crisps into a bowl before he can start eating them straight from the packet, then flop down next to him. I've been thinking about the discussion with Leon, debating the pull of first attraction, his description of when he first met Michelle.

I wait for the advert break to get Davy's attention, then ask, 'What do you remember about when we first met?'

'You was making a right fuss.' He's talking about the incident in the junior school playground; I was only ten years old and I'd just sat on a bee. 'I asked where it bit you.'

'Stung,' I say and immediately regret this picky habit I've developed of correcting him. 'You could have got a teacher to help me instead of taking the mick! I was in agony.'

'Knight in shining armour.' He chortles, screwing up his nose. 'Nah, doesn't sound like me.' Lovely uncritical Davy, who would do anything for me.

'Anyway, I didn't mean then. I meant at secondary, when we started dating. After the Christmas disco?'

Me and my friends had giggly-girly hip-swayed to a Wham song while the boys clung rigidly to the sides of the room, trying to look cool. Davy had broken ranks and asked the DJ to sell him the record so he could give it to me. Right there, on the dance floor. We'd had our first kiss that evening and started dating soon after.

He snorts a laugh and grabs a handful of crisps. 'Took me months to live that down. Wham! Couldn't have been The Specials or Ian Dury.'

'What did you think of me back then?' I ask.

'I dunno. It was years ago. You was cleverer than me and I reckoned you could help me with my homework.'

I give him a playful shove. 'Why didn't you pick Harriet, if it was brains you were after?' With a distinct lack of creativity the boys had nicknamed Harriet *Swotty Swot Girl from Swotdom*. I used to feel sorry for her.

'You was curvier.' He gives me a squeeze. 'Still are. A wiggle and a giggle. More my type.' He raises the beer bottle to the light before pouring the last drops into my glass.

'I've still got that Wham single, somewhere in the loft,' I say. 'The cards too.'

'What? All of them?'

He's right, there are a lot. Every Christmas, birthday and Valentine's since we'd first got together. Always the same. He buys the biggest cheesiest card in the shop; no message, just a hand-drawn bee and z z z where the kisses would usually be.

The adverts finish and Davy's attention is drawn back to the telly by the theme tune. A programme about two guys on a road trip, Route 66. He's entranced, hooked by the blokey chat and the cars rather than the scenery.

I watch him rather than the TV, feeling a surge of warmth. That sense of comfort brought on by your favourite sweater, a mug of hot chocolate, the smell of an old book you've loved since childhood. The safe and familiar.

He must feel me looking at him because, eyes still fixed on the screen, he reaches his arm out towards me, signalling I should snuggle up to him. With his other hand he tilts the bowl of crisps on his lap towards me, offering me the last of the crumbs.

He nods towards the screen. 'What d'you say? You and me on a road trip this summer?'

'A bit of a busman's holiday for you?'

'That don't worry me. I like driving.'

He's caught me by surprise. 'Is your passport still valid? I'm not sure if we need visas for the States.'

'I was thinking Cornwall. Visit my gran.'

I laugh. I should've known.

'What's so funny?'

'Nothing. It'd be good to see her again.' I stand up and gather the empty bottles, bend to kiss him on the forehead. 'Another beer?'

In the kitchen I'm still smiling to myself. I know him so well. We'd married at eighteen. But as I looked out at the world and itched for something more, Davy grew roots and hunkered down. Neither of us can recall exactly when our marriage ended – more of a dissolving than a break. And here we are in our fifties, neither of us ever finding the right partner, despite a string of relationships. Still bouncing back to each other, even though we know it isn't the answer.

It's a funny thing, love.

At the start of Leon's second session I ask what he would like to achieve through therapy.

'Ah, a good question.' He steeples his hands at his chin. His beard is neatly trimmed, nails manicured, no rings. 'What would I like to be different as a result of coming here?' He closes his eyes, thinking. Not wanting to stare, I smooth down my blouse, straighten my notepad on my knee, ponder the decor. A plant might look good on the filing cabinet, or a large ornament.

A deep sigh signals his readiness to continue. 'I want … I want to process what happened, the suddenness of losing her. Not keep going over it again and again in my head.'

I make a note of his exact words.

'I want to be able to think about Michelle without blocking out the feelings … to be able to talk about her, about the sadness … and remember the happy times as well.'

His phrasing is interesting: *'the feelings, the sadness'*, not 'my feelings, my sadness'.

'Anything else?' I ask.

'Yes. Eventually, I want to be able to think about … plan for … a future. Not spend all my time dwelling on what might have been and what I've lost.' He looks directly at me, scans my face for a reaction. 'Can you help me with that?'

There's something about the intensity of his gaze that is discomforting and I look down at my pad. 'These are things we can work on together, yes. Where would you like to start today?'

'As you probably know, the Ancient Egyptians held a belief that as long as the deceased's name was spoken, they live on, albeit in the afterlife.'

I give a slight nod, my face impassive, but inside doubts are pushing their way up; his diversion into ancient history is an unnerving reminder of his background in academia. He works at a local college, head of faculty. An educated man. *Stay in the room.*

Leon continues, 'I digress. You asked where I'd like to start. You sum it up really well in your article – the importance of talking about the person you've lost. Keeping a connection to them. Keeping them alive. I'd like to talk about Michelle.'

I nod. 'You mentioned that you met at a charity event.'

'Yes. We bonded over a shared concern for child health in

17

Sub-Saharan Africa. I gave her my card, suggested we discuss another fundraiser …'

His description of Michelle makes her sound too perfect. From her looks and figure to her personality. Her charitable works; her curiosity and interest in learning; her calmness – he uses the word 'serenity'; her ability to get along with anyone she met. *Idolisation?* I write in my notes.

'How long were you seeing each other?' I ask. I want to know if this was the infatuation of a honeymoon period or something more.

'Not long enough. Two, three years? It seemed like I'd been waiting for her my whole life,' he says. 'She was all I wanted.'

'Did you discuss a future together?'

He does that thing he does: looks up, closes his eyes, sits in silence for a few seconds. I'm contemplating whether dried flowers might be better than a plant when he says: 'Her husband was a challenge for her.'

'A challenge?'

'She couldn't bring herself to finally leave him. She couldn't break his heart.'

That tension in my temple again. The voice in my head condemning her – *then why did she start the affair with you, if she didn't want to break his heart?* Not so perfect after all.

At the end of the fifty minutes, the date for our next meeting confirmed, he stops at the door to my therapy room.

He stares out across the garden towards the house. 'I should probably have mentioned this before,' he says.

Clients sometimes do this, drop in another piece of information as they are leaving. It even has a name, The Doorknob Comment.

'Yes?' I shut my leather folder, underlining that our time is up. I've promised my friend Jen I'll meet her for lunch.

'You knew her,' he says.

I frown, not sure I understand what he means. 'I knew Michelle?'

'That's why I chose you. I wanted to talk to someone who knew her.'

I have no recollection of anyone called Michelle, in either a social or work context, and nothing he's told me about her so far has sounded familiar.

My face must look blank because he adds, 'She came to you for therapy.' Then, in the second before I can formulate a response, he shuts the door and is gone.

I watch him leave as I stand at the window fiddling with the cord of the blind. He crosses the lawn without looking back.

Michelle came to me for therapy?

He didn't say when, so it could've been a decade ago. Why has he not mentioned this before? Has he been testing me – to see if I react to anything he tells me? Testing how elastic my claimed professional discretion is in practice.

While this is fresh in my mind, I scribble some notes for my next supervision session with Clare.

Client: Leon J—
Presenting issue: bereavement after lover's death.
Information disclosed at end of 2nd session on leaving the
    room: his lover was my former client – confirm not an
    ethical issue.

I tap my pen against my chin, thinking about Leon's behaviour. This end-of-session disclosure is quite common in therapy; a way of avoiding a reaction, dumping the information when time has run out and it's too late to discuss it. Was he unsure what I'd say? Worried I might refuse to see him, imagining a conflict of interest?

With Leon I don't sense discomfort. What is it I'm missing?

I add to my notes – *Is this about control, drip-feeding his story in a way that allows him to handle his emotions? Or is it caused by an initial lack of trust, a need to check me out first before trusting me with the whole truth?*

Back in the house, I send a message to Jen asking her if it's okay to put our lunch back half an hour. There are twenty WhatsApp messages in our group chat – Nisha went on a first date last night. I want to see how it went, send a carefully selected gif to make them laugh, but I can't let myself get distracted. I need to check if I have a record of Michelle.

In my old therapy room I unlock the top drawer of the filing cabinet where I keep my client notes. I'm old-school, one of those people who still insist on hard copies of bills and printouts of statements. No danger of losing the lot to the wrong click of a button or a nasty bug. Davy often jokes about my tendency to keep everything, from the sentimental to the administrative, but once it's gone you can't get it back. Better to err on the side of caution.

Some years ago I asked Clare, my supervisor, what she did with her old client records. She'd arched an eyebrow before telling me that – while there were no *rules* around management of client notes – *best practice suggests* they should be destroyed six months after a client stops coming for appointments. That was a bit of a shock. I stopped off at Argos on the way home and bought a shredder.

So, while the filing cabinet is no longer as full as it had once been, there's still a large backlog that I should have destroyed. And any attempt at alphabetical order has long gone. Guilt gnaws at me, that I've let my standards slip so much over the past few years. But Dad's illness, then his death, has been tough. It's hard enough to maintain the external veneer of coping, let alone worry about what is going on behind the scenes.

Flicking through the files, it's interesting how some clients' names trigger memories of their cases, others a blank. I can visualise Mark: a skinny chap who couldn't come to terms with his unexpected diagnosis of diabetes, constantly self-sabotaging by not sticking to the diet. Sabina, a glamorous woman who – despite the image she worked hard to portray – had an aversion to sex. Janine, struggling with her identity after three redundancies. I wonder how they're doing now. Do they occasionally think of me and how I helped them? Or have they moved on, completely forgetting the work we did together? 'I saw some woman once when I went through a bad patch. Can't remember her name and don't know if it helped but I'm okay now.'

I draw out the final file: *Fliss*. No memory of her despite the unusual name. My brief notes on the front flap of the folder don't help: *2014 – 6 sessions, anxiety + panic attacks.* Years ago.

There's no Michelle amongst the files.

Disappointing.

Having emptied the filing drawer, I decide to sort them as I put them back: a pile for shredding – starting with Fliss – and another for those clients who may one day return.

Part way through this process I find Michelle. A dog-eared, yellow wallet, the Post-it note glued on the front suggesting it's been reused several times. I knew her as Shelly. *Shelly H.* I've written, underneath in pencil: *(Michelle)*.

When Leon described meeting her at the charity event, I

visualised a Marilyn Monroe lookalike, all slinky curves; now I can't be sure if I'm imagining the breathless girlish voice I associate with the name Shelly H. There's a memory of a blonde mane of hair, immaculate make-up, like a beautiful doll: is this really what she looked like or am I constructing a pastiche of the famous video clip of MM's 'Happy Birthday, Mr President' and Leon's portrait of her?

The flap of the folder is held down by one of those elastic bands the postman discards on the driveway. According to my summary notes on the cover, her initial appointment was two years ago. *2017 Feb to April: attended 4 out of 6 sessions – Marriage probs.* A flicker of recall: a husband who adored her but was difficult to please. She would have been seeing Leon at this time. *2017 Aug to Nov: 3 sessions – Diff decision.* Leaving her marriage? The gap between these dates, the missing sessions, suggest she didn't really commit to therapy, drifting in and out over a long period. That could be why I don't remember much about what we discussed; we didn't have time to build a solid working relationship.

I take the file to the sofa and sit with it in my lap. There are answers in here. Further details of the *'Marriage probs'* and her difficult decision that I can't immediately recall. Information on her relationship with both her husband and Leon. I fiddle with the flap of the folder, staring into space as I ponder. Of course I'm curious, but here's a major dilemma. This is all information Michelle shared in confidence and now she's dead. I'm not sure on the ethical guidance, but I guess these notes should be shredded unread – after all, if I was on top of my admin they would be long gone. But, what if the file contains something useful? Something important that shouldn't be destroyed for ever. Something that could help my work with Leon.

When I look down, the perished elastic band has

disintegrated, leaving flaked rubber on my trousers. Standing to brush myself down, I place Michelle's file on the chair and the corner of a postcard slips from inside. *Ah, yes!* I pick it up. *La Isla Golf Resort* it says above four views: a villa complex, a golfing green, a swimming pool, the sea. A flash of memory: she sent me the postcard to thank me, months after she stopped coming for therapy. I remember now. I tucked it in the file with the rest of her notes.

I have a strong desire to turn the postcard over, to check the date, read the message. Part of me says, where's the harm? But I know it's a line I mustn't cross: if I read this, what's to stop me from poring over the rest of the notes? I need to be professional. Before I do anything else, I'll discuss it with Clare and take her guidance.

Resolutely I put the card back inside the folder, message unread, then fetch a reel of Sellotape from the desk. Like a smoker crushing the tempting packet of cigarettes, I tape the file shut. I'm not ready to destroy it, but there must be a very good reason to open it, not just idle curiosity.

I pick up my phone and scan through the WhatsApp chain. Nisha's date was another in a long list of failures. She describes it as like the disappointment of picking the wrong Revel – you're hoping for the strawberry one but you're already committed, teeth deep in the outer chocolate when you discover it's a toffee. Ali responds with an emoji – tongue out, eyes screwed up. Nisha says The Date wouldn't shut up all night, droning on about his career in packaging.

I trawl through to find an apt gif and send a clip of a little girl, head lolling as she eats her dinner, ending up asleep face down on her plate.

Nisha replies immediately: 'Exactly that!' and before I'm tempted to respond, I grab my bag and head out to meet Jen.

Chapter Three

I look forward to my monthly supervision meetings; I'd have gone to see Clare even if it wasn't a requirement of the psychotherapy council. The textbooks say the supervisor's role is to provide an impartial view, to prompt reflection, and 'reduce the risk of misjudgement or oversight', but that doesn't get to the heart of it. I don't see how anyone can work in this field without someone to turn to, who really understands. She's one of the most important people in my life.

Clare had taught me on the *Foundations in Therapy* module, all those years back in my mid-thirties when I nervously embarked on my second career. I'd walked into the lecture hall on the first day and there was this striking woman sitting on one of the desks, swinging her legs. About ten years older than me, she was dressed head to toe in a black trouser suit, short tufty hair bleached very blonde, several stud earrings in each earlobe, a ring on her little finger. Thinking she was a fellow student I went over to introduce myself, asked if she'd studied psychotherapy before. She laughed and said, 'Just a bit.'

It turns out I'd got the time wrong. I was an hour early, arriving just after the previous class had left, when she was meant to be on a break. She took me for coffee, explaining the complexities of the canteen with its one-way flow system, forcing you past the temptation of cake and dessert before you could reach the tills. She asked me questions in a way that made me feel she was genuinely interested in me, each question phrased so that I had to think. Not, 'Why do you want to study therapy?' but '*If you hadn't signed up for this course, what would you be doing a year from now?*' Not 'What will you do when the course finishes?' but '*Give me five words that summarise what you want your clients to say about you.*'

Her teaching style was the same. Throwing out stimulating questions, challenging our lazy thinking. She taught us the skills of our new profession with her own recipe of enthusiasm, real-world experience and case studies. And I stashed away the practical tools and techniques she offered, my first-aid kit to help mend lives.

I was in awe. I wanted to *be* her.

Once fully qualified, I set up in private practice and contacted her to ask if she'd be my supervisor, trying to keep the fangirl tone out of my email. And here we are, still working together fifteen years later; her keeping me from 'misjudgement or oversight', while I continue to hang on every word she says.

'Digestive?'

Clare sounds echoey calling back to me from her stark kitchen where she's making us coffee. She tears the foil of the packet, the clatter of biscuits landing on the plate, which I know will be white. Her style is minimalist. The only splashes of colour an expensive-looking painting and a pale pink orchid. She likes flowers. Likes to have her own space. She and her wife don't live together but they've been a happy couple for years.

'So, your first client after your sabbatical!' Putting the

white mugs down on the glass coffee table in front of me, Clare continues, 'How does it feel to be back in the saddle?'

'Good, good.'

She nudges the plate of chocolate digestives towards me, taking one herself. Easy to resist: dark chocolate, not so keen. 'And what is the client's presenting issue?'

'Yes, well, that's one of the things I wanted to discuss today. It's a bereavement.'

'Ah.'

Last month when my sabbatical formerly ended, Clare had inquisitioned me about whether I was ready to start seeing clients again. She was worried I was still too emotional after losing Dad. I was. I still am. But it would be too easy to run away and give up and I couldn't bear the thought of letting Dad down when he was so proud of how hard I'd worked to get here, all the people I'd helped.

Clare studies my face as she stirs two sugars into her black coffee. 'You know what I'm going to ask,' she says.

'I'm okay, Clare. Really I am.' I pick up one of the biscuits that I don't even like and take a bite. *Look how relaxed I am.*

She nods slowly. 'So you've had two sessions now. What does she want from therapy?'

'He. It's a man. It's actually a bit more complicated. That's what I want to discuss.'

I summarise Leon's story, explain his disclosure at the end of the last session; that Michelle had been my client.

'I don't remember too much about Michelle's case other than it was a difficult marriage and she was having an affair. But I found her folder. Obviously I haven't looked at it.' I need to prove to Clare that I'm doing the right things. I don't mention the postcard. 'I wanted to ask what you thought I should do with her notes.'

'Interesting. What does your head tell you and what do you feel in your heart?'

'My head says I should destroy it unread. My heart ... My heart says, once it's gone, it's gone for ever.'

'And the implication of that?'

'There could be something in there that could help me in my work with my client – Leon.' A thought strikes me. 'How is it different to working with any couple? You remember when I worked with Geoff and David. I would see them separately and then we'd have a session together, but I would never disclose what they each had said. It just helped me to understand their relationship in a more rounded way.'

'So you're suggesting you read the file, so you would know the background information, but not share it with Leon?'

'Yes, it might help.'

She ponders for a moment, tucking her legs underneath her to get comfortable, all formality between us long gone. 'I'm going to suggest a compromise. You keep the file – for now – but don't read it. That way, if something comes up in your work with Leon and you think it would be beneficial to know the contents, we can discuss it again. When Leon finishes his work with you, you destroy Michelle's notes.'

'Yes, that makes sense. Thanks.'

'Tell me more about your work with Leon. You've had two sessions now. What are your observations and concerns?'

'He's charming, intelligent, committed to working on his grief. But there's something about him I can't put my finger on. It's like he's trying to be the model client, like he doesn't really trust me enough yet to give me the warts and all version of himself.' I give a brief outline of his background. 'His upbringing suggests "insecure attachment": I wonder if

27

he's fearful of rejection. That could be why he didn't tell me straight away that Michelle had been my client.'

'Possibly – why don't you ask him?'

At the end of my supervision, Clare hands me a sealed envelope. 'I want to pass a client on to you. A woman with social anxiety. Here's some background information on the referral so you can contact her.'

I've passed her unspoken assessment. 'Thanks, that's great.'

It's Dad's birthday.

Davy's come with me to take some flowers to the graveyard, wanting to pay his respects to Dad. They were close in that way men are: no sentiment but a depth of unspoken caring. It means a lot to me that he's there with me.

So I won't get too maudlin, we're focusing on tidying up Dad's plot. I plant clumps of heather and lavender and some bulbs for next year, while Davy digs a shallow hole for a small evergreen bush, its roots contained in a pot so it can't get too large.

Our hands grimy with soil, we sit on one of the memorial benches to survey our work.

'It looks nice, Davy. Thanks for helping me. Dad would be pleased.'

'What you gonna do now?' Davy says, nodding towards the headstone.

I know what he's asking. Now Dad's gone there's nothing stopping me from getting out of Middleford, just as I've always talked about. I could sell my house and move to London ... or rent it out and travel round the world for a few months ... But, if I'm honest with myself, I'd always hoped there'd be someone having this adventure with me: that I'd have found Mr Right by now and we'd be making plans for an exciting new life together.

I shrug. 'Maybe a holiday would be nice. Somewhere hot.' Davy hadn't mentioned the trip to his gran again and "abroad" was too foreign for his liking. 'I'll see if Nisha can get some time off.'

'If you don't want no trouble, make sure she doesn't pack that *Kiss Me Quick* hat!' he says.

At the next session with Leon, I open by restating his leaving comment. 'You said I knew Michelle. That she came to me for therapy.'

'Yes. I found an appointment card with your contact details in a book she'd been reading. That's why I looked you up online. I wanted to see – work with – someone who knew her.'

'Why is that important to you?'

'I thought it would help me feel closer to her now she's gone... To talk about her with someone else who knew her.'

Even if I remembered everything she'd told me I wouldn't *really* know her, only the things she wanted me to know. Therapy gives a sliver of someone's life. I might be party to intimate facts, secrets and fears but I wouldn't know whether she prefers cats to dogs, why she chose the car she drives, her family Christmas traditions; the minutiae of day-to-day life that make up a person.

'You understand I can't disclose anything she and I discussed?'

'Of course. But the fact you knew her might help you to understand the things I tell you, put them in a broader context. It's like having the full picture of the jigsaw to slot the pieces into.' I make a note of his simile, an unusual turn of phrase for him.

★

Towards the end of the fifty minutes Leon announces that the sessions are helping; he's starting to feel different.

'Different? In what way?' I ask, masking my pleasure at this news with a neutral expression.

Leon offers a rare smile, stretching his arms along the back of the sofa. The combination of confidence and power in his movements is like a cat sizing up its quarry, waiting to pounce. He scans my face before locking eyes with me. It's unnerving to be looked at like that, waiting for him to say something, and he holds the moment several beats too long. The therapist part of me tries to stay relaxed and in the moment but, pinned by his gaze, I feel exposed. It's like he's seeing me as a woman for the first time. And I become very conscious of him as a man. A very attractive man. I sit up straighter, resist the urge to tidy my hair as a flush starts to creep up my neck. At that moment he speaks.

'I'm going to call you Eliza.'

'Eliza? Is that someone you know?'

'No. Just my little joke. The Eliza Effect.' Is there a flash of something unpleasant in his smile – smugness, arrogance? But it's gone, replaced by a warm smile as he loops back to my previous question. 'You asked how my feelings have changed since we first met. A good question.'

I'm completely thrown and he must see it. Was I mistaken about what had passed between us? And his comment about Eliza – what did that mean? The only Eliza I can think of is the cockney Eliza Doolittle in the film *My Fair Lady*. Is he comparing me to her, implying I'm uneducated? Is he picking up on my accent? Did I mispronounce a word?

A pause as he finishes speaking brings me back, makes me focus. He's been describing the changes in his mood, most of which I've missed in my distraction, and my summary comment – 'That's good to hear' – sounds pathetic to my ears.

'First steps, but signs of progress. Thanks to you.' He suddenly changes the subject. 'Did you ever see Michelle here?' His fingertips stroke the arm of the sofa as if seeking her presence. It's a gentle yet sensual gesture, making me think of him as her lover. And as his fingers leave tracks in the pile of the suede, so my own skin tingles in response.

I respond, 'No,' when the textbook therapy response – *'Why do you ask?'* – should focus on the reason behind his question. Damn, too late now. Aware that was a little abrupt I add, 'I used to see clients in the house. In my office in the house.'

'The front room,' he says.

Deep breath. 'I'm curious about why you say that.'

'Nearest to the door so clients don't have to walk through your house. Keeps your private life anonymous. Maintains those important boundaries.'

Leon has touched a nerve with this Eliza thing. My sensitivity about my lack of a degree ('chippiness' Davy says), is made worse by the fact Leon is a college lecturer and clearly well educated. He's checked out my website, which skirts around the issue of qualifications and prior roles, probably a giveaway in itself. I've never found a way to 'sell' my transition from jobbing actor/hand model to therapist. Although acting is closer to therapy than I'd initially imagined before my training: putting yourself in others' shoes to build understanding, noticing others' behaviours and phrasing, assuming a role.

Eliza. After wading through pages of irrelevant information online about some pop star, I change the search to *'Eliza and therapy'* and find it: The ELIZA Effect. Wiki and a recent podcast tell me all I need. Apparently ELIZA was a software programme developed in the 1960s, an early chatbot designed to respond like a therapist to typed comments. 'I'm feeling sad today,' would be mirrored with: 'So, you're feeling sad?' Programmed to throw in the odd 'please tell me more', the illusion of empathy was complete. Apparently it worked so well that people readily shared their secrets with ELIZA, a machine that appeared to understand them and care more than many humans.

So what did Leon mean?

Was he implying it was easy to open up to me, that he feels I care, just as people had felt ELIZA cared? Is a solid bond developing between us? Am I really helping him as I aspire to do?

Or was he suggesting my empathy is superficial? Has he realised that I'm struggling: wrestling to pack away my judgements, mixed feelings and doubts. That I'm worrying so much about what is going on in my own head, that my empathy is too conscious and feels like another part of the act?

Friday evening is pub night with the Wellies. An eclectic bunch of friends, we've known each other since we went to Wellington Drive Secondary, a school so mediocre it's famous for nothing but an ex-pupil having been on *Love Island*. Our school days were donkey's years ago but we're still bound by our shared history of growing up together; and, of course, the fact none of us have summoned the energy to get out of Dodge. Memories of the pranks played on Mr Eccle, his bike hoisted to the ceiling of the science lab; the emotional scars of first dates and *that* school trip to Brighton; trying to get into pubs and clubs when underage, sending Mick in front because he was the first to shave; all these are dredged up and relived at comfortable intervals, embroidered every time they're retold so no one really remembers whether it was Mick or Steve.

Jake plonks himself down next to me, slopping beer from his pint onto the table, before giving me a playful punch on the arm. 'Cheer up, it might never happen.'

'It just did,' I say, trying to make it sound like a joke. The pub is crowded on a Friday night when we swell the numbers and I urgently scan the backlog of people at the bar, hoping for someone to come and save me from many more of Jake's inanities.

'Gasping for a top-up are we?' he says, following my gaze. 'Just remember, good things come to those who wait. Davy might·get you a double!'

'How's your mum doing?' I ask. She's in her eighties and just had a hip operation. 'I could drop by and visit her, if you think she'd still remember me.' She used to make amazing cakes and was thrilled once when I asked for her Victoria Sponge recipe to make it for Dad. Maybe I could bake one for her as a surprise.

'Of course she remembers you. You always was her favourite.'

There had been a phase of hanging out at Jake's house in our teens, when he was dating my best friend, Jen. His mum liked me because I always said please and thank you: 'Lovely Ps and Qs' she used to say. I had to ask Dad what she meant.

Across the room, Nisha is miming at me, pointing at Jake then shooting herself with an invisible gun, brain spatter depicted with the fingers of her other hand. He has a reputation for being a bore. Well-meaning though and always willing to help with computer problems, when you can pin him down. By the time Davy appears bearing a tray of drinks, Nisha has moved on to hanging herself with an invisible noose, her head lolling, tongue out.

'I've just spotted Nisha. I need to catch up with her.' I pick up the wine glass and offer my seat to Davy.

'I haven't forgotten your website,' Jake says, giving me a thumbs-up. He offered to 'modernise the format and graphics', but it's languished unmodernised for about eighteen months now. 'I'll get to it as soon as I get a gap. You want something done, ask a busy person!'

Davy winks at me over Jake's head. 'Great,' I say.

'There's something I want to ask you.' I sit myself down opposite Nisha and she straightens up in her chair, wearing the avid expression of someone hoping for gossip.

'All ears.'

'How would you describe me?'

'What?' She takes a large glug of her Merlot. 'Have you thrown out all your mirrors? You could lose the odd kilo but you're wearing well for a woman of your age.'

'No, really. I mean as a person?'

'Okay ...' Reading my expression, she puts down her drink to show she's taking it seriously. 'You're very kind and thoughtful. Generous. Ditzy, but not in an annoying way. A bit of a worrier.' She's counting off on her fingers and starts on her other hand. 'Clever. You're fun – well you make me laugh. You'd make a great mum.'

'Yeah, yeah,' I say, making a *'move along there'* gesture. Over the years all the others in the group have felt the call of parenthood, but I used to joke that I never got the memo. In the early days the girls would try to discuss it with me, sincerely concerned and wanting to share their tips for getting pregnant, until – eventually – they got it. Like cats, I think kids are lovely; I just don't want one.

'Do you think I'm empathic?'

She touches the next finger. 'You use fancy words.'

I laugh. 'Seriously. Would you say I appreciate how other people feel? Do you think I'm understanding?'

She pulls the 'duh!' face. 'I can't believe you need to ask. Look at the work you do.'

That's just the problem.

She takes a swig of her wine, satisfied that she's dealt with my concerns. 'Now let me show you the new dating app I've downloaded. I've got two dates lined up already! You need to sign up.'

Chapter Four

I can't stop churning over my work with Leon. Running through our conversations from the first few sessions, it's clear that I've relied too heavily on comfortable counselling methods; just rephrasing and reflecting back his comments to an extent that Clare would definitely not approve of. His comparison to the robotic ELIZA is most likely a literal comment on my style of questioning. I've been letting both of us off the hook; facts and logic so much easier to handle than messy emotions.

'How was your week?' I ask at the start of our fourth session. 'Did you use the diary?' I'd emailed him some homework. Nothing too challenging but a step in the right direction, a practical exercise to explore emotions that should appeal to someone so analytical.

He pulls the daily worksheets from an envelope. They are a diary of his mood changes with a record of the thought or incident that caused the reaction. By noticing the subtle changes in his emotions, I'm hoping he gains some insight and begins to understand how he can manage his feelings without being engulfed by them.

'Up and down,' he says.

'Would you prefer to start with ups or the downs?'

He unfolds the paperwork, an excuse not to look at me as he speaks, but the edge in his voice suggests he is not his usual self. 'I heard *her* song yesterday. On the radio. That was a down. The Beatles.'

'"Michelle",' I say without thinking. I'd heard it too, in the car on my way to see Jen. As soon as the DJ announced it, 'a trip down memory lane with The Fab Four', I made the connection, a flash of memory of Michelle telling me how much she hated it, but I couldn't recall why she disliked the song so much.

'Yes, "Michelle". It was her song. She told you about it?' He stops smoothing out the pages and leans forward in the chair, eager for me to share more. I've said too much anyway, blurting it out like that.

'I'm sorry, you know I can't discuss anything she told me.' I look down at my notepad, not wanting to see his hopeful expression. 'Other than the title, was there a reason it was her song?'

He sits back again, his disappointment filling the space between us. The daily diary lies discarded on the coffee table. He's colour-coded his notes – there's a lot of blue. He sighs, drawing it out for several seconds the way people do to control panic attacks or tempers.

'The lyrics say it all. We danced to it at a dinner in a plush hotel, another money-raising function. It was our first night away together.' He pauses, lost in the moment. 'It was her song, our song. I ... Hearing it out of the blue ... It brought back so many memories I ...' He tails off. Music can do that, flip us right back to an experience. For the first time there is real feeling in his voice.

He reaches for the water glass – a distraction technique – but it doesn't help. He sniffs hard, looks up to the ceiling, trying to push down the rising emotion.

'Oh my God. I miss her. You're the only person who can understand ...'

Lowering his head he covers his face with his hands, the slight shaking of his shoulders suggesting he's silently weeping. It's so unexpected I have to swallow hard to keep from crying too, aware of the gooseflesh on my arms, my guts knotting. In every session so far I've wrestled with a niggling judgement of him, perceiving him as the guilty party, the lover who tried to steal Michelle from her husband. But in this moment I can see him for what he is: a man overcome by grief.

It's as if my dad is sitting before me. A grown man, broken-hearted.

And I have to push away an overwhelming urge to hug him; stop myself from promising to do anything I can to make it better.

That night I have the familiar dream of Mum. She is walking away from me. It doesn't take Freud to analyse that one. She left us when I was a child, chose to leave me and Dad for her lover. But there is a simple reason her back is always turned in my dreams: I no longer remember what she looked like.

I was eight when she went, too young to understand what was going on; that this was permanent. I was packed off with my pink princess rucksack and Teddy TomTom to stay with Dad's friends, Aunty Brenda and Uncle Fred.

When it was clear the one-night sleepover was turning into a week, Brenda took me shopping for some extra clothes. I wanted to buy something for Mummy, so she'd know I was thinking of her. Brenda was patient while I dithered over such a big decision, making suggestions that I was quick to reject, knowing what Mummy would like. A snow globe: lots of glitter, a few trees and a grazing deer with her fawn.

I loved Brenda and Fred but by the third day I was

homesick. We were in the local park and Brenda was indulging me, letting me go on all the rides, promising a Wimpy and strawberry milkshake on the way back. She was pushing me on the swings and I was having such fun I momentarily forgot it was Brenda behind me.

'Higher, Mum, higher,' I said, leaning backwards on the seat, throwing my head back, to see an upside down Brenda. I burst into tears. Brenda rushed round to still the swing, lifting me off and taking me in her arms, showering me in kisses while I bawled my eyes out. 'I want my mummy!'

It was then that she explained it to me: Mummy wasn't coming back.

It's funny how I can picture exactly where we were: see the green chipped paint of the swings, the wooden planks of the seat; Brenda in her pleated skirt kneeling beside me; the pink sleeve of my new cardigan used to wipe my nose. But I can't really conjure up my feelings on that day and I wonder how much I've created the detail myself, padding out the skeleton story over the years.

The most emotional and distressing part of that whole period was seeing my dad cry. They are the vivid memories that still plunge me into depths of sorrow even though I've used techniques to blunt the emotions over the years.

The first time it happened, I'd heard a strange, almost animal sound from their old bedroom. I was home early from playing with Jen. I crept along the corridor, my heart racing, unsure what was going on, scared of what I'd find. At first, I was relieved to see Dad sitting on Mum's side of their bed in the redecorated bedroom. But then I realised the keening noise was coming from him, his eyes screwed up as tears ran down his face. His arms were wrapped tight around himself, his knuckles white where his hands squeezed his upper arms. I watched through the crack in the door as he rocked backwards and forwards, whimpering.

Tears welled up in my own eyes, my throat tightening, and I wanted to rush to him, hold him, make it stop, but I was old enough to know he wouldn't want me to see him like that. Biting my hand to keep myself from sobbing aloud, I backed slowly away, only letting myself go when I was in my playhouse at the end of the garden.

I'd hidden the snow globe there, stashed it at the back of my plastic cooker. My gift for Mum when she came back to us. I was never a destructive child but that snow globe took the full force of my distress: the plastic dome shattering as I hit it again and again with a stone, the water spilling out like glittery tears. I snapped the mother deer off her plastic base, pummelled her with the stone until my anger calmed. Looking at the outcome of my frenzy, I felt uncomfortable. Needing to hide the evidence, I buried the plastic of the dome behind my playhouse, threw the mother deer into a bush: burial too good for her. The tiny fawn I wrapped in tissue and placed in my pocket. Someone had to look after her. Someone responsible who could be trusted.

'Can you reach those?' Jen is pointing to a multi-pack of washing powders on the top shelf. We are wandering round the discount store on our quarterly bulk-buying trip. Why she needs to purchase industrial volumes of loo roll, cleaning products and cat food I'll never know, but it's a great chance to catch up on gossip outside the regular Welly pub nights, just the two of us. 'You've got longer arms than me.'

'You make me sound like an ape.'

'Why don't you get some too. Look at the discount.'

Standing on tiptoe, I tug on the plastic wrapping to pull the boxes towards the edge of the shelf. 'I only buy Persil.

It's what Dad always used.' I find the smell reassuring, hate it when they muck about with the fragrance.

'I know what you mean. I always get the butter Mum used to buy, even though the own brand stuff's cheaper,' Jen says. 'And the same toothpaste. Same gravy mix too. Habit, I suppose.'

She helps me wrestle the boxes onto the flatbed trolley alongside her other purchases, wedging my impulse buy of fake flowers against the handlebar.

'Mind you, Dad would've loved a place like this,' I say. 'Always had an eye open for a bargain.'

She stops rearranging boxes to look at me. 'It's nearly a year isn't it? You must really miss him, Cris.'

'I do. But I'm lucky, I've got you and the others to talk to about him.'

'He was great, your dad. Everyone liked him. Do you remember that day he and my mum took us to the beach? We were about ten I think.'

I draw a blank. 'Was it Canvey? Southend?'

'I don't know, but I remember the shipwreck.'

I frown at her. 'Sounds unlikely. Are you sure?'

'You must remember. He spun us a story about pirates and said there was probably abandoned treasure. We searched the boat and I found enough coins to buy ice cream. You got candy floss with yours and you were sick on the way home in the car.'

It's coming back to me as she speaks, more a feeling of familiarity than true recall. Dad had told one of his Bluebeard stories, walked ahead of us and hidden his small change in the cracks and crevices of the abandoned boat. I can't visualise us there on the beach, can't now describe the setting, but there's a sense of it. I know it had been a very happy day.

'Do you remember anything else about it?' I ask her, greedy to hear more, to talk about him.

She shakes her head. 'No. But I remember he used to tell us stories like that all the time. How he'd rescued those people from the beach after they wrote HELP in the sand. He had to get them on his plane really quickly because the tide was coming in. And the one about the dog that fell over the cliff.'

'You do know he made all that up?'

She stops pushing the trolley to stare at me. 'But he was a pilot in the war wasn't he?'

I snort a laugh. 'No, he was a bloody good storyteller that's all! And before you ask, he didn't have a wooden leg either, if he told you that one.'

'Bloody hell. Of course. He was about the same age as my mum; he wasn't old enough to have fought in the war. I never even questioned it! Don't tell me the story about the cockerel and the outside lav was made up?'

'I'm pretty sure that happened.' My nan had told me that one when I was a child so there was some validation. 'Trapped in the karzy by an angry cockerel and his harem.'

'Only your dad!' The fondness in her voice is really touching, but there's no chance of a sentimental mood settling in with Jen. She's already breezed on: 'Did you hear, Mick and Angie have split up already. It was bound to happen. Mick's so unreliable. So he's up for grabs again if you're looking!'

I roll my eyes. 'Really?' Her trying to matchmake is a standing joke. Jen is another in the gang who had married a childhood sweetheart. Unlike me and Davy, they were still together. Unlike me and Davy, they have three kids, all now starting families of their own.

'Angie's okay really, don't you think? She's trying hard to fit in. Shall we ask her out for coffee?'

I nod my agreement. Angie has recently moved to the area and doesn't know many people other than us. A quick glance at my watch reminds me that time is ticking on and we haven't got to the pet food aisle yet. I gesture to the trolley. 'This baby's not going to fill itself.'

The day before Leon's next appointment, I ring Clare.

'I'm really sorry to disturb your evening and this is probably going to sound daft but I'm going round in circles and I need your opinion.'

'I assume this is a supervision issue and not a chat about the latest Twitter outrage or a debate on modern feminism. Do you need a five-minute check-in or should we fix a Skype call for tomorrow?'

'Sorry, yes, five minutes will do it.'

'The time is yours.'

'A client mentioned the lyrics of a song recently and got very emotional. It's okay for me to look them up isn't it? I mean, it's not unethical or anything?' Even as I say it, I realise how stupid the question is, how needy I'm being, not wanting to put a foot wrong.

'Okay.' She draws it out, somehow making the word three syllables. 'You know me well enough, what do you think I'm going to say?'

'Look them up.'

'Uh-huh, but you missed something. Come on, Cris, how long have you known me?'

'Tomorrow,' I say. 'Look them up tomorrow.' Clare is a strong believer in work–life balance.

She laughs. 'My work here is done! Go get a glass of wine and relax. You are a great therapist and a great worrier.'

★

'I need you.' Those little words cut to the core. You don't need to like Lennon and McCartney to be touched by their lyrics. Leon has already told me how much he needed Michelle, but he expressed about as much passion as a second understudy reading a new script. But in our last session Leon had shown real depths of emotion and, sitting opposite him, I could *feel* how much he loved her.

I know how much agony he is in. Beneath his controlled exterior is a passionate, emotional man. He sees me as the only person who can save him. And I want to do to all I can to help him through this pain.

My biro stops working halfway through our next appointment. I shake it as if that will magic up some more ink, reach for my handbag to search for a spare. Without pause, Leon takes a pen from his inside pocket and passes it to me across the table. Bending forward to pick it up, I place one hand to my chest, conscious that my new low-cut top will gape, exposing more cleavage than I envisaged. But he is staring at the paperwork resting on my leather folder, not at me.

'What do you do with these notes?' he asks, his tone flat. It's been a low-energy session – he's had more blue days lately.

'They go into your file. You can read them any time you want. I'm happy to make a copy for you. As I said when we first met, they're primarily an aide-memoire for me.'

'Do you still have the notes from your sessions with Michelle?'

My pause tells him the answer before I open my mouth. I couldn't have lied to him anyway. 'Yes, but I can't disclose anything she told me. It's confidential.'

'Ethics,' he says quietly. *'A man without ethics is a wild beast loosed upon this world ...'* He rubs his brow, his eyes weighted

44

with sadness. He looks somehow smaller, pulled in on himself. 'That's the view of Camus ... Others think you should never allow your morals to get in the way of doing what's right. Discuss.'

He doesn't expect an answer. Dust motes dance in the silence, the air feels still. I cross my legs, settle back in my chair. The chemistry between us has changed since I've let go of my misdirected judgement against him for his affair with Michelle. The tension I carried has gone, replaced by curiosity about what makes this man tick so I can help make him whole again.

Eventually he says, 'What if this was the other way round?' His deep voice is soft but earnest and I wonder where this is going.

'Carry on.'

'Sometimes I imagine what it must be like to be you.' *He thinks about me outside the sessions.* The flush of warmth creeps up my neck again and for the second time I rue my choice of top as the reddening spreads across my chest like a rash.

'Sometimes I wonder what it would be like if our roles were reversed,' he continues. 'If you were the client and I were the therapist ... If it was you who had lost someone you loved.'

But I have, I want to say. *I understand what you're going through. I have suffered too.*

'And if you were the therapist in that situation ...?' I ask, my voice faltering slightly.

'I'm not trained to know what to say. But I know what I would feel, what I would want to do ...' He shrugs slightly, a resigned gesture as if he is too tired to deal with the weight of this. 'Let me just say this. When you lose someone, you want to gather up every little piece of them you can find. It's as if collecting every anecdote, every shred of who they were, somehow keeps them here longer, in the present.'

A stab of recognition in my chest. *I know. I know.* Until that moment I haven't really registered how alike we are, how we both want the same thing. Both greedily harvesting and storing every small detail of our lost loved ones, so as not to have to say goodbye for ever, so as not to forget.

He wants to know what is in Michelle's notes. And part of me wants to be free to tell him. To read through the file and share the stories she told me about him, reassure him he was loved.

'The love doesn't die with a person. It exists even after they've gone.' I was thinking about Dad, not meaning to speak out loud. I give a self-conscious cough and continue, 'Just like a person doesn't have to be in the room for you to think of them.'

He nods but says nothing.

The energy in the room is taut now, our shared emotion heavy in the air we breathe. This silence oppressive, rather than conducive to reflection. Momentarily at a loss for what to say, I reach for my water glass but it's empty, a cherry red kiss on the rim from my new lipstick.

'Let me,' he says. He stands to fetch the jug from the far end of the coffee table, then comes round to where I sit, the tension broken by movement. Standing next to me, he bends to pour the water. And a different more physical discomfort takes precedence as I become aware of how close he is, smelling the maleness of him, conscious of his arm next to my thigh, imagining I can feel the warmth of him through the fabric of my clothes.

I smooth my skirt down to cover my knees, mumble 'thank you' without looking up. It seems to take an age for him to replace the jug and return to his seat and I keep my eyes fixed on my notepad.

'You have a huge burden placed on you each time

someone walks through that door,' he says. ' *"Save me, make me happy, make me normal."* You do a great job.'

My thoughts are a jumble and I can't focus. His pen still lies on the table and I pick it up as if to record a note to myself. But like those complicated pepper grinders that you get in fancy restaurants, I can't see how it works.

'You have to press the clip.'

I fiddle some more, to no avail. Aware he is watching me, my face burning.

'Let me help,' he says, stretching his hand towards me to take it.

I put the pen down on the table. 'It's fine,' I say, finding my voice at last. 'I'll leave the notes for today.'

Tossing and turning in bed that night, unable to sleep, I brew on the session with Leon; his desire to learn the contents of Michelle's notes. Soon after Dad's funeral when I was at my lowest point, I received a phishing email. Full of the usual misspellings and bad punctuation, the email address may as well have said @scam.com. But the message hooked me: it purported to be from one of those family tree sites, someone claiming to be one of my distant relatives sending a photo 'wich might be off interest'. The attachment was labelled 'YOU're relative', and my fingers hovered over the enter key as I battled with the temptation to look. I left it in my in-box overnight, until sanity regained control the next morning and I double-deleted so I wouldn't be tempted to risk it one drunken evening.

I'm lucky to have a group of friends who knew Dad, people I can talk to about him and keep his memory alive. Leon has no one but me.

★

47

Putting the kettle on after my restless night, I contemplate Leon. Again. When I started this line of work I promised myself I would leave all thoughts about my clients in my therapy room at the end of the day. But Leon is creeping out of his allotted time and space. I know better than to fight my thoughts: if someone says, 'Don't think of a blue banana' it's hard not to. To *consciously not* think of Leon, I first have to bring him to mind. And I definitely don't want to keep doing that.

It's time to admit that I'm developing an interest in him; seeing him as a man as well as a client. It's not surprising really, given the intensity of emotion in our work and how attractive he is, but I need to keep it in check. My guilty secret. And much as I enjoy working with him, I'll do the same as always when working with clients: review his progress after we've had six sessions and decide then whether it's appropriate to offer more.

I tip my head from side to side to stretch out the tension, register the now-familiar creaks and cracks of middle age. Checking the kitchen calendar for the rest of the week's events, I see my schedule's as busy as ever; out and about with my friends as usual, not moping about at home. It's just as Dad would have wanted. I'm surprised to see the entry for that evening: my drama group, The Middleford Players. How could I have forgotten the extra rehearsals start this week? Our next show is looming, the opening date circled in orange highlighter on my wall diary in a few weeks' Time: *FIRST NIGHT @Middleford Theatre!!!*

It's only an amateur theatre group in a nearby town, nothing special. But it's very important to me. A place I can go where no one knows me as 'Cris, one of the Wellies', with all the shared secrets and childhood history that entails. I have never been introduced as 'Cristina the therapist', so no one ever confided their problems/their views on NHS mental health support, or – even worse – said, 'I bet you know what I'm thinking.' I'm just Cristy Evans, my old Equity stage name from back when I was married to Davy. To everyone in the troop – just another actor.

In some ways it's the place I feel most like 'me', when I'm on the stage, performing. The rehearsal is the type of distraction I need. And even though I'm not really in the mood, I would never let them down.

Jilly blows me a kiss as we take our positions on stage. To make her laugh I pretend to catch it, then mime juggling as if it's too hot to hold.

She's playing Suki, my energetic young 'love rival'. The play is a romantic comedy written by an up-and-coming local novelist who is branching into theatre.

The rehearsal is underway. Jilly as 'Suki', the patient, is on stage in an argument with 'Sam', the doctor. Sam doesn't know Suki is also a medic, or that the nurse, played by me, is in love with him.

I am seated to one side of the set beside a computer, my 'hand props' are a clipboard and thermometer. My script says *'eyes only for Sam'*, so I fix a lovesick expression on my face and twiddle with the thermometer. I'm a silent observer in this scene.

Suki is sitting on a hospital trolley, peering at her bandaged ankle. 'No X-ray? Just exercise? Seriously?'

'It's my humble—' Sam starts to respond but the director is on stage between them flapping her copy of the script. Suki has fluffed the line more often than she's got it right, mixing up the order of the words so she no longer knows which is correct.

Suddenly it dawned on me. 'Sex!' I say. 'That's the answer!' Everyone turns to look at me, laughing.

'What's the question?' The lighting guy calls out from the wings.

I hold up the script pointing to the line. 'Suki's line spells SEX *"Seriously? Just Exercise and no X-ray?"* It's a mnemonic.'

Suki claps her hands, grinning. She raises her arm in a virtual high five across the room and I mirror it. 'Now, why didn't I think of that!'

'Because you are pure of heart,' The director says, waving her into position. 'Back to one.'

In the cramped dressing room after the rehearsal, Jilly attempts to hug me as I shrug myself into my jacket.

'I never got a chance to thank you properly for your help last time! It really worked,' she says when she eventually releases me from her grip. She'd had a wobble at one of the early rehearsals, shaking with nerves and saying she couldn't perform 'ever again!' I offered to work with her on it and we met up a few times over coffee at my house. I walked her through a few techniques – things I learnt from therapy training and my own drama mentors when I was her age: breathing exercises, reframing the feeling in your stomach from stage fright to excitement, mental rehearsal of the performance. It was a pleasure to be of help, her enthusiasm a reward in itself.

'You're welcome. Any time.'

From the corridor off the dressing room someone shouts: 'Drinks at the Fox?'

'You need to ask?' The standard reply. Call and response. There is something relaxing about the familiarity, a feeling of belonging.

The pub is next door and it's hard to resist staying half

an hour longer when we are all bubby and energised. Over all, the rehearsal went well and whenever we've pleased the director, our proxy audience, we're on a high.

'I propose a toast.' 'Sam' raises his beer glass. 'Comedian of the night award goes to Cristy!' Glasses are raised and clinked and various cast members re-enact the jokes of the evening. I've been relaxed and on a roll all night. My exaggerated shadow-mime taking Suki's temperature behind the screens had gone down well. Then my impromptu Eric Morecambe impression when I delivered my line had caused Sam to corpse with laughter before our stage-kiss.

I look around at the smiling faces and it feels safe, like home.

Chapter Five

My car was stolen once many years ago. I'd attended a training conference at a hotel – Acceptance Commitment Therapy I think it was – and it was dark and raining when I left the venue. My head brimming with new ideas, my arms laden with books and handouts, I headed for the car park and home. I was already planning how I could apply the theories, my head off somewhere else, never in the moment.

Across the car park, in the place where I thought I'd left my old Astra, another was parked. Same make, same colour, but the driver's door was open, the car was empty and the engine was running. Studying it, for a split second I thought, 'How did I manage to leave the engine running all day?' It was only when I checked the number plate I realised it wasn't mine, then noticed the paint was metallic, there was a dog blanket in the back, and a pair of driving shoes in the passenger footwell.

Strange what the brain can do, trying to make sense of an unreal situation. It turned out it had been dumped and my car taken, a chain of vehicle thefts to mislead the police after a robbery. A logical explanation that had escaped me in my confusion.

That is what it is like the morning of the break-in.

★

It's a week after Leon's fifth session, when he had offered me his pen. I'm determined to stay focused in our meeting today, not allow myself to be distracted by the mix of emotions he is stirring in me.

I'm running slightly late this morning. Last night I went out for a pizza with Jen and Nisha, which had led to another restless night; the 'double cheese crust' heavy on my stomach. Walking across the path to my therapy room to set up, a fresh jug of water in my hand, I ponder when exactly I stopped measuring sleep in hours and started using units of 'loo visits', 'bedding adjustments' and 'podcasts played'. Last night's tally is one trip to the bathroom, three duvet shuffles and two podcasts – one of them something quite interesting about Cleopatra. Not such a beauty apparently, but a very intelligent woman.

My hand raised ready to insert the key in the lock of my therapy room, I'm distracted by the greenfly on the climbing rose and resolve to spray it with soapy water later. The door swings open at my touch. Must've forgotten to lock up after my last client yesterday afternoon. Menopause brain Nisha calls it.

But the door won't open fully, blocked by one of my new cushions, which is on the floor, its stuffing spewing onto the painted floorboards. The neighbour's tomcat must've got in, taking advantage of the open door to have somewhere cosy to sleep. Sniffing, I'm grateful I can't smell anything; he has a habit of marking his territory as I discovered when he once got in the kitchen. Took half a bottle of bleach to get rid of eau-de-Tom.

Putting down the water jug, I bend to pick up the cushion and spot my filing cabinet, until then out of view behind the sofa: it's lying on its side, the drawers open. Trying to work out what has happened, I move closer. My heart starts thudding. The drawers are not just hanging open but bent out of shape.

I don't understand.

My gardening gloves, secateurs and the plant labels are strewn on the floor, a ball of twine unravelled, disappearing under the sofa. The brown envelope of poppy seeds has been ripped in half, the small black dots scattered over the matting like thousands of full stops. My neighbour Susan harvested them for me last year for my proposed wildflower garden. I've already prepared the plot.

Kneeling to salvage them, I try to sweep them into a pile with my hand, but I can't see clearly for the tears welling in my eyes. *Why would someone do this?* Such a pointless horrible act. The thought of an unknown intruder here in my space makes me shudder.

Something rips across the side of my hand, drawing me back from my thoughts – a shard of glass has torn into my skin and lodged there. I tentatively pull it out and immediately the blood drips onto my pale pink skirt, forming red polka dots. The throbbing increases, my tears now running freely down my cheeks, my skirt now patterned with dark pink tears and darker blood.

A knock on the window makes me jump. The burglar returning? My pulse racing, I cower low behind the sofa, holding my breath as the door creaks open. One footstep, two, I close my eyes ostrich-like, ducking lower. Has he noticed movement? Can he see me?

'Hallo?' A male voice. Concern, rather than threat.

A familiar voice.

'Leon,' I say, my voice a whisper, the tears now a combination of shock and relief.

Seeing me huddled on the floor he rushes over, crouches beside me, kneeling in the mess with no care for his smart suit. 'Cristina!' He reaches out to take my injured hand and I flinch.

'Oh my God, you're hurt. Let me see.' He gently turns my palm so he can see the damage. 'This looks nasty. Here let me help you.' He puts his arm out to steady me as I shakily get to my feet and it is as much as I can do not to cling to him and weep in his arms.

I let myself be led to the sofa, still crying. He places a cushion under my elbow – 'Keep it elevated' – and rips open the cardboard box of tissues to grab a wad, pressing it on the wound to stem the bleeding.

'It's okay. I'm just a bit shocked, that's all.' My words understating the case as tears pour down my face, my body shivering uncontrollably. Seated, I can now see my certificates have all been smashed: their frames broken, the glass ground into the flooring. All the evidence of the qualifications I worked so hard for, trampled with muddy footprints.

'I just wasn't expecting ...' I tail off, mopping at my face with my sleeve.

'Do you have a clean tea towel? I could do with something to bandage this.'

'Not here. In the house.'

'We should phone the police.' He has his mobile out ready.

'You won't get a signal out here. They won't be interested anyway. Nothing's been stolen ... There was nothing to steal.' My voice is shaky; I'm too tired to cope with this. I can't pull myself together.

He looks around the room. 'I suppose you're right. It was probably just bored kids. Such a nasty shock for you. Let me get you to the house and I'll phone someone to come and sit with you.'

I let him guide me across the lawn, taking comfort from his arm around my shoulders, the warmth of him, relieved he's taken control. I can't think straight, don't know what to do.

'I'll boil the kettle,' he says, steering me towards the kitchen. 'Sterile water for the wound and a cup of tea for the nerves.'

Sitting at the breakfast bar, I'm no longer crying but still can't stop shaking. I watch him moving around my kitchen as if this is all natural. He clicks the switch on the kettle and turns to ask me, 'How's the hand doing?'

I lift the tissues cautiously but it starts bleeding again. It might need a stitch.

'Throbbing.'

Suddenly conscious of my smudged make-up and dishevelled hair, I push a strand back behind my ear, straighten the neck of my blouse.

'Should I call your husband?' Leon asks, pouring water into the mugs that he's taken from the draining board. He'd selected Davy's West Ham mug and the Scrabble one.

'No, I'm not married.' I shouldn't have said that, shouldn't have volunteered personal information. 'It's just the shock. I'll be okay.'

Leon is politely trying to make conversation as he adds the milk – 'Didn't have you down as a football fan' – but I need him to leave. He really shouldn't be here in my private space; shouldn't know this much about me, about my private life. The recipe for tonight's dinner is on the kitchen unit, the shopping list of ingredients half-written beside it. By his elbow, the cereal packet and milky bowl from my breakfast stand, left exactly where I used them. Pinned to my corkboard there are old photographs, cards and handwritten notes – 'Thanks to a Special Friend'. Shoved in the toast rack unopened post and bills waiting to be paid. My social life laid out on my wall calendar – coffees with the girls, curry night at Ali's, regular meet-ups at the Lion, evenings out and rehearsals.

I can almost feel Clare on my shoulder, imagine her disapproval at this breakdown in boundaries between the personal and professional; the therapist and the client. Boundaries I'm expected to maintain.

'I'm sorry, Leon. You've been so kind, but I just … I need to make some calls.'

He puts the mug down in front of me, then reaches forward and I freeze as he gently touches my cheek. 'You've blood on your face. Here, I'll get you a wet tissue to wipe it off.'

'It's okay, I—' He's already turned his back to me, busying himself pouring hot water into the washing-up bowl, adding cold then testing the temperature. I can't think what to say, my emotions a maelstrom − confusion, gratitude, embarrassment, shock, tumbling one over another as I try to regain control of myself and the situation.

He puts the bowl on the breakfast bar and I let him take my hand and place it in the warm water.

'That looks nasty. Do you have any Dettol or TCP? We ought to get something on that cut.'

'There's probably some upstairs in the bathroom.'

'Left or right at the top of the stairs?'

I have to get a grip. 'It's okay, I can get it later.' I try to sound resolute.

He takes a step towards the hallway. 'It won't take me a moment to pop up there. Which cupboard?'

I really have to regain control. I take my hand from the bowl and lay it on the towel he's brought over. 'Leon, you've been very kind but this isn't appropriate. I need you to go. Now.'

'Of course. Yes.' He looks me up and down, assessing the situation. 'As long as you're okay.'

'I am. Thank you.' I start to stand from the stool but he stays me with a hand on my forearm, my skin responding with goosebumps.

'No need to get up. I can see myself out. I'll phone you later to rearrange the appointment.'

I am mortified.

All the effort I've put into being professional, ruined in one morning. What will he think of me? How can he respect me as his therapist now he has seen behind the curtains?

And how can I ever explain this to Clare? There were so many points where I should have drawn a line, pulled myself together; remembered my duty of care to Leon as my client, not piled my emotions on his shoulders. I can't face Clare's disapproval on top of my self-castigation.

Having cancelled my next two client appointments and bandaged my hand, I'm still brooding on these unhelpful thoughts when Jen rings to remind me of my promise to email the details of my show. The Middleford Players ... so far from my mind right now. She's coming to see it and has promised to tout tickets at the school where she works.

'Jen, I can't really chat now. I—' At that point I burst into tears, the real boo-hoo type.

'Oh my God, Cris. What's happened? Are you ill?'

I sob my way through the story and, of course, Jen says she's coming straight over when she finishes work.

By early evening the jungle drums have rung out round Middleford and Jen, Ali and Nisha arrive, all keen to offer their help with clearing up and cheering up. As I serve mugs of tea and Jen cuts the homemade cake she's brought with her, Nisha dons her *CSI* baseball cap.

'At last, a fitting occasion to wear it!' It was our gift for her forty-fifth birthday, her obsession with the American TV show legendary. Over the years the black has been sun-bleached and the peak has lost some of its perk, but she still loves it.

'Who needs the police to investigate when we have Nisha in her hat?'

Nisha checks herself out on her phone, sucking in her cheeks and posing as she takes a selfie. 'Don't you think I look a bit like that dark-haired woman in the original series? The one with the strangely spelt name.' This isn't the first time she's fished for this compliment, and certainly won't be the last, and we all pull confused expressions pretend-ing we don't know who she's talking about. These running jokes between us are part of what binds our friendship and I immediately feel safe again.

Cake devoured, we go over to my therapy room where we all stand in silence as we contemplate the damage. It's worse than I thought. There are dents that look like hammer blows in the walls where the filing cabinet had stood. All four cushions have been ripped apart. And what I'd taken to be mud turns out to be spray paint. A trail arcs across the back of my chair then meanders pointlessly to the floor finishing in a dark puddle, the empty can moored on its surface.

Ali prods the can with the toe of her boot. *Midnight Sky*, it reads. 'Teenagers.'

'Pretty angry ones judging by the amount of damage,' Jen says, picking up the remnants of a cushion.

'Probably looking for something they could sell and got pissed off when they found nothing.' Nisha retrieves the vase from the floor, the fake flowers in her other hand. 'Not Ming, I assume?'

'Costco's finest.' I laugh. 'Let's just get the worst of it cleared up then crack open a bottle of wine. Davy can help me with the heavy lifting when he gets back from his road trip.'

That gets unanimous approval and Jen gets us organised and we all set to our allotted tasks of mopping up paint or sweeping up wood, glass and feathers. I stall Ali with her broom while I carefully retrieve my certificates from the scattered glass and broken wooden frames, each move as considered as if I were playing Jenga. Kneeling to one side to allow Ali to sweep through, I place one on my lap: *Brief Therapy Diploma,* it says in blue cursive font; a gold-coloured rosette embossed with the name of the college. *Cristina Hughes – Distinction.* Dad was so proud of me. Each certificate like his own personal triumph. I try to smooth it out, flatten the creases, but make things worse adding smears of blood where it has seeped through the makeshift bandage on my hand.

'Chuck that out,' Ali says, holding a black sack open before me. 'You can send off for copies if you need them.'

I watch her tie the neck of the rubbish bag in a knot and take a deep breath. Now is not the time for sentiment. 'Wine, anyone?' I say.

The Monday after the break-in I see Clare for my monthly supervision. My account of the incident now has an edge of humour. 'I'm surprised the little hoodlums didn't take the poppy seeds to see if they had any street value!'

Clare smiles politely; she won't let me hide behind jokes. 'It must've been quite unsettling at the time.'

'Yes. It was really.' Her fluffy white cat, Fritz, pushes its way through the half-open door to join us, like a heat-seeking missile for a warm place to sit. I pat my lap encouragingly, ignoring the fact I am dressed in *professional therapist* black. 'I had to cancel all my clients for the day, which I hate having to do, but they all understood.'

She knew I was trying too hard to make light of it. 'How did you feel, Cris? You're allowed to be upset.'

'Shaken. It was very disturbing at the time.' Fritz pads my knees, getting comfortable. I don't usually encourage him but it gives me a distraction and a reason not to look at Clare. 'But I'm okay now. I know that it wasn't personal, just an opportunist prank. I'm only pleased that all my client files were locked up safely in the house.'

'Very sensible.'

I lean round Fritz for my coffee mug and take a sip. 'One of the people I was due to see that morning was a new client. I managed to reschedule her for the next day and it's an interesting case. I'd like your opinion on whether I should suggest couples therapy. And, if we have time, I'd like to discuss an article on existential therapy, which I saw in the journal.'

'Fire away.'

I launch into a description of Pam, the sprightly seventy-five-year-old who wants to explore leaving her third husband 'because he's not the man he sold himself as'. She found him on a dating site and they've been married two years.

The hour of supervision is soon up and, claiming a hairdresser appointment, I leave without even brushing the cat fur from my trousers.

Lying by omission Dad used to call it; I'd avoided all discussion of Leon and the boundaries that were crashing down around me. I just don't want Clare to think badly of me, to think I'm not coping. But that doesn't stop the guilt of not telling her.

★

After seeing Clare I check the code of ethics, hoping to find answers to all the things I should have explored with her in my supervision session. While I find nothing explicit, nothing remotely similar to the incident with Leon, professional misconduct cases have been brought against therapists for far less. Inappropriate clothing; hearing a washing machine running through the therapy room walls; family photos on display – all had apparently been raised as grievances by disgruntled clients. The therapist's life spilling into the session.

While I'm on the website, I'm drawn to read the current complaints. Seven therapists currently under investigation. Inflating practice hours during training. Failing to complete the Continuous Professional Development and supervision requirements and renewing membership with false documentation. An affair with a current therapy client… I scan through the summary case notes on that one: 'abuse of power', 'failure to maintain a professional distance', 'inappropriate intimacy'. The final line reads, 'Accreditation removed. No longer deemed fit to practice.'

For the rest of the week following the break-in, I avoid speaking with Leon. I email him to arrange our appointment, sending a calendar invite, keeping it formal. He responds with a message enquiring after my wellbeing, but I don't reply.

On the day he is due to see me, I revert to my standard therapy uniform: minimal make-up, no perfume, plain black trousers and top. I'd let my standards drift. I am ready for the appointment ten minutes early and stand in the hallway, counting down the minutes until the doorbell rings. As usual, he is bang on time. A deep breath before opening the door; getting into role.

'Hallo, Leon.'

'Good morning. How are you?' He glances towards my hand where I cut it last week.

I nod in acknowledgement but don't respond to his question. 'We're meeting here today.' I open the door to the front room, my old office, to show him in. I've removed the ornaments, photographs, even the prints that were on the walls, transforming it back into the bland therapy room it had been before.

Leon and I sit in silence for a moment before I launch in. He's waiting for me to take the lead as I normally do. I've prepared what to say but now it doesn't feel right. I should've discussed it with Clare, sought her advice. But I couldn't admit to her how much I'd let myself down.

'Last week … thank you for your support but I'm sorry that—'

'Don't be,' Leon interrupts, holding up one hand, his palm towards me signalling stop. 'It's okay. I was pleased to help.' His smile is kind, his voice gentle but firm.

I carry on. 'It was unprofessional of me – the way I handled the situation. I think we should discuss what happened.'

He shrugs, snorts a laugh. 'Well, I don't. So it's stalemate.' He smooths the leg of his immaculately ironed trousers, then looks out of the window. 'Don't you think we adapt our plans to fit in with what life throws our way?'

'Is that what you believe?' Part of me is grateful for this potential diversion.

He looks at me steadily. 'Sometimes things happen for a reason.'

'Give me an example?' I'm ill at ease about where this could lead us.

He steeples his hands to his chin, contemplating me. 'An attractive woman meets an attractive man. They find a shared interest – photography let's say – and they start to spend more time together. Things develop, if you'll pardon my pun. He appreciates her for her skills as well as her beauty.'

Locked in his gaze, my face is definitely reddening. Is he flirting with me?

'The man encourages and develops her talents. She comes to depend on him, love him. Maybe talks of leaving her husband.' He claps his hands, the sound louder for being unexpected, and I jump. 'Then she is gone. Just like that.'

Michelle. He is talking about Michelle.

'And all that are left are the photographs.' He leans back in the chair. 'Maybe *that* happened for a reason.' A flash of memory – Michelle loved photography. I recall telling her I'd been a hand model, her asking if she could photograph me … She studied it at college. Of course, Leon was probably one of her tutors.

I take a deep breath, about to follow this line of thought, but before I can say anything he continues.

'Take another example. A man approaches a professional for help. He is impressed by her expertise, her dedication, her sincerity. She helps him move forward and he trusts her. One day, the mask slips and he sees her humanity. The woman beneath the mask. Would he think any less of her?'

He doesn't expect an answer.

'There is nothing either good or bad, but thinking makes it so,' he says.

That should have been my line. It's a quote from *Hamlet*, a quote I have printed on my business card.

'One can be driven mad by grief,' he says. I assume he's thinking of Hamlet.

'That's true.'

'You must miss your father terribly.'

'I'm sorry?' Did I hear that correctly?

64

'Your father. It's a good job you have your therapy training to help you come to terms with it.'

I'm confused; part of me sure I've never talked about Dad, part of me wondering if I inadvertently mentioned his death to show empathy. Is there something in my bereavement blog that alludes to it?

'We have a lot in common, you and I,' Leon says.

I bite back the stock question: *Why do you say that?* Not wanting to hear more, to get led down that path when I'm trying to maintain professional distance.

'How old are you in the photo?' he asks. 'You look so happy together.'

I realise what he's seen. I don't need to look. On the bookshelf behind me, the one personal item inadvertently left in the room, my favourite photo of me and Dad. It's a blow-up of an old Polaroid. We're in a park, both of us on one of those witch's hat rides in the playground area. I'm standing up on the seat and he has his arm round my back, stopping me from stepping backwards and falling, protecting me as always. He's shading his eyes with his other hand, the sun bright on our faces. We're both grinning broadly at the camera. I am nine or ten. Mum had been gone over a year.

'Did you complete the homework task?' I ask. 'How did it go?'

At the end of the session he stands, patting down his jacket pockets. 'Ah, yes. Before I go. I brought this along for you last time, but there wasn't an appropriate moment to give it to you.' He bends to place a clear oblong box on the table before me. It holds an elegant black pen. 'A Montblanc. A replacement for yours.'

I don't move an inch.

'Thank you for the thought. It's very kind but I can't

accept it. As your therapist I'm not allowed to accept gifts.' Even to my own ears I sound pompous.

He makes no move to pick it up. 'A pen runs out of ink. Another is bought. Cause and effect. Things happen for a reason. If it seems unprofessional to keep it, please pass it on to a charity.'

I pick it up and his smile broadens but, determined not to fail this test, I hold it out towards him. 'Thank you, but no. I can't take it.'

A vague flicker of something crosses his face – annoyance, frustration – but he reins it in, taking the gift box with a theatrical bow saying, 'Your wish is my command.'

A quick recovery, but he is a man not used to being thwarted.

Chapter Six

'You didn't mention Leon last time we met. Is he still coming for therapy?' Clare says at our next supervision meeting. I've brought her some tulips from my garden and she's arranging them loosely in a large glass bowl so they droop artistically.

'Yes. It's been going well.' I'm alert and focused, determined not to let myself down.

Clare sits on the sofa, tucking her legs under her. 'Hmm?'

'He's less stuck in his head – more in touch with his emotions. You remember, at the start he found it really difficult to talk about Michelle; he'd get overwhelmed.' I check the notes I'd brought along with me, anticipating this conversation. 'To be precise, he said it was like "the way champagne sprays from the bottle after its been shaken; everything nearby gets damaged and there's no way to get the cork back in".'

She smiles. 'A creative analogy for an amygdala hijack. Not bad for a man so literal.'

'We've worked on strategies to manage it, so he doesn't get overtaken by emotion. And he's realised he can choose when he takes the metaphorical cork out and do it carefully, in his own time.' I laugh, cueing her that I know I'm about to stretch the metaphor too far. 'He can even recork the bottle if he wants to! He says he feels much more in control.'

'Good work.'

I pull my shoulders back, sit straighter. After all my doubts recently, it's reassuring to have her praise, to know she still thinks I'm a capable therapist. I want more validation. *Look at me the professional.* 'He tried to give me a gift last time we met but I told him I couldn't accept it.'

Her brow furrows and I immediately regret mentioning it, even though it's something I would normally be happy to discuss with her.

'Walk me through what happened,' she says.

The exchange that follows includes phrases like boundaries, power games, vulnerability, ethics.

'Keep an eye open, Cris. That's all I'm saying. Remember what Freud said about analysis: it's "a cure through love". You've observed that he has attachment problems – he's vulnerable, wants to be loved. You're the professional here and you need to manage this so it doesn't get out of hand. Call me any time if something happens that makes you uncomfortable.'

It's the first night of our show. There's a wonderful feeling backstage just before a performance starts: a tingling excitement that grips everyone. I tried to explain it to Davy once. 'It's like pouring Prosecco on sherbet and then adding glitter and balancing a sparkler on the side.'

'You mean like Space Dust?' He was referring to that synthetic sweet we used to buy at school that would pop and fizz on your tongue and make your mouth sore.

'Yes, something like that.' In a way, his was a better description – it's a feeling on the edge of too much. Balanced carefully at the right peak, it feels great; too high and the cast become giddy, like kids with too much sugar. And that threatens diva tantrums or dreadful overacting.

Davy and Jen have seats reserved for them in the front row. It's not really Davy's thing, but he and Dad always came to my opening nights for as long as I can remember. This is my first performance since Dad died. Just as Davy had accompanied Dad, Jen is now accompanying Davy.

Don't think about Dad. Not now. I give myself a quick talking-to: *Focus outwards on the here and now, not inward on your memories. Be present. Feel the buzz.* The auditorium is filling up, echoing with chatter and the bustle of people as they file in, drinks in hand. All dressed up for the evening out, even though it is just a local theatre, an amateur performance. Tickets have sold well, the play having featured heavily in the local press; the writer already established as the town's one claim to fame, due to her best-selling chick-lit novels. There is talk of a TV series that she's developing with an established comedian.

A voice pulls me back – 'Places please' – and I slip to my position in the wings ready for my entrance. My stomach a flutter of excitement, I tug the chain around my neck and raise Dad's ring to my lips, my lucky charm. He's there with me: *Break a leg, kiddo.*

The performance has gone well – broad grins, hugs and high fives all round. We take our curtain call and I search the audience for Davy and Jen and anyone else I might recognise. That's when I see him.

Leon. Five rows back towards the centre seats. Taking my bow along with Suki and Sam, the three main parts, I wonder if I've made a mistake. But no, a glance as I straighten confirms it's definitely him. At his side, a woman in a green dress. As I watch, she leans in close to him, whispering in his ear, but he doesn't turn towards her, merely inclines his head. He is looking directly at me.

In the dressing room I scrub at my stage make-up until my face is sore. This has to be a coincidence. That's all it is. It's possible he didn't even recognise me, what with the thick grease paint and the accent I adopted for the part. And in all

69

the promotional material they've used my stage name, Cristy Evans, not Cristina Hughes as he knows me.

I continue arguing with myself as I struggle out of the nurse's outfit. I haven't done anything inappropriate or un-professional – lots of therapists have other careers where their clients might come across them. And some have been actors or comedians, look at Ruby Wax or Pamela Stephenson.

My arm catches half in/half out of the puffy sleeve of my costume and I'm tempted to rip the thing, stopped only by knowledge of the temper this would invoke in Mavis who does Wardrobe. It's part of the running joke that my character tries to attract Sam's attention by wearing a range of different nurse uniforms in each scene. This one was indecently short and very non-PC, reminiscent of Benny Hill crossed with Carry On.

At that moment Jilly appears with a huge bouquet of roses, which she thrusts towards me, ignoring my plight. 'For you, hon.'

'For me? Aw, thanks,' I say, automatically adopting the upbeat slightly 'lovey' character the others assume. I take the flowers with my one free hand and am about to add *you shouldn't have* when she interrupts me.

'Don't know who they're from. There's a label.'

They are too posh for the local Tesco so I guess Jen had a hand in it. I put them on the dressing table and give the costume a final wrench to free myself. Once I've pulled on my jeans and jumper, I stuff my other odds and ends into my bulging rucksack, pick up the bouquet to hurry round to the lobby bar where Davy and Jen will be waiting.

'Lovely flowers,' Jen says, grabbing me in a body hug. Following her lead, Davy gives me a chaste kiss on the cheek, not one for public displays of affection.

'Yes, they're gorgeous. Thanks. It was a lovely surprise.'

They look at each other blankly. 'They're not from us,' Jen says, reaching for the small envelope attached to the cellophane. She tries to pass it to me but my hands are full.

'You open it,' I say.

'Wow. It's very small writing. *Congratulations. Leon.*'

'Let me see.' I thrust the roses at her so I can take the card and read it myself. 'Oh.'

'A fan?' Jen asks, sniffing the blooms. 'They smell nice.'

'No, someone I work with.' That's vague enough. My stomach is dancing and I'm getting hot. I pile everything on the floor, the bouquet on top. 'I need a drink. Is the bar still open? My round.' I stride off before they can argue, the two of them shouting their orders after me.

The flash of the green dress catches my eye before I spot Leon. He's steering the woman through the thinning crowd towards the door, one hand in the small of her back. The dress is low-cut at the back, her exposed skin a beautiful mocha colour. Tall and slim like a model, her head is on a level with his. They pause in the entranceway – it's drizzling outside and neither of them have coats. He says something and she turns to him and laughs, showing perfect white teeth, her lips a deep red. He takes off his suit jacket and raises it over their heads and she slips an arm around his waist, the move casual and familiar.

I check her left hand. She isn't wearing a ring.

He turns his head to look around the lobby before they leave and I step sideways behind a pillar, breathing hard, hoping he's not seen me. Watching.

I take the drinks back to Davy and Jen but tell them I've developed a splitting headache and need to get home and sleep it off. I make Jen take the flowers, claiming their perfume makes my head worse. But I keep the card.

Davy walks me to the car park, oblivious to the fine rain settling as a mist on my hair, marching us straight through the puddling water. 'I could drive you back ... if you like,' he says. 'We could get your car tomorrow?'

I kiss him on the cheek. I hate lying to him. 'Thanks, but I'll be okay. You know I need to be on my own when I feel like this.' Davy will take what I say at face value, even though I rarely get headaches.

I take the long route back. Driving helps me think, gives me space to analyse what's happened tonight. My happiness at our great first night has dissipated to be replaced by this discomforting feeling that the play was a small, shallow thing. Of course, I know the cause. Spotting Leon in the audience unexpectedly, then the bouquet; flowers that he had to have purchased in advance, meaning he *knew* I was in the production. But before or after he bought the tickets?

And then there was the woman in the green dress.

Much as I hate to admit it, this churning and burning in my guts is not just about professional boundaries.

It has a name: jealousy.

Technically my feelings for Leon would be called *erotic countertransference*. That's how the psychoanalytic bunch would define it: 'romantic, sexual or sensual reactions towards a client'. Too embarrassed to admit this to anyone, let alone Clare, I look for advice online. It seems odd to be consulting Wiki rather than Clare – hoping to find *'How do I stop myself falling for my client?'* buried in amongst guidance on *'How to bake bread'* and *'How do I stop my mobile deleting messages?'* Despite my initial reservations, my search proves helpful.

It appears it's not that unusual. In fact some psychologists think it's only natural to develop this sort of bond in a therapeutic relationship – 'a cure through love' as Freud and

72

Clare said. But I can honestly say I've never felt this way about a client before.

On reflection, there are a number of factors that make it more inevitable with Leon. From the start he got under my skin. He's challenged me intellectually in ways I've not experienced with many clients, the feeling akin to when I first studied with Clare. And just as she enthralled me back then, Leon entrances me now. And our work on love and loss has meant exploring feelings we both share, so it's normal that I should care about him. However, when I saw him at the theatre, with that woman, it was clear there is more to it than that. I've become a lovesick teenager again; all bubbling hormones and jealousy. Not such a good look on a middle-aged woman.

I have to do something about it.

Apparently, there are three recommended ways for a therapist to deal with 'erotic countertransference'.

The preferred textbook option is to talk it through openly with the client, *'particularly if there are signs the feelings might be reciprocal'*. I try this on for size, imagining myself in the therapy room with Leon and how I might broach the subject. In my mind's eye, I start by explaining that 'feelings of attachment' are in fact quite common, particularly when working this intensely. To illustrate that this is a well-established phenomenon, I then mention Freud and Breuer, and the latter's infatuation with his client Anna O.

But my confidence fades as I imagine Leon's response: his fingers steepled at his chin, contemplating me in silence as I redden under his scrutiny. Listening in horror as *he* then expounds on Freud's theories, showing a depth of understanding that puts me to shame, baffling me with his know-how whilst I glow with embarrassment, a schoolgirl put on the spot by her teacher.

Or worse still, maybe he is taken aback by my confession: 'I assure you these feelings aren't reciprocated. I can only apologise if anything I have said or done has led you to the conclusion that I may have a romantic interest in you. I can see that you may have misread my gift of the pen, the flowers, for more than they were ...'

My God, the embarrassment.

The second approach would be to ignore it: to control my reactions to him and keep my feelings well out of the sessions. Whilst this has the benefit of allowing me to keep my secret, it would be too uncomfortable continuing to see him in this professional context. I would be even more self-conscious and would be bound to make silly mistakes that would give away my feelings. And too many boundaries have already been breached.

The third choice is avoidance: stopping our work together and cutting Leon from my life.

Years ago my own therapist observed that I hate endings. He said it was to do with Mum having left so suddenly, cutting all ties. He theorised that this was why I would do anything for my friends, so they know I love them and, hopefully, love me back. After all, you don't abandon someone you love. It's why I try to please people and hate arguments, avoiding anything that could upset someone and result in them leaving for good. He was right. It is reflected in my psychotherapy work now. I usually allow my clients to decide when their therapy is complete and always leave the door open for them to return, in case they need me.

But this time there is no choice. There is no other viable option: if I want to retain my professional career – and my sanity – I will have to wrap things up and let Leon move on.

Even if it is with the tall slim woman in the green dress.

★

At the start of the next session with Leon, I thank him for the flowers he sent backstage. It doesn't seem worth reiterating my comment on boundaries, given how many have been crossed. Instead I launch straight into my prepared lines, not giving him time to start a discussion and knock me off track.

'In our first session we agreed that we'd review progress at this point.' Not waiting for his response, I pull out the paperwork and lay it on the coffee table between us.

'Your stated goals for therapy are written here.' I tap with my finger, drawing his attention to the outcomes we agreed. He leans forward to look and I pull back, conscious of his closeness, the peppery lemon scent of his cologne. My high-necked sweater is too hot for this mild spring day.

'Firstly, you wanted to process what happened. And then – once you could control your emotions – you wanted to be able to think about the happy times you both shared without becoming overwhelmed.' Realising that was unnecessarily formal, I force a lighter tone. 'Finally, you wanted to look to the future and not keep dwelling on your loss. Let's take them one at a time. On a scale of one to ten, how much progress do you feel you've made on processing the events?'

He contemplates the paperwork, looks up at me, smiling. I sense he sees through me, but is willing to play along.

'That's gone well,' he says. 'The memories of that day don't catch me out any more.'

He's referring to the day he heard of Michelle's accident. The administrator appearing at the door of his lecture room, bringing news of the accident. He'd been playing this memory on a loop ever since, berating himself for all the things he might have done, that might have been, the times they should have spent together.

'The techniques you gave me work really well. I can remember it, but it's less emotional. I don't keep rerunning it.' He's leaning forward, his head lowered to read the paper-work, and he raises his eyes to look at me: hazel-brown, his lashes dark. 'Ten.'

'That's good. And the next goal – understanding and processing your emotions?'

'I'd say nine out of ten.'

'What would make it a ten?'

He sits back, relaxed. 'I can still get tripped up – "trig-gered" to use your term – if something comes out of the blue. But I can at least manage it now.'

I record '9' on the paperwork. 'And looking to the future?'

'The same. The techniques you've given me have helped a lot. I've been thinking I might take a short holiday. Go abroad for a few days, change of scenery.'

I've helped a lot. I retrieve the paperwork, placing it in the folder on my lap.

'As you know, my approach is brief therapy. I typically see clients for six to eight sessions before a taking a break. This ensures you don't become overly dependent on the therapy sessions or on me.'

Come on, you're an actress – sound more natural. 'It's to give you a chance to try the different strategies on your own.'

'I understand perfectly. I can't be deemed independent until I let go of your hand.'

His metaphors have improved if nothing else. 'A good way of putting it. We can use the time today to review the tools and techniques. If, in a few months, new issues arise you can book further sessions.' I didn't intend to say that last sentence.

I have prepared a handout for him, a summary of all the techniques we've used and a list of relevant websites. Wanting to ensure our final exchange shows me as a professional, I hand the document to him as he is about to leave. He thanks me, shaking my hand, a mirror of our first meeting. I'm not sure what else I expected but it seems uncomfortably cold and formal given the emotions we've shared over the past months.

Seeing him out at the door I'm overcome by a wave of sadness, but there is also relief that our final session has gone so well. That I've lived up to my professional values. There were no challenges, no unexpected reactions. But then he spins round on the steps, his lips twitching with a grin.

'By the way, you should wear heels more often.' And with that he is gone.

I am wearing flats. He is referring to the final costume I'd worn in the play: the skirt short, the heels high.

Chapter Seven

Over the next days and weeks I try to push him from my mind. Engage fully with my other new clients: Sajid, who's worrying about his recent promotion; Lizbeth, the woman referred by Clare, who is suffering with anxiety. Take pride in the work I'm doing with them.

On Jen's half-day we go for a coffee at our favourite venue, Bag a Bagel. A regular haunt for me, Jen and Nisha. The venue offers a unique combination of qualities we deem desirable: cool in summer/warm in winter; they serve warm cinnamon bagels with cream cheese and honey; and the loos are well stocked with hand cream. Plus their trump card, the aisles are too narrow for buggies, so it is delightfully child-free, meaning we can talk without yelling above the hubbub.

Jen rubs her stomach and pushes her empty plate to one side, 'Hmm, yum.' She starts rummaging in her cavernous bag for her purse. 'I have to dash soon to get the bus. I'll leave you the money for my share.' She pulls a crumpled leaflet from the depths and tries to smooth it out before thrusting it at me. 'Look, here, take this.'

Introductory Defibrillator Course, it reads. She's mentioned it before, warming us up to the idea. She's organising the training at the school where she's a teaching assistant. They are trying to raise interest – and funds – to install one.

'Say you'll do it! Seriously. It's a thing. Defibs are every-where these days,' she says. 'You see them in every phone box in the countryside.' She doesn't need to twist my arm; as soon as she mentions it I decide to donate some cash in Dad's memory.

The leaflet shows a diagram of a woman giving CPR to a dummy. 'Do you remember learning how to do it at Girl Guides?' I ask. 'Part of first-aid training? I wore my uniform all night afterwards to watch telly with Dad, hoping he'd notice my new badge.'

'I bet he was proud of you.'

'You know Dad. He couldn't just say "well done". He pretended to fall over on his way to the kitchen and rolled around on the floor shouting, "If only there was a first-aider in the house!"'

Jen snorts a laugh. 'I've never done CPR. It looks hard.'

'It's all right when you get the rhythm. And the dummies don't complain. Did you know, they call them Annie?'

'No?'

'That's what the Michael Jackson song is about. You know the one – "Annie are you okay?"' I sing a few lines doing my best impression of MJ. 'I can do the dance too.' That's a lie, but I tip an invisible trilby down over my eyes and make as if to get up from my seat. I'm willing to give it a go – it can't be that difficult. 'It's just an exaggerated Tennis Ball Rise coupled with a crotch grab.'

Jen holds her hand up to stop me and gives a hiccupping giggle, trying to swallow her last mouthful of coffee without spitting it out. 'Don't you dare do that at the training! I'll never be able to do the resuscitation if you make me laugh.'

It's then that I spot Leon. He is sitting across the café, his chair directly facing our table. Although he seems engaged in his newspaper, he is near enough to have heard our conversation and seen my performance had he been looking our way. *Oh my God. Did he see me acting the fool?* He's wearing

79

his usual suit and white shirt, immaculate as always, while I look like I spent the night on the streets. My curls are tumbling from a scrunchie, my face bare of make-up, my top the nearest thing to hand when I realised I was late to meet Jen. Thankfully my baggy tracksuit bottoms and trainers are now hidden beneath the table.

Jen's gathering her things. A kiss on the cheek and she heads for the exit, nearly colliding with Leon who has stood up to leave. He holds the door open for her, saying something I can't hear but I can tell she's flattered by the way she blushes and fiddles with the strap of her bag as she thanks him. He heads to the right, towards the car park. And Jen turns left for the bus stop, pausing at the window to mouth 'wow' at me with a nod towards his retreating back.

She is, of course, completely unaware of who he is.

That night, unable to sleep, I replay the scene: imagining Leon watching me act like the class clown; wondering whether he was flirting with Jen as she left; picturing how plain and unkempt I looked. Eventually, the sheets in a knot from my twisting and turning, I stop wallowing and use one of the therapy techniques I taught Leon to remove the emotion. I bleach out the colour from my memory of the scene, turning the café and all us customers pale sepia; change our voices so they are distorted like a slow-running recording; make the whole image a still snapshot, then shrink it and float it away into space ...

That's enough to get me off to sleep. But I wake some hours later when the pillow falls on the floor. I'm at the tail end of an unsettling dream in which Leon and Jen get married and I am one of a flock of bridesmaids in green dresses. I had pushed the wedding cake off the table.

★

Another couple of weeks pass and even though my diary is pretty full I still manage the odd visit to Bag a Bagel on the off chance I might bump into Leon. I'm curious as to how he's getting on; it would be nice to say hallo and have a quick update, see if he's still using any of the techniques I suggested.

When Clare suggests that she and I have an informal catch-up, I propose we meet there. She recently attended a conference on 'mental wealth' and thinks I might be interested in some of the material.

We're at our table deep in conversation, when the retro bell above the door tings, drawing my attention, and my heart lurches as I see it's him. He chooses a seat near the entrance and I rest my forehead on my hand, peering through my fingers to study him. He looks even lovelier, his hair slightly longer, the top button of his shirt open beneath his jacket. Clare is delivering a cynical soliloquy on the use of lucid dreaming as a therapy and I find it hard to focus, nodding in the right places. 'It takes months to train clients apparently,' she says. 'So unnecessary, when there are far quicker approaches available – but he was an enthusiastic young researcher and clearly thought it worthwhile. His paper …'

I'm juggling a far more immediate conundrum than the best trauma treatment: how to get Clare out of the café without her meeting Leon. Whilst I've been hoping to bump into him again in the café ever since the last time, my invitation for Clare to join me was clearly not thought through.

In the normal scheme of things it wouldn't matter, but I'm concerned about Leon saying something inappropriate, asking how my hand has healed or giving away something else I've avoided telling Clare. Or what if I catch him looking at me and start to blush? Or my behaviour doesn't seem natural and Clare puts two and two together? If Clare and I leave together, I could keep her engaged in conversation and ignore Leon as I march her past him. Or if he does speak to me, I can keep it to a brief 'good morning' or fudge the introductions, not mention his name. Or maybe it would be better if she left on her own – he wouldn't have a reason to speak to her … And then maybe I could go over and politely say hallo, ask how he's doing.

Best to concentrate on the discussion with Clare, ask some questions to show my interest, string the conversation out. Hopefully Leon will leave before us and the problem will disappear. 'I heard a programme on a similar theme a few days ago,' I say. 'What was the name of the speaker at the conference? It might have been the same guy.'

She laughs. 'Welcome back! You were miles away, day-dreaming. Which I suppose is a form of lucid dreaming.'

'Sorry. I was trying to remember the key points from the podcast.' I catch movement in the corner of my vision; Leon is at the cash desk talking to the young waitress. Thank goodness, he is leaving. There's a brief exchange and he returns to his seat. The waitress picks up the filter coffee pot and heads towards his table. She is around twenty, a very pretty brunette. Is she topping up his mug?

Clare follows my gaze and my stomach knots. 'Sorry. Distracted,' I say.

'Do you know him?' she asks, getting straight to the point, as always when she observes something unspoken.

'I …' My pause gives me away. 'I think he might be one of my old clients.'

'Hmm. And judging from your reaction I'm thinking there's some unfinished business between you. Maybe a topic for our next formal supervision?'

My reddening confirms her suspicions. 'Yes, that would

be good. It was a bit of a messy ending.' *Don't say any more. Don't dig a hole for yourself.*

At that point Leon gets up to leave. He must have been asking for his bill. I quickly lower my gaze, determined not to let him catch me looking.

A few days later Leon leaves me a phone message. 'I have a huge favour to ask. Could you call me to discuss, when you have a moment?'

Of course, I am hooked. Replaying the message, I listen for clues in his tone: there's a hint of warmth in the way he says 'call me to discuss', but is this negated by the business-like brevity? What could he possibly want? Another session or two couldn't be classed as 'a huge favour', neither could therapy for a friend, or a recommendation of helpful reading matter.

It's a couple of days before I feel controlled enough to phone him back, but I freeze and hang up when his mobile goes straight to voicemail. All evening I check for missed calls and fiddle distractedly with my mobile, making sure it hasn't dropped the signal, but he doesn't return the call. By ten o'clock I've downed the best part of a bottle of Pinot fantasising about where he might be, who he is with. Sensibly I decide it's time for bed and leave my phone downstairs so I'm not tempted to drunk-dial.

My curiosity is well and truly piqued by the time I get through to him on my fifth attempt, early the following evening.

'Leon. Hallo, it's Cristina,' I say. 'I got your message.' *Duh!* 'A statement of the bleeding obvious' as Dad would've said.

'Ah, yes. Thank you for calling me back. I appreciate that this is a huge favour but I don't know who else to ask.'

I steel myself, unsure what to expect. 'Carry on.' A therapist's response. *Lighten up!* 'I'm intrigued.'

He explains that he has tickets for a matinee and his usual theatre partner can't make it. 'My cousin, Sophie, usually joins me – she came with me to your performance. She's moved to Paris on business, leaving me with tickets for events booked months ahead. So I thought, who would be the one person I know who would appreciate theatre as much I do?'

My heart is pounding. 'I … I'm not sure—'

He cuts me off. 'I'd be delighted if you could join me. I know I'm putting you on the spot so let me give you the date and you can think about it. It's the matinee of *Hamlet* at the Globe.'

I write the date on the palm of my hand using the purple felt pen discarded on the sideboard – *23rd*. 'Thank you for asking me. I'll get back to you tomorrow. You understand that I—'

'Of course. We'll speak tomorrow.'

Hamlet, my all-time favourite play. At the Globe. A theatre I've always wanted to visit. It's as if he knows me better than Davy, better than Jen.

I check the date on my kitchen calendar: the 23rd is a Saturday – the Saturday the Middleford Players have set aside to discuss options for our next performance, do some initial read-throughs of possible plays. I'm hoping for one of the lead roles again.

A glance at the kitchen clock tells me I'm late for Quiz Night at the Lion. I'll postpone my decision until later when I get home.

★

At the pub the quiz has already started. The bar is full and there is such a good turnout in our corner they've divided us Wellies into two teams. Nisha has saved me a space next to her and I clamber over a pile of jackets and bags to squeeze in.

'No Mick tonight?' I ask, scanning the group and not seeing him.

'No, but we have "not-the-full-penny" Angie as a substitute.' Nisha nods towards Mick's ex at the other table. In the short time we've known her, Angie has become famed for her malapropisms and misquotes. According to Nisha's version of the story, Angie had announced their break-up saying: 'Don't tell the world and his oyster but Mick and me have split up.'

Jen pushes the team's Quiz Question Sheet towards me, along with a glass of wine. 'Are you any good at capital cities? We've only got three between us so far.'

I call to Ali across the table. 'Didn't you do geography at school?'

Ali flicks a V sign at me laughing. 'Your point being?'

I stretch both hands in front of me as if limbering up. 'Pass me the pen!'

As the evening progresses there are no signs of Angie's claimed 'break-up bruise', her laughter bouncing across the room. She seems to be getting on very well with Davy and Jake, mapping something out on the table using crisps and the drink mat; trying to throw peanuts into Jake's open mouth.

Davy looks relaxed, content; in his favourite place, surrounded by his favourite people, a pint in his hand. As Angie stands on the seat to climb across Jake's lap to get to the bar, Davy clocks me watching them and winks, his broad smile exposing his gappy front teeth, his cheeks rounded, his eyes crinkled almost shut. When he looks happy like that I can still see traces of the young lad I'd first fallen in love with. I once made the mistake of pointing it out to Nisha, how he sometimes looks like his younger self. Not being a romantic, she sarcastically observed, 'And at four stone heavier there's so much more of him to love.'

Surrounded by our friends, settling into familiar routines, jokes and stories, *contentment* feels a good place to be. But then, reaching for a handful of peanuts from Ali's open packet, I catch sight of *23rd* scribed on my palm and a wave of certainty spreads through me. There's still more I want, more adventures to be had.

I am going to say yes.

It's towards the end of my next supervision session at Clare's that she raises the subject of 'the man in the café'.

'There's one more topic on my list,' she says, looking at her notebook, which is more of a prop than a tool. She has an astounding memory. 'Let's spend the last five minutes discussing the man you described as "an old client". The rather good-looking man who held you spellbound in the café.'

'Okay.' Knowing Clare would see through any lies, I've not prepared an elaborate cover story.

'I'm going to go out on a limb here. Was that Leon?'

'Yes … He's an ex-client – you know I finished working with him a couple of months ago.'

She nods slowly, several times. 'The same Leon who bought you a personal gift. The one who you described as a fascinating man to work with. Whose grief you likened to your own father's when you were a child. The Leon who you were desperate to help.' I'd forgotten that I told Clare I found him fascinating. 'Answer this next question without too much forethought: how do you feel about him now?'

'I'm pleased we've stopped working together; it was getting a bit uncomfortable.' I pause and decide to be open. 'I'd become too emotionally attached to him. If I'm honest, I guess I looked forward to seeing him more than was healthy. That's one of the reasons I ended the therapy.'

'It's good that you can acknowledge that to yourself and to me. It's also a positive that you acted quickly to draw a line.' She studies me a moment and then asks, 'Did he ever mention a wife in any of the sessions with you?'

'No, he's not married. He always hoped Michelle would leave her husband for him, they planned to move away together.' She's triggered a flash memory of something Michelle had told me. 'Michelle and Leon wanted to go to Spain – he wanted to retire and live on a golf resort. She sent me a postcard from Spain sometime after we finished therapy. I assumed that meant she'd decided to move there to be with Leon.'

'But she wasn't with him when she died?'

'I could be wrong. As we agreed, I've not reread Michelle's file so I'm going from memory ... Maybe they just went there for a quick holiday?'

'Possibly. It can take years sometimes to act on a decision, as you well know.' She's referring to me and Davy; she knows all about the extended running down of our relationship before our eventual divorce. How we still bounce back to each other when we're lonely.

'Maybe she was comfortable with her husband – better the devil you know? Or couldn't afford to leave?' I shrug a 'who knows'. 'It's irrelevant now. What makes you ask if Leon has a wife?'

'He was wearing a wedding ring.'

I sit up straight – how have I not noticed this? 'Are you sure? I know he doesn't live with anyone now. Maybe it's a memento of Michelle – something she gave him.'

'Could be.'

The dull buzz of Clare's intercom signals the arrival of her next appointment and, responding like Pavlov's dogs, we both stand up. She presses a button to let the person into the hallway downstairs.

At the door to her apartment she gives me a hug and says, 'Be careful, Cris.'

Clare is the closest I've ever had to a mother figure and I take her comments as the protective concerns of a parent. But she can rest easy: while Leon is no longer my client, I don't imagine a romantic relationship with him, now or in the future. A supportive friendship will be more than enough.

Chapter Eight

It's the Saturday before the matinee with Leon. I've bribed Nisha into coming clothes shopping with me in exchange for helping her prepare a menu for a dinner party she's planning for some of our crowd next weekend. She knows I'll have to miss it because I'm not sure when I'll be back from the theatre trip, but I've been vague about who I'm going with. She assumes it is one of my colleagues from the Middleford Players, which is fine for now.

'Yes, but is it a *date*?' she asks. She's sorting through the racks of clothes in the department store looking for inspiration.

'No, he has a spare ticket and thought I'd like it. That's all.'

'So why the new outfit?'

'Have you seen my wardrobe lately? It's all pjs and sweat pants. Anyway, people dress up these days – I need something halfway decent to go to the theatre.'

She holds up a bodycon dress. 'This is your style. You may as well work your curves since you've got them.'

'Okay, I'll try it on. Grab me a size fourteen and a sixteen in navy.'

By the time we leave I've bought the fitted dress, a pair of cream and navy heels, a matching handbag, and an emergency loose frock in case I'm having a fat day.

'You'll be the bee's knees,' Nisha says. And the unexpected mention of bees leads to Davy and brings with it a strange pang of guilt.

Leon collects me for our trip to London in his BMW. He opens the door for me and helps with the seat belt, in the same way I would help Davy's mum, and I'm not sure whether to feel patronised or cared for. The bucket seat is fairly low, which means that my legs are at an awkward angle, exaggerated by the height of the heels on my new shoes, and the tight stretch fabric of the fitted dress pulls up my thighs, exposing my knees. There's a ring of it bunched up, clinging to my tummy in an unflattering way and, with little success, I try to tug it looser before Leon settles in the driver's seat next to me.

His car is of course spotless and I'm relieved he's never seen mine; Jen calls it a waste bin on wheels. It only gets emptied when the chocolate wrappers and water bottles threatened to overspill the footwells. And Leon's car smells *clean*, not like those artificial tree-shaped car fresheners that Davy hangs in his truck.

As he drives, Leon holds the steering wheel with both hands perfectly placed at twenty to four. He isn't wearing a ring on either hand so Clare must've been mistaken, which is a relief. It's complicated enough without an ex in the picture. It's strange to be with him in this context, where I don't have a clear role to play. Whilst I know him well as his therapist, I don't know him as a friend and it's hard to introduce topics of conversations that don't sound too inquisitive or trite.

'How's Sophie settling in?' I ask as he takes a turning onto the A1.

'Who?'

'Your cousin, in Paris.'

'Oh, yes.' He checks the wing mirror before changing

lane. 'I assume she's fine. Haven't heard anything from her, which is always a good sign.'

He clicks a button and classical music fills the car, the volume sufficient that we don't have to engage in any more small talk. Beethoven apparently.

Eventually Leon pulls into a numbered bay in an under-ground car park at the Barbican Estate and we sit there as Leon waits for the crescendo of Beethoven's fifth. With his eyes closed I have time to study him, see the few small bristles that he's missed when tidying his designer beard, the slight pulse in his temple, the delicate curve of his ear. I look away quickly as he sits upright, turns the electrics off and sudden silence fills the car.

'My friend lives here,' he says, although I haven't asked. 'Very convenient for me when I come into town.' He pockets his keys and reaches for the door handle. 'Nearly there.'

From the moment the play begins – *Who's there?* – all my self-consciousness evaporates and I'm completely absorbed. The wooden outdoor stage, just as it would have been in Shakespeare's day; the costumes and scenery understated, al-lowing the dialogue and the actors to fill the space. Hamlet's emotions played with subtlety, Ophelia's descent into mad-ness a counterbalance. We are in Act Two and Rosencrantz and Guildenstern have just arrived at the palace, when I am drawn back to reality by Leon's hand on my forearm. His touch is so light, almost a caress, and I can't be sure if my skin rises in goosebumps because of the chill in the air or the gentleness of his fingers.

'You're cold,' he whispers, wrapping his suit jacket around my shoulders. 'I'm sorry. I should have warned you to bring a wrap.'

'Thanks.' I smile my appreciation, then turn my attention back to the stage but I can feel his eyes on me.

'You've been mouthing the lines.' He is watching my lips and, self-conscious, I clamp them shut, hoping my lipstick can stand up to such close study and he doesn't notice the fine lines that have started developing above my upper lip. He sweeps his forefinger across my cheek as one might do to a child, but it seems to briefly linger at the side of my mouth. 'Relax. It's sweet.'

I attempt a casual laugh, but I am melting inside.

It's during the interval that his mood changes. We've just collected our pre-ordered drinks when a fat, balding man in a suit comes over and shakes hands with Leon.

'I thought it was you. Saw you on the way in but lost you in the crush.' His voice booms; well spoken, like Leon, and I wonder if he is another academic. 'What happened about the German project? Did you manage to salvage anything? Will you still be able to exhibit?'

Since Leon hasn't introduced me, and the other man hasn't even acknowledged my presence, it seems a good time to find the toilets. I put my hand on Leon's arm to get his attention. 'Excuse me, I'll be back in a minute.'

I may misread his reaction, be oversensitive, but he appears to shrug me off without an acknowledgement, turning his back on me as if to shut me out. When I return five minutes later the fat man is nowhere to be seen. And Leon's good mood has departed with him.

We leave sharply at the end of the play and it isn't until we have started for home in the car that Leon defrosts.

'I'm sorry if I appeared rude,' he says. 'My colleague was

92

inappropriate. I don't like to mix work with pleasure and some people don't get the message.'

'That's okay. Is he a colleague of yours at the college?'

'I don't like to mix work with pleasure,' he repeats, his tone friendly but firm, closing off any further enquiry. 'Let's talk of happier things. What did you think of the production?'

We discuss the performance the whole journey back. He asks my opinion of the lead actors, what I think of the set and how it worked for the performers, whether there is anything I might change if I were directing, who I would cast as Hamlet given the choice of every actor past and present. When he comments that I'd make 'a lovely Ophelia', I find myself telling him about parts I've played, my corporate training videos, my hand modelling – it all comes out. I even confess my dream of being a professional stage actor, a dream I've finally accepted isn't to be.

'You carried the play I saw you in at Middleford,' he says. 'You have huge talent; we just need to find you an opportunity. You're wasted on these bits and pieces.'

'You're too kind,' I say. My face glows; I've registered the 'we'.

He pulls up outside my house and all my previous thoughts of inviting him in for a coffee disappear. In the familiar environment of my lounge and kitchen, we'll switch back into our previous roles of therapist/client and the day would be spoilt.

'Thank you, Leon. It was a lovely afternoon.'

'So you will accompany me again?' he asks. 'It's not the same watching a performance on one's own; so much better if there is someone to share the pleasure.'

Butterflies dancing inside, I say, 'But next time you must allow me to pay for the ticket.'

He smiles. 'Sweet dreams, Ophelia.'

★

I'm going to Jen's for our girls' night in. Jim's out with his mates so Jen's home with the dog, a loyal mangey old Labrador that doesn't like to be left alone for too long. A bit like Jim, Nisha says. She would have joined us but she's out on a second date with one of her online dating catches.

A search of the kitchen cupboard turns up an unopened bottle of sweet sherry that I 'won' in the Santa Swap at some point; a ritual where all the Wellies palm off their unwanted Christmas gifts on each other. That was years ago, but while there is no use-by date I'm not sure anyone would voluntarily drink it. Apart from that, the only wine in the house is half a bottle of Chardonnay in the door of the fridge. I'm not sure either are an ideal contribution to the evening.

On the way over to Jen's house, I stop at Tesco. Browsing the white wines, looking for something medium dry, I'm distracted by Davy's voice from the next aisle.

'Nah, not that stuff. It's weak as gnat's piss.' Davy's opinion on the required strength of his beer is as firm as on the strength of his tea − a glass/mug of 'gnat's' being the worst designation.

I seek him out in the beer area and there he is − with Angie, a six-pack of the despised lager clutched in her boxercise-muscled arms.

'Hey Davy, look it's Chrissy,' she says, as if introducing us for the first time, getting my name wrong in the process. 'Sorry we beat you guys at the quiz. It's a doggy dog world!'

'No worries.'

'Just getting some beers,' Davy says. His expression reminds me of the time he got caught sneaking Pick'n'Mix from Woolworths back in the day. So vulnerable I want to hug him. 'Her car's got a flat so I drove her.'

'We're going to watch the footy. West Ham at home,'

94

Angie says. She's returned the beers to the shelf, points to a box of Kronenbourg. 'What about this?'

'Got to dash,' I say. Then, to signal to Davy there are no hard feelings, 'Have a good evening. See you both Friday at the Lion.'

Driving to Jen's I ponder how good they look together.

Of course, Davy turns up at my house the next day. We know each other too well.

'I was going to tell you,' he says. 'It's not really anything. She just asked me about the footy and I said I'd got Sky.'

'It's okay, hon.' I place a mug of builder's tea in front of him. 'We're not married any more.'

'Yeah, but I know you don't like people messing you about. I wouldn't do that. You know that, Cris.'

Messing you about, a catch-all shorthand for a partner flirting, seeing someone behind your back, having an affair.

'Davy, you have never messed anyone about. You don't have it in you.' He couldn't lie to me if he wanted to – that's one of the many reasons I love him.

It takes me half an hour to reassure him that, whatever happens, we will always be 'the best of mates' – he was never one for the L★★★ word.

'You know you're my number one,' he says, as he leaves with my blessing to pursue whatever kind of relationship he wants with Angie.

'You too. Always.' And I mean it.

A week passes and I hear nothing from Leon. It's like being a teenager again: the fizzing excitement when the phone rings followed by bitter disappointment when it's not Him; the hours spent staring into space willing Him to call, before the ritual 'how dare he treat me like this' and the resolute decision to Forget Him For Ever. Repeat …

Despite recognising this childish pattern, when Leon does call to invite me to an art gallery for a 'Private View', I forget all my qualms and jump at the chance.

'Sorry, it's so tedious,' he says. I've forgotten how deep and sexy his voice is, like honey dripping from a spoon. 'I have a plus-one invite and, if you will do me the honour of being my partner, I will take you to dinner afterwards.'

It's only once I hang up I realise this is definitely 'a date'.

What have I done?

I stare at myself in the hall mirror, my hands clamped to my cheeks. I am flushed, heady with excitement and guilt. My professional head tells me to call him back immediately to cancel. You can't go, you really can't. You CANNOT date a client.

But … This is all so exciting, such a change from my usual routine.

I negotiate with myself: nothing untoward has happened yet. I will go on this date in order to get to know Leon better, just the once to see how we get on. That is all. I am merely accompanying him to an art gallery. As a female friend.

Ahead of me and Leon, the people in the queue are undergoing bag checks and handing in coats and jackets. I've borrowed a black boiled-wool wrap from Nisha, which looks sophisticated and stylish with my black strappy sandals. It's what's underneath that concerns me. I've followed online advice and gone with 'kooky art school': a blue polka dot 1950s-style frock, acquired from Mavis in Wardrobe. Looking around, most people are wearing posh suits or little black dresses, while I am togged up like an extra from *Westside*

Story. Taking off my wrap I blush as Leon surveys my outfit, his face expressionless.

'You forgot the exotic bloom in your hair.'

Unsure how to take that comment, I laugh rather loudly, but he's already moved on, leading the way through the first of several galleries.

I assumed he knew one of the artists, that this was indeed 'an honour' To be invited as one of their personal guests. But it turns out the whole invite was a misnomer – it is neither private, nor can you view much for the hordes of people that are crowding the space. The path only clears when one of the waiting staff sail past with a drinks tray or canapés, everyone trailing in their wake like seagulls following a ship.

As we manoeuvre our way through the rooms, a woman hails Leon over but he shakes his head, mouthing something and she laughs, throwing her head back, raising her glass. Flipped into schoolgirl thinking, I assume the exchange is about me – imagining he is embarrassed to be with me, that they'll have a joke about it at the college in days to come. 'What was she wearing? Did she think it was fancy dress?'

But meanwhile Leon has moved on again. He appears to be on a mission, weaving through the clusters of people, only nodding to acknowledge greetings but never stopping to talk. I try to reason with myself as I trail behind him: he invited me to be his 'plus-one', he can't be that uncomfortable to be seen with me.

The waiter is just leaving Gallery 10 as we arrive, his tray fairly full. Leon removes two glasses of wine, passing one to me.

'Lose the hoi polloi. Always head for the furthest gallery and work backwards.'

'A good strategy,' I say.

He reads the signage on the wall then surveys the room. 'Hmm. Photorealism.'

I step closer to read the explanatory text. 'Gosh. I thought they were photos but they're paintings! They're so realistic.'

He laughs. 'Hence the term photorealism. It was very popular in the late 1960s and early seventies, after the Pop Art phase – Warhol and his ilk. You'll have seen the soup cans and Marilyn I'm sure. This is what came next.' He gestures theatrically to the framed pictures around us.

'They're amazing.' I study a lifelike portrait of an elderly woman, every wrinkle brought to life. She has kindly crinkled eyes, the brown pupils rimmed with the blue of old age, just like Dad's. 'Look at her eyes, they seem to follow you.'

Leon comes to stand behind me, bending down to see what I see as I move from side to side. He is so close the warmth of his breath is like a kiss on my bare shoulder as he speaks. 'It's the steadiness of the gaze. A phenomena that's named after Mona Lisa herself.'

'Oh yes, I read about that,' I say, eager to make an intelligent contribution. 'The *Mona Lisa* is actually one of the portraits that's an exception.' He takes a step back from me and I turn to face him, warming to my theme. 'They've researched it and found she's looking too far to the right for it to work. Something like that … It's to do with the angle of the gaze.' My explanation peters out as Leon's expression momentarily changes, a flash of anger in his frown?

'Have you actually been to the Louvre? Have you seen the work itself, not just a copy in a magazine? If not …' He catches himself mid-sentence and takes a deep breath, as if suddenly aware of the curtness of his tone. 'If not, you really must go sometime. Yes.' He nods, smiling at me, charm itself. 'Have a chance to appreciate the original. It's worth it.'

'Yes, that would be good,' I say. 'One day.' But I feel like a precocious child that's overstepped the mark, embarrassed by my vain attempts to impress him, the expert in the field.

He gestures towards the next gallery. 'Come, let's move on to work with more creativity. Other than its technical ability, this work has little merit. These artists are no Gerhard Richter. I want to show you one of my favourite pieces.'

We leave soon after.

The restaurant is nearby, for which I am grateful as the ankle straps on my sandals are starting to rub and Leon is marching at quite a pace. This isn't like our theatre trip where we were in my environment, where I knew the play and had the expertise to hold up my end of the conversation. In the art gallery, surrounded by his colleagues from the college, I've been conscious of my lack of knowledge and felt out of my depth all evening.

Leon asks a waitress to escort me to the table while he hangs back to speak to a black-suited man who I assume is the head waiter, a small, rounded chap a bit like Hercule Poirot. I have plenty to distract myself while I wait: everything about this place looks costly, from the wall art and the metre-high exotic flower arrangements, to the other diners who are all smartly turned out.

When Leon returns he is in a good mood again. He seems to know the place well as he waves away the waiter proffering menus and places an order for us both. 'A bottle of the Château Pape, 2009. Sparkling mineral water. Seafood platter for two. No bread.'

'Can I confirm if madam has any allergies?' The waiter asks.

Leon looks across at me and raises his eyebrows. 'You do eat shellfish?'

'Yes. I love it.'

'Good. So do I. Their seafood platter is the best in town.'

The waiter finishes fussing with the candles and leaves us alone, but Leon seems lost in thought and there is a slight uncomfortable pause before I ask, 'Is this somewhere you come often?'

'I used to. With Michelle.'

'Oh, I—'

'I like it here. The food is good. I'm sure you'll enjoy it.'

I look around the place, imagining them here on their dates, knowing they'd be safe from prying eyes in the bustle of central London. They could have sat at this very table. Leon gives me a stern-parent look as the waiter arrives with water and wine and I realise I've been fiddling with the cutlery, a nervous habit. I lower my hand to my lap, sit straighter in my chair. I've always been a fidget. I use my hands to communicate like an Italian; Dad used to say if I sat on my hands I wouldn't be able to talk. It crosses my mind to share this with Leon, tell him about my therapy training; how I eventually mastered the ten-minute practice sessions where we were taught to sit perfectly still and just be present. But I say nothing, uncertain if it would sound childish or paint me in a bad light.

The wine poured, Leon raises his glass to mine, a warm smile back on his face. 'To plans for the future.'

'The future.'

He rolls the wine around his glass, studying it in the light like I've seen wine buffs do on TV. As he takes a sip I watch his lips, imagining their softness, what they would be like to kiss. Placing the glass back on the table he looks directly at me and I worry that he's noticed my stare. 'Tell me,' he says, 'what are your dreams for the future? What plans do you have?'

An image comes to mind that I can't voice. *Don't blush. Let it go. Focus.*

'Well ... I'd quite like a holiday this summer, if my friend Nisha can get time off work. I didn't get away last year ... And I'd like to build up my therapy practice. I'm considering branching out a bit, doing a course in drama therapy so I can use my acting experience.' I shouldn't have mentioned therapy. 'And you?'

'Hmm. I want to look up some old friends. There are some people I've lost touch with over the past year. With everything going on, you understand.'

Old friends. I wonder if they are ex-girlfriends.

When it arrives, the seafood platter requires rather more complicated cutlery than I'm used to. An array of tools are set out by the tray, the fish itself displayed on ice like at the fishmonger's, scattered with sprigs of herbs and halves of lemon wrapped in gauze at either end. The waiter talks through the spread then proceeds to serve us both. I watch Leon closely to see which implements to use and how. His hands deftly manipulate crab shells and lobster claws as I clumsily copy.

'Like this,' he says, his attention drawn by the clatter of metal on ceramic as I drop the tool I was using to wrestle the meat from a crab's leg. 'It's a knack. Pass me your lobster claw and I'll crack it for you.'

'My dad used to take me for shellfish at Southend when I was small,' I say as I watch his hands move with firm precision. 'There used to be a seafood shack near the pier and he'd buy a tub of prawns and we'd eat them on the beach. The smell of shellfish still reminds me of holidays.'

Leon dips the tips of his fingers in a bowl of tepid water

to rinse them, dabbing them dry with his napkin. 'You never mention your mother.'

'She left us, when I was young.'

'When did you last see her?'

'I was eight years old. We didn't stay in touch.'

'Tell me,' he says gently, his expression soft and concerned.

'Mum was meant to collect me from a schoolfriend's party but she didn't turn up.' I've told this story many times, polished it into a suitable anecdote for public consumption. 'I was left sitting there with the fractious party girl and her equally fed-up mother. It was long before mobile phones, of course, so it took a while to get a message to my dad to come and fetch me. I never saw my mum again.'

'That's very sad.'

'At the time I was more upset that I'd let go of my helium balloon. I didn't understand what was going on. That she'd left us.' I can still see the balloon bobbing around the ceiling of the village hall. In my mind's eye it's pink and the string hangs just beyond my grasp. But that can't be true, else one of the adults would have reached it for me.

'I was sent to stay with some friends of my dad's. By the time they took me back to our house, there was no sign of Mum anywhere. Her clothes and jewellery, everything, had gone. My dad had even removed all the framed photos. Years later I found out he'd destroyed the family photo albums too.'

'Do you know where your mother is now?' I shake my head and he asks, 'Don't you want to find her?'

'I've not really thought about it. Dad would probably have disowned me if I'd tried. He cut off all contact with that side of the family when she left and we never heard from any of them again.'

'But aren't you curious? Wouldn't you like to get to know her if she's alive? Find out how her life turned out?'

I shrug. 'I would never have considered it while Dad was alive ...' An unexpected wave of sadness sweeps through me – of course, I've wanted to know. I've wanted answers all my life. Wanted to find her and ask why. Before I can get too maudlin, I force the actress in me to the fore and bluff: 'She's not been part of my life for over forty years, so it's not as if I miss her.'

'Yes. Missing someone. That's the key to heartbreak.' And I know he is thinking of Michelle.

When Leon selects a cheese course for us both without consulting the menu, I wonder how often he must have come here with Michelle. Is he comparing us? Would she have given insightful comments about the art exhibition as she dextrously tackled her lobster? Would they have had a stimulating debate, Michelle holding her own as she defended *photorealism* against his critique, while I don't even know how to frame the questions? I must seem so shallow in comparison when all I've managed to contribute is childhood anecdotes. My wine seems to be disappearing faster than the waiter is topping it up and I fiddle with the stem, hoping he will spot that my glass is empty.

Leon reaches across the table and places his hand over mine, which appears an affectionate gesture until I realise he's stilling my nervous movements. His long slim fingers are cool to my skin.

'I can see why you were a hand model.' He strokes my palm, his fingertips tracing my lifeline before turning my hand over and holding it in both of his. 'Such beautifully shaped fingers.'

My pulse quickens at his touch, my imagination taking things further.

'Let me treat you to a professional manicure next time.'

He places my hand back on the table, turning to summon the waiter. 'A dessert wine for the lady. Not too sweet. I'll have a port.' He pauses seeing my expression, raises his eyebrows. 'You'll have a dessert wine?'

'Thank you, yes. That would be lovely.' I move my hands to my lap, too late to hide my Midnight Blue nail polish that I smeared by putting my shoes on before it was dry.

The waiter brings the bill in a leather wallet, which he places in front of Leon, and I grapple with my handbag, an idiotically small thing with a twiddly clasp, trying to reach my purse. Whether I can afford a place like this Lord knows, but I'm still intent on paying my half.

Leon waves away my credit card. 'No need – it's covered. I hope you enjoyed the food.'

'It's been a lovely evening,' I lie. Next time, if there is a next time, I'll do some work on my nerves beforehand, ensure I can relax and not make a fool of myself again.

And maybe double-check the dress code.

Chapter Nine

'Hey, where were you last night? I popped over to see you.' It's Jen on the phone, the morning after the art gallery trip with Leon.

'Out with some of the acting crowd. Shame I missed you.' Much as I'd normally love to give Jen a blow-by-blow account of the evening, I can imagine the look she'd give me if she knew Leon was once my client. She's perfected her 'Disappointed Mum' expression over the years, practising on her kids, and isn't afraid to turn the cold laser eyes on us. No, until it's more certain that there's any kind of future, I plan to keep this secret.

'When can we meet up?'

The following Saturday we end up at an 'almost new' sale at the Assembly Hall. We're good at this; having grown up with jumble sales we both have an eye for colour and fabric, diving into the piles of clothing to extract an item that is just right for one or other of us.

'Any good?' I hold up a pale pink summer top, Jen's favourite colour. She grabs it from me to add to her stash, the items hanging over her arm all shades of pink.

'Hey look!' Jen points with her free hand towards a stall near the exit. A homemade banner above reads: 'Costume jewellery by the kilo'.

'What's not to love?'

The woman hands us small plastic bags to fill with what we want and we happily scour the piles of necklaces, bangles and brooches, not being overly fussy given how cheap they are.

I hold up a dark green necklace against my face. 'What do you think? Does it go with my colouring?' I'm not usually a green person.

Jen nods her approval and passes me some earrings that as good as match. I end up buying them both and a selection of necklaces in different lengths and colours, hoping I'll have plenty of opportunity to wear them over the coming months. Not bad for under a tenner.

'Why do you sign yourself *Cris*?' Leon asks. We've just entered the British Museum where he wants to show me some specific artefacts.

It's two weeks after the Private View and our third social event together. I insisted on paying for the tickets this time and his comment is prompted by seeing my full name on my bank card. After our previous outings I sent him thank you emails, my sign-off – *Yours, Cris* – a conscious decision. I need to separate the 'me' he is getting to know from the person who has been his therapist.

'It's what my friends call me. That or Cristy.'

'Cristina is much prettier. More feminine. Is it a family name? It's an unusual spelling.'

'Dad chose it. He thought it looked Spanish. He always wanted to go to Spain but never got much further than Southend.'

'And you? Have you been to Spain?'

'Only to Palma in Majorca.'

'Interesting history, but you picked *the* major tourist spot in Mallorca,' he says. He pronounces it mah-lyawr-kah and

I rehearse it in my head to ensure I get it right next time. 'There are still some beautiful places in the Balearics that are well off the beaten track. And on the mainland the mountain villages are largely unspoilt.'

He's never mentioned Spain before; that was something Michelle had told me. Their dreams of retirement there. But now he's brought the subject up, I feel free to explore it. 'You seem to know Spain well,' I say.

'Some areas, yes. Michelle and I travelled there. She was fluent in Spanish.'

'Ah, of course.' So she's here with us again. 'Golfing resorts, wasn't it?'

He smiles as if I've said something funny. Another mispronunciation? 'Ah yes. One of many different places.'

It doesn't take long for memories of Michelle to be dispelled. Here in the museum Leon is in his element, naturally falling into the role of educator, while I am genuinely curious to understand and discover.

Together we look at hand axes, spear points and chopping tools housed in glass cases. He explains to me about the Clovis people – the ancestors of modern Native Americans – and the tools found in the Olduvai valley that are over a million years old.

He steers us to another room. 'You'll recognise this game,' he says. We are standing by a display of carved chess pieces.

'The queen looks a bit fed up,' I say without thinking. Does that sound stupid? It looks like her crown is too heavy for her, the way she's resting her chin on her hand, mouth pulled down with the grumps. I don't say that bit out loud.

'So she should be. She had little power in the medieval version. Unlike today when she's the most powerful piece on the board. It's my favourite game. Do you play?'

I shake my head and he laughs. 'Maybe a good thing. The French say you can't play chess if you are kind-hearted. Like war, you need strategy and a killer instinct to win.'

When we break for a coffee he suggests we share a cake. Cupping my chin with one hand he feeds me most of his half with his fork and it is a strangely intimate and sensual experience.

'Come, Cristina, there's another treasure I want to show you. My favourite in the whole museum.' He holds out his crooked elbow towards me and I link arms with him, resisting the urge to snuggle close, not wanting to misread the runes.

He leads me to a display case holding a small grey-beige stone. 'What do you see?' he asks.

It doesn't look like anything much to me. It's nothing like the tools we saw earlier and I can't see any obvious purpose it might have. If you saw it lying on the ground you wouldn't look twice. Standing behind me, Leon places his hands on my upper arms, gentle but firm, and a thrill runs through me. He moves me to a position where I can see the object directly from the side.

'It is not just a pebble you are looking at,' he says. 'Soften your gaze and look again.'

He carefully lifts my hair, bunching it in his hand, then lowers his head towards my ear and whispers so no one around us can hear, 'Look carefully and you will see.' He gives me a moment to study the piece but I am too aware of his closeness. 'It's a carving of two naked people.' The warmth of his breath on my neck, the smell of mint on his breath, his familiar cologne, seem to flood my brain. 'See their foreheads pressed together ... their arms and legs wrapped around each other ... They are entwined in an embrace, making love ... an embrace that locks them together ... together, for ever.' Flustered and hot, I distract myself by reading the text beside the case, *Ain Sakhri Lovers Figurine, 9,000 years BCE.* Leon continues explaining, his voice, slow and deep, almost hypnotic. 'Look closely, Cristina, and imagine the man who carved this, his thoughts as he worked.'

I let his voice wash over me as he shows me how the carving takes on different forms from different angles, looking like parts of the human body: 'penis, breast, vagina'. The words those of a biology lesson but somehow, from his lips, whispered so close in this dry, sterile museum, they are incredibly erotic.

I move my hand to my throat. I want him to kiss my neck, to touch my cheek, to hold me to him – anything that would signal that he feels the same way. But he lets go of my hair and I take a deep breath to calm the feelings building inside me. Whilst the figurine itself has left me distinctly underwhelmed, I am uncomfortably aroused by Leon.

'Enough for today?' he asks. *Oh my God.* He must know what he's just done; has to be able to see the state I'm in? 'I'll show you the Maya Relief another time.'

'You are positively glowing!' Nisha says as I arrive for drinks on Friday. 'You've either started drinking kefir or you've met someone. Spill the beans.'

'I am seeing someone, actually.'

She widens her eyes dramatically. 'Duh! How come I'm the last to know?' She turns to Jen, accusing. 'Why didn't you tell me?'

Jen shakes her head. '*I* didn't know!'

'Whoa, slow down. It's not serious. We've only been on a few dates so far.'

'I can't believe you didn't tell us. What's his name? What dating site did you use?'

'When do we get to meet him?' Jen asks.

You already have. 'I need to know if it's actually going anywhere first. He's quite private. Don't say anything to Davy yet.'

'Scouts' honour,' Nisha says, saluting.

'Cross my heart.' Jen holds both hands to her chest, concluding the ritual pact we've jokingly followed for every shared secret since our teenage years.

'Remember, I know where you live,' I laugh. 'It's my round. What do you want to drink?'

Returning from the pub later, slightly tipsy, I pour myself another glass of wine and take my iPad up to my bedroom. Settling on my bed, curtains closed, a candle lit, I nestle against the pillows to get comfortable. I google the Ain Sakhri Lovers and stare at the image, conjuring up the memory of Leon. He lifts my hair, whispers in my ear; the warmth of his body so close to mine, the musk undertone of his cologne; the sensuality and command in his voice; us as voyeurs of the entwined lovers ... the melting inside ...

The next day, happy and hungover, I sift the evidence that Leon feels the same way, sorting through his words and behaviour for confirmation. I replay the visit to the museum, the previous two trips. Hanging on the intensity of a look, those times when his eyes lock with mine as if wanting to see my soul. The questions he asks me, showing an interest in everything that makes me 'me'. The sensual way he touches my arm, my face, my hands. His references to 'we', his toasts to the future. It seems plain to see: he wants a relationship as much as me. He is just taking it slowly, getting to know me properly.

I allow myself to indulge in fantasies of a future together

– to play with the idea that I might, finally, have found the man who wants to share adventures with me. That this could be the first step into the exciting new life I've dreamed of. But then the sane part of me pours cold water on the whole idea. *He was your client.*

His dead lover was your client.

Leon. Leon and Michelle.

My thoughts dart off down another dark alley. He knew all about the Ain Sakhri Lovers, knew where they were in the museum, described them as his favourite piece. Had he shared that same experience with Michelle? After the art exhibition, the restaurant we went to, he told me they used to go there. How many of our dates have been a replay of experiences he had with Michelle?

Is this just his way of keeping her alive, living it all again through me?

Once again he doesn't contact me all week. I am determined not to phone him; we are not in a relationship and realistic-ally we may never be. However, by the following Saturday my resolve crumbles. The weather is glorious so I use it as an excuse to get in touch, inviting him for a pub lunch in the countryside. A venue I know he will not have been to with Michelle: the Fox and Hounds, which purports to have *legendary* fine ale and ploughman's lunches.

Over lunch Leon asks about my 'relationship history' and I end up telling him about the years Davy and I were to-gether, how young we were when we met and got married. I mention that we've been divorced for years now, but leave out details of the on-off nature of our relationship since then and the men I dated in between. I don't tell him that I've never been on my own for more than a month, always had a boyfriend. Or Davy.

When I mention that Davy is still one of my closest friends, he seems surprised. 'You're still in touch with your ex-husband?'

'Yes. In fact I see him most Fridays, at the pub, with my other old school friends. He's got a new girlfriend I think.'

'Doesn't that feel strange to you? Him being with another woman?'

I laugh. 'In some ways, but a lot of time's passed and we've both dated other people since we were married. We're not the same people we were when we got together at fourteen.'

He asks to see a photo of Davy. The one on my phone is a group shot of the Wellies in the Lion. It was taken around Christmastime, everyone sporting the most ridiculous novelty jumpers – another tradition. Passing the phone to Leon, I explain the unusual dress sense of my friends.

'That's Davy.' Seeing him through Leon's eyes, I realise that Davy appears quite ungainly, the combination of the thick woolly and his rounded tummy not doing him any favours. His gappy smile and balding head make him look older than his years. 'He doesn't get as much exercise as he should, but he used to play a lot of football.'

'And the others? Did you all go to school together?'

'Most of us. There are a few honorary Wellies.' I point out certain people in the group even though I don't expect him to remember the names. It's nice that he's interested in getting to know my friends.

He enlarges the image, focusing on Jen. 'She looks familiar,' he says. 'Good bone structure.'

My stomach flips. *I knew it. He had noticed her in the café.* 'Do you have a picture of Michelle?' I ask, taking my phone back.

'Of course. But you know what she looks like.' He turns on his mobile and as it comes to life she's there – his screen saver. She is posed against a white wall, her long platinum hair parted on the side, highlighted with several tones of blonde, the ends curling over her bare right shoulder. Her lips are parted slightly and her teeth have that whiteness only achieved by bleaching. I know she was approaching forty but she looks younger: her forehead wrinkle free – Botox? – her eyebrows tinted, make-up immaculate. High-maintenance.

He flicks through, showing me several more images, holding the phone up so I can see rather than passing it to me to hold. Petite but curvy, a chest too large for her figure, probably implants. A figure she clearly liked to show off with tight-fitting clothes; although, curiously, always high-necked and below the knee. An illusion of modesty. A woman who would attract male attention.

If she is Leon's type, he won't be interested in me for long. I suck in my tummy, pull back my shoulders.

'You remember her,' he says, a statement not a question.

I nod. I can visualise her now. And with that memory comes a sense that I hadn't liked her. But I still can't recall much about her case beyond the hints on the cover of her folder – *relationship issues* and *difficult decisions*.

'She looks familiar but it was some years ago now and I see a lot of clients. Remind me what it was she did for a living?'

He laughs. 'She was a kept woman, didn't have to work! Not stupid, mind you … She read a lot.'

'Hmm. She was interested in photography. You taught her, didn't you? She was so good at posing for the photos she must've understood lighting.' *Did that sound snide? You cannot possibly be jealous of a dead woman.* 'She seems to know how to stand, like a model.'

He closes his phone, his mood suddenly changed. It's so easy to upset him when talking about Michelle that I try to avoid it, but it's clear he thinks about her a lot. Her ghost always seems to come along for the ride. We finish our coffees and go our separate ways soon after, with a standard kiss on the cheek and vague murmurings of 'speaking before Friday'. Leon has proposed a cinema trip, a new French film; hopefully with subtitles.

It is only later that evening, back at home, that I realise what has been nagging me about the photos. While the jealous part of me was caught up with assessing her beauty, the therapist side of me has noticed something else.

She was smiling in every photo, but she didn't look happy, her eyes blankly focused on the' camera. It was all quite staged.

I pour myself a large glass of wine and take it through to the front room along with the bottle. My curiosity is roused. I sit on the sofa and stare hard at the chair she would have occupied when she came for therapy here in this room, trying to conjure her up. What do I recall about her?

A people-pleaser. Or am I inventing that, reading a need for approval, a need for attention, into the way she dressed? I sip my wine as I try to remember; picture her arriving late for sessions, cancelling at short notice, full of apologies and excuses, too gushy, too fake for my liking – is that true? Some clients are hard to bond with at first, particularly if they're not committed to therapy. And sometimes they don't want to work on their problems, just talk about them, hoping you can magic them away without them putting in any effort to change. Maybe we didn't bond. But then, when I think of the postcard I have a sense of warmth towards her; maybe I did grow to like her, had helped her in the end. Certainly a degree of gratitude is implied by her making the effort to send a card after the therapy had finished.

But these things are peripheral to my real concerns. I'm not really interested in my emotional reactions to her – it really doesn't matter if I liked her or not – it's the details of *their* story I want to recall. If Leon and I are ever going to have a closer relationship, Michelle can't remain a ghost we try to work around – the spectre at the feast. I want to understand their relationship, to understand why certain things trigger him, to help find ways to talk about her naturally without setting him back. He's come so far and I need to help him stay well and happy if we are to find a way forward together.

My glass of wine empty, I pour another. There may be things in her file that can help me to understand better. Give me both sides of the story and allow me to tread more carefully. And, if I am honest with myself, I am curious about this woman and her ability to hold both her husband and her lover in her thrall.

Half an hour later I find myself still sitting there in the darkened room, but now the bottle is empty. And I am nursing Shelly's file on my lap.

I click the lamp switch on the table beside me. Time to stop dithering.

I cut the tape.

Chapter Ten

There is a split second of professional guilt as I put the scissors down. But my need to know takes over as I lift the contents from the wallet file and spread them out on the coffee table – a jumble of paperwork.

There are a couple of items that immediately catch my eye in amongst the notes: the La Isla postcard and a photographic contact sheet.

The postcard tells me little: *'I made my decision! Thank you for all your help and sane advice. Shelly xx'* There's a childish doodle of a smiling sun, the rays spreading out to fill the gaps around the writing. The postmark is impossible to make out.

I tap the card against my hand as I think. The detailed logistics of the relationship between her and Leon had never been discussed in my sessions with him – they were not relevant to Leon's bereavement or his therapy goals. This card, however, raises more questions than it answers. Sent from La Isla, it implies that her final decision was to be with Leon, living their dream of a move to Spain. But they weren't in Spain when she died; she was with her husband, not Leon. Maybe they just went on holiday. Making plans for Leon's early retirement, exploring where they might live; returning to England to sort things out, and then – out of the blue – the horror of the accident.

All those dreams gone in a moment.

But she remains. Frozen in time. In his memory she'll

never age. The memories will be embellished each time he thinks of her, the sun always shining, both of them always happy. She'll always be the perfect angel that he's lost for ever.

How can I ever compete with that?

I need fresh air.

Outside in the garden I pace around trying to clear my head. It's a cloudy starless night. Staring at the crescent moon, I ponder. Leon came to me for help. He chose me because he knew I'd understand.

He chose me. I must hold onto that.

As Leon said, things happen for a reason. He chose me.

New beginnings.

I need to know more. Returning to my task with a strong black coffee, I kneel on the floor next to the table. The photographic contact sheet shows a series of black and white images of an older man. Michelle told me about her nascent photography career … It's coming back to me – she'd asked if I would pose for photos. She'd given me this contact sheet to illustrate her skills at portraiture, to try to persuade me. Some studio head shots would have been useful for my acting portfolio. But tempting as the offer was, of course I said no; she was my client. It wouldn't have been appropriate.

I study the images, holding the sheet under the light. The man has a kind, avuncular face. A bald head fringed with faded grey-blond hair, dark-rimmed glasses, open-necked shirt. He looks relaxed, his soft smile conveying warmth. There's no annotation on the back, no clues as to who he is; possibly her father or another relative, an older friend? But it could be anyone, no one important.

I set the contact sheet on one side with the postcard and

search through the papers for my Client Summary Record. A useful document that captures background information and summarises key points from each session; a skeleton diary of our work together.

> **Name**: *Michelle Harrison, prefers Shelly*
> **Age**: *39*
> **First session**: *February 2017*
> **Goals for therapy**: *Client unclear.*
> **Key relationships**:
>> *Matthew H – husband 4 years, together 6. No children. (Both previously married but divorced when they met.)*
>> *LJ – lover. C 3 years off and on. Works at a college. Won't give his name or disclose more.*
>> *Lisa – sister. Doesn't see often. Lives near mother, 3 hours away.*
>> *No close friends now. Moved away with husband after marriage.*

So far, nothing of note. I take a sip of my coffee; at this rate I'll need it to keep me awake. The summary of the session notes tells me a bit more.

> *Feb 8th 2017, Session 1 of 6:*
>> *Arrived 10 mins late. Not sure what wants from therapy. Concerns re confidentiality. H/band travels a lot for work. Unhappy/lonely. On antidepressant. Feels lonely/ isolated. No income – h/band gives allowance, is paying for photog courses and therapy.*
>> • *Homework: clarify goals for therapy*
> *Feb 23rd 2017, Session 2 of 6:*
>> *Not done homework. Left session early. H/band wants child, but she's not sure about relationship. He buys*

expensive gifts but does he really love her? Seeing 'LJ'
but nervous re h/band finding out.
• *Does lack of commitment to therapy reflect lack of*
  commitment to both men in her life? Discuss with
  Clare.

I skim through the rest of the notes.

By the August she was at a crossroads: her husband keen for them to have a baby, plying her with vitamins and sexual attention; her lover – Leon – asking her to move to Spain with him. It seems she wanted a child but wasn't sure who with.

I'd set her a homework exercise to help her think about the pros and cons. She'd made a token effort at completing it. On the sheet of A4 she recorded her husband as 'generous', 'adoring' and 'decisive'. There's another sentence that she's scribbled out with a black marker pen and I can't read what it says even when I hold it up to the light. I smile at her description of 'LJ', recognising Leon in the words 'intelligent', 'fun' and 'likes to enjoy life'. Only three descriptors for each of them – it appears she gave the exercise little serious thought, spending more time on bubble-writing doodles of the words *Baby* and *Spain*, colouring the letters in alternate pink and blue.

It seems I never really got to know her. There's a clear pattern of booking sessions and cancelling, turning up late, leaving early. She cancelled and rebooked the fifth session several times, then disappeared until August that year. Maybe this is why we never formed a good working relationship? Or was it that I likened her to my own mother? Placing her own wants first and trampling on anyone else's needs?

I try to imagine Leon with this woman depicted in my notes, to see them as a couple. She seems so selfish and shallow and Leon so intelligent and cultured. Opposites attract? Maybe he was captivated by her looks initially, but they saw each other for years, planned a future together ...

The last time I had seen her for therapy was eighteen months ago, November 2017. The peak of Dad's illness. At that final session she told me her husband had begun to suspect something was going on; asking questions and checking up on her. She was worried he would find out she was seeing someone and she planned to talk with her lover about what they should do. Maybe break it off for a while. Another appointment had been booked for early December but she cancelled and never rebooked. And of course my head was elsewhere by that point, too wrapped up in my own sadness to have space for an unreliable client, with no bond between us.

Reading the summary of those last sessions I have a tug of guilt that I could have done more for her: made more effort to understand what made her tick and help her explore the difficult decisions she faced. But the postcard suggested that she was happy. *Thanks ... sane advice.* I wouldn't have encouraged her to leave her marriage for her lover – it's not my role to give advice in that sense. It's more likely I edged her towards making a decision – any decision. The rest was down to her.

The first signs of cramp in my calf warn me I've been kneeling on the floor by the coffee table for too long. Standing to stretch my leg, I catch the edge of the empty folder with my knee, the folder on which the remains of my tepid coffee is precariously balanced. I grab at the mug but not fast enough to stop a mini tidal wave of black coffee engulfing the nearest session notes. Dabbing at the papers with a handful of tissues I'm making things worse, smearing the ink across the pages, fibres of Kleenex adhering in clumps as the tissue disintegrates. I sweep the other notes off the table onto the floor, out of the path of the coffee then run to the kitchen for a dishcloth.

Berating myself for my clumsiness, I swab at the paperwork, wipe the table and dab at the carpet. It must be karma for succumbing to nosiness; if I'd stuck to my ethics it wouldn't have happened. And as much as I tell myself I'm only trying to help Leon move on, I know that's an excuse. By understanding Michelle and what she meant to him, I might understand how to make Leon fall in love with me.

'Yo! Chrissy!'

Oh no.

Angie's voice rings out across the parking area and I keep my back turned, pretend to search for something in my handbag. Leon is retrieving a bottle of sun cream from the car boot and doesn't react. It's Friday and such a beautiful day I've suggested a walk in the forest rather than our planned cinema trip. Unaware of my crisis, he squeezes some of the Factor 30 into my palm. 'Put some on your nose. I'll do your shoulders.' I've never been sunburnt in my life but he is concerned about me getting skin cancer. He's even made me wear a hat.

'Chrissy, over here!'

'There's a woman trying to attract your attention,' Leon says, looking over the top of his designer sunglasses. Coupled with his dark good looks, they make him appear mysterious and sexy.

Angie is standing by one of the wooden picnic tables, her arms above her head in a one-woman Mexican wave. Ignoring her is clearly not going to work. She beams a broad smile when I acknowledge her with a queen-like wave of my hand.

'I'd better go and say hallo,' I say. 'I know her from the Lion.'

I lead the way, keeping a safe distance from Leon just in case he chooses that moment to reach for my hand. I don't want Angie spreading gossip prematurely. It seems she's on her own, a large bulldog tied by his leash to the table leg next to her.

'Hi, Angie, this is a friend of mine.' I deliberately don't say Leon's name. 'I didn't know you had a dog.'

'Hey. Nice car. This is Churchill.' She roughs the top of the dog's head and it slobbers happily. 'He's over there.' She nods towards the ice cream van where there are about ten people waiting, the children hopping back and forth between the picture menu of ices and the adult in the queue with them. A man and small boy peel away from the van, the kid already tearing at the wrapper of his lolly. And Davy steps forward to the window.

Oh no. Leon and Davy are going to meet.

'Look, he's at the front,' Angie says, as if I won't recognise him. With no warning she put two fingers in her mouth and whistles loudly. The dog stands up alert, taking it as some sort of signal, but Angie ignores him. 'Dave! Dave! Get two more!'

'There's no need,' I say, but Davy has already acknowledged her call. Unfazed when he sees us standing with her, he gives me a thumbs-up.

'We don't want to interrupt you,' I say.

She laughs as if I've made a joke. Leon says nothing but studies Davy as he strolls across the car park towards us clutching four 99 cones, the ice cream already starting to dribble over his fingers.

'Can't shake hands, mate,' Davy says, holding out the ice

creams for us to take. 'The ones with two flakes are for the girls.'

He always gets me two flakes, mitigating the risk that I might steal his.

'Thanks,' I say, taking a cone, not knowing what else to do. My guts are churning. I search Davy's face for signs of a reaction at seeing me with another man, but he looks as calm and unruffled as always. I feel I have to introduce them. 'Davy, this is Leon, a friend of mine. Leon, this is Davy.' I'm too nervous to look at Leon, not wanting to know how he is taking this unexpected turn of events.

Once he's passed out the cones, Davy wipes his free hand on his jeans and, for a moment, it looks like he is going to extend his sticky hand towards Leon, but he takes his baseball hat off and wipes his brow. He looks hot in his football shirt, dark patches already forming under the arms.

Angie breaks the end from her cone and throws it on the ground for the dog, oblivious to any potential awkwardness. She has a tattoo of a face on her calf, possibly young Elvis but it's not well executed and she's a chunky/muscly girl so it looks more like the Vegas years.

'I was only saying to Dave last night it's a while since we saw you down the Lion.'

Dave. He hasn't been called that since we first started at Welly when there were two Davids in the class and Dave Evans became shortened to Dave E and from there to Davy.

Angie continues, 'Yeah, we've not seen you for ages and I said, "Chrissy must've given up beer for Lent", didn't I?'

It is early summer; she clearly has no idea when – or maybe what – Lent is.

'You coming to the quiz this week?' Davy asks. I scan his face for any emotion but he seems as happy as usual, whilst

123

I'm now wondering if I put antiperspirant on this morning, the amount I'm sweating.

'I'm not sure,' I say, hoping Leon won't chip in with some off-beat plan involving him and me. 'I hope so.' Angie's ice cream is now melting from the bottom of the cone and the dog stands on Davy's foot to get to the drips.

Beside me, Leon pulls his sleeve up, looks at his watch then smiles at everyone. 'We best get going, we have a table booked for lunch at one.' That isn't true. He puts his hand on my elbow to signal his intent to move us on, a perfectly valid gesture between two friends. 'Good to meet you both and thank you for the ice creams. A treat on a hot day like this.'

We say our goodbyes and for once I'm relieved Davy isn't a natural hugger.

When we're out of earshot, Leon says, 'Sorry to break things up, but you looked so uncomfortable I felt the need to save you.'

'I don't know what to say really. Angie is new to the group. The others aren't like her.' I realise how snobbish and mean that sounds so try to add something kinder. 'She's well-meaning but—'

'They seem nice. Very friendly.' That wasn't at all what I expected him to say. 'I only dragged you away because I want you to myself!'

I laugh with relief. How could I have misjudged this gorgeous, charming man?

He puts his hand out towards me. 'If you pass me your ice cream cone I can throw them both in the bin over there.'

The following evening we meet at 'our' country pub. Knowing he hates lateness, I make a lot of effort to arrive early and find a good table with a view of the door so I can watch out for him. I tug the neck of my dress slightly lower and fluff up my curls, then lean back against the cushions trying to look relaxed and sexy. Not used to being early, I fidget about and have just given my wrists another spray of my 'lucky' honeysuckle perfume when he comes through the door.

He makes his way across the bar and a flicker of pride runs through me. He is dating *me*. His good looks set off by his light golden tan, he attracts appreciative glances from several women he passes, their eyes momentarily following him, then appraising me as he bends to kiss my cheek.

He sniffs the air, turning his nose up slightly.

'Smells like the staff have been a bit liberal with the air freshener.' He pulls aside the curtain behind me. 'If there's one of those diffusers hiding somewhere, either it goes or we do.'

'Were you out playing golf today?' I ask, rubbing my wrists on the fabric of the banquette under the table. 'You've really caught the sun. Where was your Factor 30?'

He frowns at me, a flash of frustration. Or am I being paranoid? It could just be concentration as he tries to work out my leap in conversation.

'Golf?' He sits down opposite me.

'I thought you played. When you and Michelle went to Spain. To the golf resorts?'

'Golf! I wish! Not today, no.' He takes my hand, slowly folds my fingers down one by one into my palm, enclosing my whole hand in his. It brings back memories of my small hand clasped in Dad's, the warmth and security.

'I was watching a cricket match. A corporate event,' he says. 'A sponsor of the college. Tedious things but they have to be done. I'd much rather spend time with you.' I sigh quietly, reassured that all is well, as he continues, 'Tell me about your day. I'm sure it was much more interesting.'

He sips the bottled lager I bought for him – I should have asked for a glass, but he's not complained. He watches me intently as I try to make anecdotes out of anything that has happened since I saw him the day before.

'Oh, and next week they are starting auditions for our new production. I spent hours reading the play, trying to memorise the lines for the part I want.'

'Please tell me it's Shakespeare or Stoppard or something else worthy of your talent.'

'I wish.'

'Do you have an agent? If so, they aren't doing their job. Probably time to change.'

'I used to … but we parted ways …' I tell him about my decision to give up the corporate/paid work so I could spend more time with Dad as he became more infirm. 'I lost confidence for a while, but Davy encouraged me to join the local theatre group.' Lovely Davy, who thinks the pinnacle of acting is a part in *EastEnders*. *Leave it, Alf. He ain't worth it!*

'Well, I'm encouraging you now! We need to get you treading those boards and into some serious roles. Project "Find an Agent" starts today.'

I laugh, holding my hands up in a whoa gesture. 'I need to update my acting website before I approach anyone again. And sort out my showreel. And get some new headshots.'

'And the problem is …?'

His sincerity and enthusiasm start me thinking it could be feasible.

'Well, maybe … Do you think you could take some photos for me?'

'You are very photogenic.' He holds his hands up, framing my face in a thumb-and-finger square as if sizing up the shot.

126

I play along, turning my head this way, offering different facial expressions – a come-hither smile, a wink, a pout.

'I'd love to work with such a beautiful model. But sadly I no longer have my own lighting kit. I use the studios at the college.'

'I could come down and meet you one day. It would be fun to see where you work.'

He shakes his head. 'I'm afraid not, my love. Students only. It's not professional to use the studio for personal projects.' He lifts my chin slightly, turns my face to the side, contemplating the best angle. 'Disappointing for us both, but you of all people understand the importance of not mixing business and pleasure.'

'Of course, sorry.'

'Professional boundaries.' He taps the end of my nose gently, slowly strokes his finger down to the Cupid's bow, then outlines my lips. My body responds with that now-familiar tingle. I arch my back, leaning towards him, aching to be kissed.

'Now, let me get you another white wine,' he says.

Chapter Eleven

The next morning my mobile rings and I rush to pick it up from the kitchen counter, hoping it will be Leon. But it's Clare's name on my screen.

'Hi, Clare, how are you?'

'I'm well. I was just wondering how *you* are?'

'Hmm, good, good,' I say, turning on the cold tap with my free hand then reaching for a glass.

'It was disappointing not to see you yesterday.'

'My supervision session's next week, isn't it?' I spin round to check the calendar. It's written there in purple ink. 'I'm looking forward to it.'

'I expected to see you last night. My talk at the monthly meeting of the Counsellors and Therapists Group? I sent you an invitation.'

She's right. I'd pinned it to the fridge so I wouldn't forget. There it is, half hidden under a recipe for herb-baked cod and a magnetic Humpty Dumpty that Davy gave me.

'Oh, Clare. I'm so sorry.' I'd gone out with Leon and completely forgotten my commitment to Clare. 'I hadn't put it on my calendar. I did plan to come – I really wanted to hear you present.'

'I can email you the slides.' There's a momentary pause, then she says, 'Are you sure you're okay?'

'I am, I am. Just being more scatty than usual. The heat isn't helping with my sleep problems.'

'Tell me about it! Bernard was sorry you weren't there. I'd told him you were coming.' Bernard Jones works at a local health clinic. He has a great reputation and Clare has previously mentioned that she wants the two of us to meet. Matchmaking or networking, I'm still not sure. 'He wants to refer on a client who's asked for a female therapist. I thought it might be a good case for you.'

'Thank you. That would be great.'

'I told him we'd arrange another date for the three of us to get together. If he gets to know you and your work, it could lead to further referrals. It would be a good way for you to build up your client list again.' The pause again. 'But I think we should discuss it in supervision first. Just to confirm you're ready to take on more clients. I don't want to put you under unnecessary pressure.'

It's only later that it dawns on me: is she protecting me or the clients? It seems I've given her yet more cause to doubt me.

If there's a possibility that Bernard Jones might refer more clients to me, it's definitely time to repaint the garden therapy room. I've been seeing clients in the house since the break-in, but it would be nicer to have views of the flowers and trees, rather than the pavement. And *if* Leon might ever be a guest in my house I'll need to turn the front room back into a lounge; no reminders of our previous, more formal relationship.

Davy's already done the heavy lifting, patched the wall and taken the broken filing cabinet to the dump. All that's left is to wash the floor and the remaining soft furnishings, get the stepladders out and start painting. It's a sunny day so there really is no excuse not to get started.

I smile to myself remembering the original clear-up with

the girls after the break-in: Ali's promise to send her daughter round with her crystals 'to cleanse the room of bad karma' once I was ready to use it again; Nisha suggesting we have an official opening ceremony where I cut a ribbon and Jen volunteering to handle catering if we get the rest of the Wellies over to join us. Not such a bad idea; maybe I should think about it – any excuse for a party.

Making space so I can lay out dust sheets, I give the sofa a shove with my hip, trying to edge it further into the centre of the room. Reluctantly it budges forward an inch at a time, exposing a few spiders, what turns out to be a B&Q receipt for the lock and more glass from the smashed frames. On my hands and knees with the dustpan, I spot the edge of a something white pinned under the leg of the sofa. Once I've eased it out, I'm completely thrown by what I see. It's the certificate announcing my formal registration as a therapist. But that's not what makes my spine tingle. There's something sellotaped to the back; Davy must've done it when he framed the certificate for me. A congratulations card from Dad. The two men who have been in my life the longest, who have always shown me unquestioning love; now Dad's gone and Davy's with Angie.

Hey Kiddo, Dad had written. *You've made me the proudest man in the world. You show them how it's done! Love you to the ends of the earth and back. Dad xxx*

I hug the card to my chest and burst into tears.

It's as much as I can do to take down the curtains. I'll come back to it later in the week.

In the house I wedge the receipt under the coffee pot on the kitchen worktop, unable to remember if I paid Davy back. Cramming both curtains into the washing machine, echoes of Davy's voice ring in my head: 'That thing's going to give up the ghost one of these days the way you stuff it in.' He always rebuffs my plea that it's an economy measure. 'You won't say that when you need a new machine.' It's been odd not having him drop in for a cuppa when he gets back from a long haulage job ... or when he wants an official document explained ... or when he needs a button sewn on.

Angie's role now.

The last time I saw him was weeks ago, when we bumped into them at the forest. It's the longest time we've not spoken in years. Even when we were dating other people we've always had our regular catch-ups. Fancying a chat I give him a call, but there's a twinge of disappointment when his mobile goes straight through to the factory-set voicemail message.

'Hey, you,' I say. 'Long time no see. Just thinking of you 'cause I'm finally redoing the shed. Did I ever pay you for the lock? Anyway, come round for a coffee sometime soon. Catch you tomorrow evening at the Lion. Save me a seat.'

The following afternoon, the doorbell rings just as I'm getting ready to embark on the painting stage of the garden office refurb.

'Coming,' I shout, shoving stray locks of hair into the makeshift bandanna, made from a twisted T-shirt. It must be Davy, wanting to see me before we meet up with the whole gang this evening. I open the door with a broad smile on my face but it isn't Davy.

It's Leon.

I haven't seen or heard from him since our evening in the pub. I'd not been worried; he'd told me he was travelling to some foreign conference but he wasn't due back until next week. 'Is something wrong?' I ask. My heart is hammering but I can't tell if it's nerves or excitement. He hasn't been inside my house since his final therapy session.

He laughs. 'Take that frown off your pretty face. You'll be needing Botox for the wrinkles if you keep on like that.' He steps forward, clearly expecting to come in. 'I've a surprise for you.'

'Oh. In that case I'll make us some coffee.' I can't stop myself beaming as he follows me through to the kitchen, a fluttering in my stomach signalling how pleased I am to see him. He parks himself on the breakfast-bar stool, completely at ease and this time he really belongs here, in the kitchen, with me. I assume he wants 'proper' coffee, not the instant. Luckily I keep some in for Nisha. Aware he's watching me, I search the saucepan cupboard for the cafetiere, finding it stuffed at the back unused since I last had the girls round. Swilling it out I manage to get water all over me and while wiping my hands dry on my paint-spattered work overalls, I embark on an unnecessarily detailed explanation of my decorating plans, trying to cover my embarrassment.

Leon waits for me to finish then says, 'That's not a job for you. What do you think tradesmen are for?'

I laugh as I open the biscuits, supplies bought in just in case Davy calls round. 'Are you questioning my prowess with a paintbrush? I'll have it done in an hour or two.'

'Climbing up ladders when no one's here could be dangerous. What if you had a fall? I'd never forgive myself for not looking after you better. I'll get one of my people – someone from the college – to come and do it next week.'

'That's not necessary. It's a waste of money. I can easily—'

He holds his hand up to silence me. 'No arguments. Please, just let me sort it out. Now, you didn't ask me why I came round. I'm taking you out this evening.'

Before he can say more there's the crunch of feet on

132

the back path and then a face pops up at the open kitchen window. It's Jilly from the Middleford Players.

She waves her arms above her head as if she is a mile away and needs to attract my attention urgently. 'Hey, babe! It's me!' I raise a hand in acknowledgement. 'Loving the outfit,' she says. 'Takes leisurewear to a whole new level.'

She leans in through the window, eyebrows raised in an unspoken question, checking that it's okay as she grabs a biscuit out of the open packet. 'Hmm, yum, shortbread.' Resting her elbows on the kitchen counter, half in, half out of the window, she takes a huge bite then covers her mouth with her hand and carries on speaking, 'Soz, I'm absolutely famished. Missed lunch again.'

'This is Jilly,' I say. 'Jilly, Leon.'

She leans forward further and extends her hand towards Leon, her hips now balanced on the windowsill and her feet off the ground, paddling the air behind her. Her flowery perfume wafts in with her, plus an undertone of armpits; not shaving or using deodorant is her 'feminist statement'.

'Jilly, for goodness' sake, just come in through the door like a normal person.' She's just as likely to climb through if I don't stop her. While she usually makes me laugh with her exuberance and playfulness, I'm unsure how she will come across to Leon and feel I need to manage her excesses.

'I'm not staying. I'm on a mission from She-Who-Must-Be-Obeyed.' She means the director. 'Oh, and I wanted to ask you a favour.' She wriggles backwards, trying to reverse herself out of the window but gets the waistband of her utility trousers caught on something. 'Help! I'm hooked.' She turns half on her side exposing a pale, washboard stomach and the smoothest of skin and I'm aware of Leon watching her.

'Hang on, let me come round and help you,' I say, heading for the back door.

A few minutes later she is untangled and I've helped her down. Standing in the flower bed she lifts her top to examine her lower rib where there is a small reddening graze. 'Wow, I could've died,' she jokes.

'Do you want some Germolene on that?'

'God, who are you – my gran?' She takes a scrunchie from round her wrist and pulls her hair back in a high ponytail. 'I do think health and safety would have something to say about it though.'

'I'm on it. I'll get a sign made.' I mark out an invisible square where I'll place it. '"Do not use window for entry unless back door is blocked by large dog, uncollected recycling or floodwater." Then a second one here: "Ensure you are wearing appropriate safety gear before attempting entry."'

'That should do it.' She retrieves her large canvas bag from where she'd dropped it and hands me a dog-eared copy of the script we're auditioning. 'She's made some annotations to your part.'

'What? Why?'

Jilly puts her hands up. 'Don't shoot the messenger. Oh, and can you spare me an hour or so to rehearse and help me go through those techniques you taught me? I sooooo want to get the part of Cassandra!'

We agree that I'll email her some dates.

'Best be off,' she says. She turns to the window and waves to Leon who has taken over making the coffee. He nods in acknowledgement.

'Bye-ee. Hope to see you at the show.' Her arms around me in a bear hug, Jilly gives me a loud theatrical kiss good-bye. 'Mwah, mwah.' It's a standing joke amongst the Players, but as I join in I do it quietly, not wanting to seem childish in front of Leon.

I go inside and drop the script on the countertop. 'So, *that* was Jilly.'

'Yes, so I gather.'

'A bit of a whirlwind.'

'She seems very young. How old is she?'

'I don't know. Twenty-five? She's been with the Players for three or four years now. Very keen.'

I step past Leon to take over the serving of the coffee, opening the cupboard to find the best matching mugs.

'If you'll forgive me saying so, *that* illustrates how far you are punching below your weight with that group. I understand that it's been fun but you deserve to be working with professionals, not wasting your time with amateur dramatics.' He reaches out to me and strokes a lock of my hair, twining it loosely around his fingers, before cupping my chin and staring deep into my eyes. 'I sometimes think I believe in you more than you believe in yourself. Promise me you will focus your efforts on getting another agent. It should be your main priority, not frittering away time and effort on getting a part in their next *amateur* production.'

'When you put it like that …'

'I know you would want to make me and your dad proud.'

'Of course. I—'

'Well, tonight's adventure will inspire you to greater things, I'm sure.'

'Oh, yes. Where are we going? I was thinking of going to the Lion tonight … It's quiz night. But I guess they won't miss me.'

'To the opera. The tickets are as rare as hens' Teeth so I was lucky to get them.'

'Gosh, I feel spoilt.'

'Cinderella shall go to the ball.' He gesticulates to my dungarees then kisses my forehead. 'Wear something special.'

That evening *Carmen* holds me spellbound. The singing isn't really my thing but the costumes and the sheer drama of the performances are fascinating. And the actress playing Carmen oozes sexuality with every move. Leon whispers a translation of some of her lyrics: 'Love is a wild bird that cannot be tamed … If I love you, watch out …'

Her acting is mesmerising and there's really no need for dialogue – her body conveys it all. Sitting so close to Leon, our thighs almost touching, watching as her passion plays out on the stage, that familiar tingle starts running through me. To be wanted that much …

At the interval, Leon hums one of the opening arias as we make our way to the bar, his hand on my arm: 'de dum de dah, de dum de dah'. *Habanera*, he tells me. I love it when he is like this, relaxed and warm, the real Leon. While he joins the ranks vying for attention from the bar staff, I wait at the back of the lounge area, staking my claim to a clear space. Surreptitiously easing off one of my shoes to rest my arches, I catch the eye of a young man standing next to me. He gestures to a stool where he's been resting a bag and I gratefully bagsy the seat.

'Thanks,' I say, removing the other shoe to massage my foot. 'Are you enjoying the performance?' It turns out he is in a similar boat, brought along by his girlfriend, knowing nothing about opera yet warming to the experience.

I spot Leon easing his way through the crowd with our drinks and quickly replace my shoes. The man is still standing next to me, raving about the singer playing Carmen, as Leon passes my wine. 'Hallo,' he says to the young man, but his tone isn't friendly.

'Hi, I was just saying to your wife—'

'Oh, we're not married,' I interrupt, embarrassed in case

Leon thinks I've implied we we're a serious couple. 'We're friends. Good friends.'

But the young man has resumed talking and didn't hear the last part, chatting away oblivious to the look on Leon's face, which clearly signals how unwelcome his conversation is.

It's only when the young man's girlfriend arrives that Leon thaws. She is about thirty years old and quite plain-looking; her mousy hair cut in a chin-length bob, she's wearing an unbecoming floral midi dress and flat shoes. Leon beams his full attention on her, smiling warmly, asking questions, eyes for no one but her. I watch as she blooms before him, batting her eyelashes, stroking the strap of her handbag, relaxed and chatty, drawn out by his interest. The therapist part of me remains dispassionate, able to observe without emotion, suspecting this is some kind of power game he plays – anything you can do, I can do better. A control thing. I smile to myself. I've made him jealous! However, the twitching in my guts tells me I wouldn't have felt so calm had she been single and pretty.

The young man doesn't seem to notice. 'Where did you travel from?' he asks me. 'We're from Harpenham. Bit of a trek.'

'Oh, my friend works in the college there,' I say, gesturing to Leon. 'He's a lecturer.'

The young man turns to Leon, interrupting his girlfriend mid-sentence. 'You lecture at the college? What subject?'

Leon and I both answer at once, Leon saying, 'Let's not talk shop,' as I say, 'He's Head of Fine Art Photography.'

The young man continues, 'Wow. You must know Ian – he's been a technician in Fine Art for years.'

'Of course,' Leon says hurriedly. The interval bell rings

signalling the five-minute warning and Leon puts his hand on my back. 'Let's return to our seats.'

'Poor old Ian,' The young man says. 'Terrible what's happened to him. Give him my best when you see him.'

As we work our way back to the stalls, I ask what's happened to Ian, the technician.

'He's seriously ill. I went to see him last week at the hospital.'

'How awful. Are you very close? You should've told me.'

'I don't tell you everything, my sweet. Ah, here, this is our aisle. Let me hold your drink so you can squeeze past these people.'

Chapter Twelve

The rest of the evening passes pleasantly and Leon is charming and attentive. It has all been so romantic that I wrestle with the temptation to ask him in for a nightcap when he drives me home. I don't want to risk him misinterpreting an invitation as more than a drink as I'm still trying to adhere to the professional standards – there must be a gap of six months between finishing work with a client and starting a sexual relationship. Otherwise it is a breach of ethics. Professional misconduct. Grounds for being struck off.

I doubt I would be able to resist if he kissed me properly.

As it is, he leaves with our usual peck on the cheek; a perfect gentleman.

Wide awake, it's pointless to go to bed, so I click through to YouTube and watch a Royal Opera recording of *Carmen*. The lyrics scroll across the bottom of the screen – *'If I'm in love with you, don't ever try to reject me …'* Replaying Leon's behaviour with the young couple, I'm sure Leon's flirting was prompted by jealousy that I was talking to the young man. If so, it suggests he wants me for himself. That he really does want us to have a relationship. It isn't my imagination. He does fancy me, just wants us to get to know each other better before making a move.

I replay the song from the start, imagining I'm the sexy

Carmen on a path of seduction. If he is thinking the same as me, it won't be long before we move to the next stage.

And I'm ready.

The next day, after a particularly erotic dream about Leon, I can't get him out of my head. But I can't ring him for a chat – he has a busy schedule and doesn't like to be bothered with phone calls or pinned down with dates. He often has to travel to lectures at other colleges, give talks or visit art exhibitions, so I never know when we will meet up again until he contacts me.

I should iron the curtains for the garden office, but instead watch the *Carmen* videos again. And again. Then, in the hope of finding a photo of Leon to moon over, I google Harpenham College, registering a pang of guilt, which gives me pause for a second. Is this inappropriate? Most of my dating life has taken place long before the internet made this kind of thing the norm and with my therapy background, I'm cautious about these sort of boundaries. But I'm not spying on him, not digging around, only looking at readily available information on a college website.

Disappointingly, the college doesn't list faculty members, only the vice chancellor and dean, neither of whom are particularly interesting to me. So there is no photo for me to get dreamy over. I look up the photography courses and toy with signing up, imagining his surprise if I were to turn up in his classroom. What would he be like as a tutor? Would he put on a different persona to help him play the part? I doubt it. He is like Clare: far more self-assured than me with no need to pretend to be anything but himself.

On the college website there are pictures of the main building: Georgian, set in its own small campus. With nothing better to do with my day, I check out the location on the map of Harpenham. There's a river only five minutes or so from the college itself and I play with the idea of dropping in to see Leon one day, taking a picnic lunch for us to have between his classes. Given his spontaneity – calling at short notice to invite me out, buying tickets for events and springing surprises on me – I wonder if he might appreciate the same. But it will have to be something more aligned to my budget – a romantic picnic when he was anticipating the canteen sandwiches again.

Warming to my idea, I decide to go to the college on Monday to find out from reception what days he teaches. Discreetly of course, I don't want to spoil the surprise.

Since I am online, I allow myself one more search. Selecting the *Images* tab I enter *Leon Jacobs photographer*. The usual string of unrelated pictures appear. Amongst these seemingly random images there are probably photos he's taken, his professional work that others have posted online. Spotting the cover image of a book on photography, I click the link. '*Fresh Focus*: Leon Jacobs' listed along with three others under the title. Excited to see his work, with just a few more clicks I've ordered a copy for next-day delivery.

I've frittered away too much of the day already. Time to do something useful. I pick up the phone and call Jen. 'Sorry I missed you all last night at the Lion. Do you and the dogs fancy a walk and a chat? I've loads to tell you!'

Of course, I'll leave out any reference to Leon having been a client.

The reception at the college is the old-fashioned sort. No barriers, pass cards or lanyards, just stroll up to the desk. The nominal security chap puts down his crossword as he hears me approaching, my heels clattering on the flagstone floor.

'Hi. I'm enquiring after Leon Jacobs, Head of Fine Art

Photography.' There's a note of pride in my voice when I say *Head of*, basking in reflected glory.

'You're a bit late for that, I'm afraid.'

'Oh. Has he left for the day?' It's only three o'clock.

'You could say that. He retired over a year ago.'

'Retired?' It doesn't make sense. Have I got it wrong? 'So he's part-time now?'

'No. He's long gone, I'm afraid.' The security guard laughs.

I don't understand. Why would Leon say he works here if he doesn't? Maybe I'm at the wrong college ...

'Did you do a course with him? We often get people stop by to invite him to their shows and exhibitions. He was always very popular with his students.'

'Oh. I ... Yes, I used to do photography here.' *Concentrate. Act the part.* 'That's so disappointing. I was really hoping to see him. Do you know where he works now?'

'Can't help there, I'm afraid. Ian might know how to get hold of him if you want an email address or something. You must remember Ian? He's outside having a cig break.'

'Oh, he's in today?' Ian, the technician mentioned by the young man at *Carmen*. 'I heard he's been really ill.'

The security man snorts a laugh. 'Nothing wrong with him that a square meal wouldn't sort out.'

Outside a tall skinny man leans against the wall smoking, his nervous energy apparent in the way he drums on one leg with the fingers of his free hand. Since he is the only person who fits the description, I'm safe to assume he is Ian.

'Hi, I'm Cristina. Someone told me you've been off work recently. Are you feeling better?'

He frowns. 'I wasn't ill. My car got nicked – a bloody write-off now. They totalled it.' He takes a deep draw on his cigarette. 'Are you a new student here or faculty?'

'Neither actually. But you might remember my friend Shelly? She was a photography student.'

He shrugs, uninterested, blows the smoke out slowly in a steady stream.

I persevere. 'She did one of Leon's courses, a couple of years ago. Long blonde hair. Very pretty.'

'Oh yeah. I remember her. *Friendly* sort.' He smirks as he speaks.

I chose to ignore the implication. 'Yes, she and Leon were good friends.'

He raises an eyebrow. 'More than that, from what I saw. They had a bit of a thing going, her and Leon.'

'Yes, I guess you could say that. She was very fond of him.'

'Married though, wasn't she? Some bloke came here once after Leon. Made a hell of a scene.'

'I didn't know that. What happened?'

'They got in a fight. The bloke got a few punches in before security intervened.'

I don't have to act; I'm genuinely shocked. It wasn't in her therapy notes and surely I would have recalled such a significant incident if Michelle had told me about it. And Leon has certainly never mentioned it. 'Was Leon hurt?'

'Black eye, broken nose. Could've been well nasty if the guy had had a knife. I think it went to court. Police got involved anyways.'

'How frightening.' Poor Leon.

'That shit happens if you muck around with other people's wives. So, what was it you wanted?' His cigarette is now a stub in his paint-stained hand.

'Sorry. Yes. I was hoping to catch Leon, but I didn't realise he'd retired already. Do you know where he works now?'

Ian looks me up and down, assessing whether I'm another potential groupie, contrasting me with Leon's usual type.

'No, can't say I do. He just up and left. What do you want him for?'

'I wanted advice about an evening photography course.'

'Depends what you're into, but Interpretive Photography gets rave reviews. Or City Skylines.' He drops his cigarette end on the floor and turns away from me towards the college. 'The course descriptions are online.'

I head for the river where I'd envisaged our romantic picnics, following the signposts around the campus but still managing to take a wrong turn. Parking myself on a bench beside the well-used towpath, I try to clear my thoughts.

Why would he lie to me about still working at the college? Of course I understand the psychological reasons he might not want me to know – his ego wrapped up in the identity of Head of Faculty. His dignity compromised in front of his students after the fight in reception. The affair with Michelle made public knowledge. He was probably asked to resign for having an illicit relationship with a married student; crossing boundaries. That must've been why he left the college, covering it up with 'early retirement', losing his job and his reputation in one go.

Is this why he didn't want me to know? Not wanting to dredge up the assault, in case I see him as unmanly, a victim. Wanting me to know him as the successful professional he has been throughout his career, not tarnish it with a brawl in the foyer. And once he's started with a lie, each lie in turn leads to another – making excuses as to why he couldn't use the studios there to take my portfolio shots; claiming he had recently seen Ian, the technician.

Maybe all he really wanted was for me to see him in a positive light … not to judge him …

I want to hear his side of the story, but most importantly

I need him to know how I feel about it. This is my line in the sand.

I need him to understand how important it is to have complete honesty in a relationship.

No secrets, no surprises.

Determined to have it out with him, I propose we meet at 'our pub', as I've come to think of the country inn we've visited a couple of times already. Neutral but familiar territory for us both. Even though I've carefully planned my strategy, I know he might not take it well, however delicately I approach the discussion. He doesn't like too many questions and can sometimes be a little chippy if he feels ill-judged.

It is six-thirty when the doorbell rings. Looking out of the bedroom window, I see that Leon's car is on the drive. He was meant to meet me at the pub and we aren't due there for an hour. My make-up is thankfully finished so I don't look too much of a sight, but when I open the door I'm still wearing my cotton dressing gown and my hair is wrapped in a towel-turban.

'This is early, even for you.'

'I couldn't wait to see you. And it's greener if we go in one car.' He hugs me to him, kisses me briefly on the lips. Some sort of progress but I can't believe we still haven't properly kissed. There's something respectful and charmingly old-fashioned about the pace we're taking things.

I usher him into the front room while I go to dry my hair and get dressed.

'That was the most speedy turnaround I could manage,' I say, coming back into the room twenty minutes later. He is sitting in my therapy chair, his book *Fresh Focus* open in his hands.

'When did you get this?' he asks. He doesn't look happy.

I'd stashed it under the coffee table earlier in the week, not intending to tell him I'd bought a copy. The photography in the book is amazing, but his section is full of photos of Michelle – *My Muse* – and I didn't want to run the risk of upsetting him.

'I saw it online and couldn't resist buying a copy to see your work.' I turn my back, pretending to look on the bookcase for my keys, not wanting him to pick up on my nerves, anticipating the conversation I plan to have later. 'If you sign it for me it could be worth something!'

'Have you been stalking me, Cristina?' His voice has an edge and it's hard to tell if he is joking or really cross. 'That's not the behaviour of a professional therapist is it now?'

I force a laugh and go over to perch on the arm of the chair. 'None of this is terribly professional, but you're not my client any more, remember?'

The book lies open on his lap at a moody photo of Michelle in a Monroe-style pose; hair dishevelled, one strap of her dress slipping off her shoulder. My heart beats a little faster looking at the image, imagining Leon snapping hundreds of photos as Michelle flirts with the camera and him; both of them working their magic to end up with these sensual poses. She looks so happy, confident and relaxed. The images so natural, they could only be taken by a lover. I feel like a voyeur. Once again a third party to their relationship.

'I'm sorry,' I say. 'I hope it's not too upsetting for you to see these photos.'

He shuts the book firmly. 'You just reminded me that you're no longer my therapist, so don't come over all concerned for my emotional state.'

'I just thought—'

'You just don't think,' he interrupts. 'How would you like it if I was to ferret around in every aspect of your past? Is

146

it not enough that you know almost everything about me from the therapy? Oh no, clearly not. You now need to do your online investigating too. And since you asked, yes, it is upsetting to see the pictures of Michelle. Bloody upsetting. How would you feel to open a book and find photos of your dead father staring up at you? How would that feel, Kiddo?'

How does he know Dad's pet name for me?

The book lands with a thud against the leg of the coffee table as he shoves it from his lap onto the floor. He leans forward, holding his head in both hands, covering his face, and I perch perfectly motionless next to him on the arm of the chair, my breathing shallow, unsure what to say or do next. His neck is red and he is breathing heavily, but I can't tell if he is crying or trying to regain his composure. How did we get to this? How stupid of me to leave the book where he could find it and upset him like this.

Eventually he lifts his head, rubbing at his eyes. 'I'm so sorry, Cristina — that was so unforgivably rude of me.' He reaches for my hand and holds it tightly. 'You caught me unawares, but it was unforgivable to speak to you like that. I am a complete and utter arse.'

'No, I—'

He picks up the book from where it has fallen and places it on the coffee table, smoothing the dust jacket, which has torn where it hit the table. He gives a fake laugh as he waves his hand at his co-authors' names on the cover. 'And I'm sure they're all grateful someone's still buying it — royalties on every copy.' He swallows hard and leans his head against my side. 'Do you mind if we reschedule tonight? I'm not feeling quite myself.'

'Of course. I am so sorry, Leon. I never meant to upset you.'

'My dear sweet girl. Of course you didn't mean to. You are an absolute innocent.' He raises my hand and holds my fingertips to his lips. 'I am so glad I found you.'

So, we had our first argument that evening. Just not in the way I'd feared. And now I am even more anxious about how to broach the discussion I want to have.

Meanwhile, I hide Leon's book away so it can do no more harm.

Chapter Thirteen

It is a couple of days before Leon and I have our postponed date. He comes to pick me up, bang on time, and is charm itself: complimenting me on my appearance, holding the car door open for me as my nail varnish is still tacky 'and you wouldn't want to spoil it', carrying my jacket.

My nerves are jangling and I've decided it's better to tackle the issue early in the evening, get it over with. While Leon's at the bar I run through the lines I've been rehearsing in front of the mirror. As soon as he returns with the drinks I'll launch in, not give myself a chance to back out, or allow him time to raise another topic.

I look up expectantly as I sense someone approaching the table, ready with my opening line – 'There's something I want to discuss' – but it's a barmaid clutching a pile of leaflets. She places a lurid A5 promotional flyer on the table: *'Our S&M Night: Two-for-One Sausage and Mash combos TONIGHT!!!'* it proclaims in bright red text. Who on earth is their target market?

'Thank you, we—'

'Menu's on the back.' She flips it over to show me. 'Your choice of sausage – the pork, onion and apple is lovely, but a lot of people go for the venison because it's a bit different, but to be honest I find it too dry.' I try to interrupt but she's not looking at me, busily organising a wooden rack of cutlery, paper napkins and condiments on the table. The forks have got mingled with the knives and she's not happy about it. 'We've even got Quorn if you're that way inclined, but why would you go for that when there's so many other choices? Three types of mash – there's your standard buttery mash, the herby one although if you're not keen on coriander I'd...'

Leon arrives back with the drinks as she is midway through the gravy options. He raises an eyebrow and she takes this as an invitation to start at the beginning. 'I was just saying to your wife, the sausage and mash combos are on special offer tonight—'

'Thank you,' I say firmly, picking up the menu to signal that I've understood the delicious range of options. 'We'll have a look.'

'Place your order at the bar. Remember to tell them your table number.' She heads for the next couple with her stack of leaflets, her voice drifting back. 'Two-for-one offer on...'

'With such commitment to the sale, she has to be on commission,' Leon says.

I'm about to join in his banter, make a joke about use-by dates on the sausages requiring this BOGOF, but I catch myself. I mustn't get distracted.

'There's something I want to discuss actually,' I say, taking a sip of my white wine.

'Ah, that sounds serious.'

'I went to the college this Monday. Harpenham College.'

Leon runs his hand through his hair, frowning slightly the way he does when he is concentrating. 'The college? Are you signing up for a course?'

'Actually I went to meet you.' I keep my voice calm, my speech well modulated, just as I've rehearsed. Behind me the waitress has reached the *mustard mash* part of her soliloquy. 'I thought we might go for lunch together – a surprise picnic.'

'Ah.'

'You weren't there.'

'No.'

'I spoke to the chap on reception. He told me about your retirement.'

'I see.'

'Leon, I know you've not worked there for over a year.'

He looks the picture of innocence, like the doe-eyed child in one those tacky 1960s paintings. 'What do you want me to say?'

'Well, an explanation would be good.' Even to my own ears, I sounds surprisingly calm. I'm channelling Clare, as best I can, rather than wronged girlfriend.

He takes a sip of his red wine, then another. 'I'm not sure that I actually said I still worked there. I think you assumed it and I didn't disabuse you of the notion. When I was having therapy with you, it never seemed that relevant to what we were discussing. And then, it was too late.'

'You could have told me when I asked about the head shots for my portfolio.' I keep the whine out of my voice, my tone reasonable.

'Yes, I should have. You're right. But I didn't want to risk spoiling a lovely evening with you.'

I'm thrown by his calm admissions. I wait a moment for him to say something else but he picks up the sausage and mash flyer and peruses it intently, like it's one of the menus in the posh restaurants he usually frequents.

Does he think that's enough? Much as part of me would love to let it go, avoid conflict by burying my head in the sand, I know I can't leave it there.

'They told me about Michelle's husband assaulting you.' I speak gently, hoping to tease information out of him, like I would with a reluctant teenage client. 'That must have been really upsetting. Was that why you left? Because your relationship with Michelle was made public?'

'One of the reasons,' he says. 'Look, I'm really sorry. It was stupid of me not to have told you. And, for what it's worth, I'm glad you've raised it and we've cleared the air.'

He seems to think that's all that needs to be said, as he's now studying the desserts at the bottom of the flyer – '*Traditional British puddings ADD your choice of cream or ice cream in 5 flavours!*'

His avoidance is frustrating and a tone edges into my voice. 'So. Do you still work? Are you lecturing somewhere else now?'

'Yes. I mean no. I don't work at another college. I'm freelance, my own business.'

I nod, raise my eyebrows, signalling I expect more.

'Calling it a business sounds a bit grand I suppose. It's just me, an administrator and a couple of student interns. I realise I should have told you but it just didn't seem that relevant to us. There were always more important things to talk about.'

'You're away a lot. That man at the Globe mentioned a project in Germany. Are you lecturing abroad?'

'Sometimes, yes, I travel for work – keynote speaker on several courses, photography commissions for people who want a known name, that kind of thing. My reputation goes before me.' He reaches for his wallet in his inside pocket, intent on replacing the credit card he used at the bar but as he removes it, a coin falls to the floor and rolls under my chair.

Reflexively I bend to pick it up and inches from my fingers I find not a pound coin but a ring. A gold wedding ring.

Clare was right.

'And what is this?' I hold it up close to his face, my hand

trembling with anger. 'Something else you conveniently forgot to tell me?'

He goes to take it from me but I hold it out of reach, clutched in my fist, like a child-bully.

'Michelle gave it to me. A symbol of what we meant to each other.'

'Really? Do you think I'm a fool!' The woman at the next table nudges her husband, who turns round to look at us, as if our argument was a performance piece. Seeing my furious face, the man turns back but she keeps taking surreptitious glances, using her menu in place of a lace curtain. I lower my voice, my bitterness now a vicious hiss. 'How do I know you're not married to someone else? That woman you were with at my play – *"Sophie"*. You seemed to know her well! Is *she* your wife?'

Leon places his hand on my arm. 'Darling, how can you say that? I told you she's my cousin.'

'You lied to me straight-faced about the college. How can I trust anything you say any more?'

'Do you think I lied when I poured my heart out to you in therapy? You've seen all my emotion and vulnerability. Do you doubt everything we've shared over the past months?' He shakes his head, his eyes sad and sincere. 'It's almost impossible to prove something doesn't exist – I can't *prove* there are no unicorns but we both believe there aren't any.'

'Don't try to turn this into a philosophical debate. All I'm asking for is honesty.'

'I don't know how I can reassure you. Look, I'll phone Sophie right now.' He pulls out his mobile.

'No, I—'

'I can't have you upset like this.' He presses a contact name, holds up a hand as I go to speak then says, '*Bonsoir mon amie*, Sophie.' He speaks quickly in French and laughs at something she says in response. '*Bien sûr, je vais te payer!*'

He smiles broadly as he passes me the phone, as if it is all no more than a minor misunderstanding. 'Speak to Sophie, she'll reassure you.'

I shake my head, no. My cheeks are flushing and I feel like the butt of some kind of joke between them.

He holds the phone to his ear continuing a brief conversation in French – I pick out the word *Paris* and a date. He reverts to English to end the call: 'Let me know when you will next be in London. The three of us can meet up, have dinner … Bye. Have a good evening.'

He smiles, pleased, believing he's solved everything with this one call. 'There. I've arranged dinner for the three of us. Is that proof enough for you, darling?' He reaches out to pat my hand but I pull it away.

It proves nothing. Maybe Sophie is his cousin, but that doesn't mean he's not married to someone else. And even if he's not married, why is he still so obsessed with Michelle that he's carrying the ring she gave him? She is dead. Why can't he move on? There's a pounding in my temple as I place the ring on the table and stand. 'I have to go.'

'Yes of course, let's go somewhere quieter. I'll settle the tab and drive us somewhere where we can talk.'

'No.' I need to be on my own. To get away from him. To think. 'I want to be on my own.'

'Please don't walk out.' His expression has changed, his confidence evaporating at my unexpected reaction.

'How can I trust you not to lie to me again?' I modulate my voice, speak slowly, try to sound calm and rational. 'If you can have one affair you could have another. I will not be your bit on the side.'

'Wait. Don't go.'

I hurry away from him, pushing past tables towards the bar. 'Excuse me,' I interrupt a woman asking the barman if she can swap one sausage for extra mash. 'I need a cab as soon as possible, please. Do you have a number I can call?'

He passes me a battered business card: *Clive's Cabs – affordable luxury*. 'You'll get a better signal in the car park.'

Outside I stand in the shadows under the trees, jabbing at the numbers on my mobile. It takes several attempts because I can't see properly for the tears. What a bloody fool I've been. Like a teenager, flooded with hormones and willing to believe anything I'm told for an *I love you*.

'Could be ten minutes, love,' The woman says, once I give the name of the pub. 'The car's got to come from the station but I'll tell him it's a rush job.'

If I stay where I am in the car park, Leon is likely to come out and find me, maybe try to reason with me. My heart pounding, I set off in the direction of the station. Unsteady on my high heels on the uneven surface of the country lane, I haven't gone far when I hear him calling me.

'Cristina? Are you there?'

I pull back into the hedgerow, my pulse thumping in my ears, breathing hard.

'Cristina? Please.' He sounds desperate. 'Please, don't walk out on me. You can't leave me like this.'

He stands silhouetted in the middle of the lane, near the pub, looking in both directions searching for signs of me. Long grass scratches against my bare legs; the bushes prod my back as if pushing me forward, towards him. I fight the urge to run to him; to pound on his chest with anger until, my fury exhausted, he would hug me to him and make the last half hour disappear. But I've always sworn I would never let myself be lied to.

'I'm sorry,' he shouts into the darkness, unconcerned

about the couple leaving the pub behind him. 'I've been so bloody stupid.'

The sound of a car approaching draws my attention. A taxi rounds the bend travelling slowly, the yellow roof sign declaring *Clive's Cabs*. The driver is chatting on his mobile and when I launch myself from my hiding place in the undergrowth he's forced to brake suddenly. I run towards the cab, stumbling on the uneven surface, almost falling.

Leon shouts, 'Wait.'

As I fumble with the door handle, Leon strides towards me. And part of me is still hoping that he'll reach me, stop me leaving. Somehow make it right again. But once in the back seat I find my resolve and slam the door shut. 'Please, hurry,' I say to the driver. 'I'll give you directions.'

Leon is now alongside the taxi but doesn't try to open the door. He presses his palm to the glass. 'I love you,' he says, his eyes locking with mine. '*That* is the truth.'

'Want me to go?' The driver asks, looking at me in the rear-view mirror, eyebrows raised, waiting for a signal that I still want to leave. I nod, tears welling in my eyes.

As the car pulls off I turn back to look at Leon. He hasn't moved from the spot but it is as if he has caved in on himself, his shoulders slumped, head down, disappearing into the shadows.

In the taxi my tears give way to rage. The man I have allowed myself to love is not what I thought. He has lied to me.

How dare he treat me this way. What a fool I've been.

Before I change my mind, I take my phone out and delete his number. Then turn the mobile off, shoving it deep into my bag.

By the time I get home I'm shaking so much my key judders around the lock as I try to open the door.

My anger is a visceral thing that runs from my fingertips to my toes and seems to have a life of its own. As if something wild has been unleashed, my mind and body taken over by a force outside me, a thing I can't control.

I try to calm down. Cuddling a cushion for comfort, I walk myself through what's happening in my brain and body: this is no more than a surge of stress hormones from the amygdala causing a chain reaction, shutting down my frontal lobes, literally stopping me from thinking rationally. I try to distance myself from the feeling, observe it rather than experience it, but as the cushion flies across the room with all the strength I can muster, I admit defeat. I cannot focus on anything but my rage, cannot recall a single technique that might help.

So I pace then, worn out, sit and stare lost in thoughts that aren't thoughts but a car crash of emotion, then I pace some more.

As the sun comes up I think I have control. I decide to do what I always tell clients to do: write things down. If I can get events, emotions, reactions, into some sort of order I can get some perspective. I fetch a notepad and pen and go through to my lounge. But as I write *'Leon'* at the top of the page I glance across at the chair he sat in only days before and the anger surges through me again. The pen becomes a weapon and I score out his name, ripping through the pages beneath, not satisfied until I have destroyed every page in the pad, a confetti of torn paper around my feet.

Exhausted, I go to the kitchen for a glass of water and in a trance state stare out at the garden towards my therapy room. I remember that first session with him, his calm confidence, his intelligence, his good looks; these things compelling enough on their own. But coupled with his need for my help, he had me hooked from the start. *But he lied to me.* Cold water spilling over my hands draws me back to the present. I've left the tap running. My hands shake so violently I try to place the too-full glass down on the kitchen counter and the water slops out and my brain tells me: *Nothing will ever go right again. You are a failure at everything you do.*

Without forethought or plan, I purposively tip the glass over, watching the water flow towards the box of teabags where it soaks into the cardboard. Another rivulet finds the novel I'm reading, the spine cracked open, lying where I'd left it while waiting for the kettle to boil at some point yesterday. A lifetime ago. I cannot recall what the book is about. Some water drips into the cutlery drawer, where it can mingle with the teaspoons and the inevitable bread-crumbs that find their way there. Not content with this act of destruction, I watch dissociated as my forefinger prods the glass several times until it rolls off the countertop and hits the floor, a thud and a slight chip in the rim rather than the dramatic smashing I'd hoped for. *You can't even get that right.*

The cutlery drawer is provoking me. I open it wide then slam it with as much force as I can muster. But it merely glides into place on its 'soft close' mechanism. The comedy of this strikes me and suddenly I am laughing. Laughing so much I cannot stop until, once again, I start to cry.

I need Clare.

Chapter Fourteen

On the drive to Clare's, I ponder what I want from her. Do I want her to reassure me and tell me … tell me what? That I'm not stupid for falling for him, not spotting his lies and evasions? That it could be so much worse?

No. What I need right now is a hug from someone I love. And trust.

Clare opens the door and immediately clasps me to her, without need for explanation. All I'd said to her on the phone was that I needed to see her and she didn't ask why, reading the tone, knowing I'm not one to cry wolf. She answers my unspoken need with her unconditional love, my surrogate mother, always there with a metaphorical plaster, a glass of lemonade and a hand to my forehead. We stay locked together in her hallway until my sobs quieten, my breathing slows.

'Okay?' she says.

I nod. Keeping her arm around my shoulder, she guides me to the sofa where she sits down next to me rather than in her usual chair. A slight breeze from an open window makes the hairs on my forearm stand and, noticing, Clare moves to shut it but I stay her with a touch. *Don't leave me.* I cannot bear her to move even the few yards to the window. We sit in silence and she waits, breathing slowly until my breath matches hers and I am calm.

'Thank you,' I say.

She places her hand on my arm. 'We have as long as you need. There is no rush.'

'Leon lied to me,' I say. She will know who I'm talking about.

She nods her head slightly in acknowledgement of what she's heard.

'He lied to me from the beginning.'

'Ah.'

'He's not a lecturer like he said he was. He might even be married.' And I spill the whole story.

I disclose that I've started to see him socially, noticing that I am too numb and too emotionally tired to *feel* the guilt that I carry deep inside. She doesn't react. There is no blame, no criticism for my evasions and omissions. She merely listens without judgement, as I aspire to do. I admit to how things have developed over the months to be more than supportive friendship on my side, that I find him attractive. Tell her I had started to hope it would become something more. That I thought we might have a future together.

Clare is everything I could have asked for and more. Her calm presence, her patience, the way she listens without me having to put everything into words; all these things help me to see each step. How his lies built.

How my own lies and evasions built.

How I've risked everything for this.

'So you were right to doubt him from the start,' she says. 'You always said there was something you couldn't put your finger on.'

She is saying this to reassure me, but I am still glad that she said it – that in some things my judgement is valid.

★

This must be what it feels like to go to a confessional, an unburdening. I feel lighter, almost spacey. In her bathroom I wash my hands, splash my face with cold water. Catching sight of my reflection I momentarily wonder at the tired, sad, middle-aged woman staring back at me with heavy-lidded eyes. I haven't seen her since the weeks after Dad died.

When I return, Clare offers me a drink: 'Water, coffee, tea, something stronger?'

She brings two tall opaque glasses of iced tea and I think of the glass I pushed to the floor earlier.

'How can I best help you process this? What do you need?' she asks.

'I want to understand why I got in this mess. Why I fell for a deceitful liar when I always promised myself I never would.'

'Where would you like to start?'

'Why would he lie to me? Why couldn't he tell me the truth?'

She shrugs. 'To hide something? To gain something? Let's think more widely about why people lie.'

'To deceive others.'

'Too simple. That's a tautology. Would you say you set out to deceive me when you didn't tell me about Leon?'

'No. I ...'

'So what was your positive intent? What was the purpose of the lie?'

'I wanted you to see the best of me. Not to fail in your eyes.'

'So we mustn't leap to conclusions. Let's think broadly; what purpose might someone have for not telling the whole truth?'

'To present a positive picture of themselves ... Maybe

161

waiting to find the right time ... To protect someone, so they don't hurt or harm someone else ...'

'Like your father did when your mother left. He lied to protect you. What I'm saying is, it is complicated and there are many sides to every story, as we both know.'

I nod, take a sip of iced tea. 'So, I shouldn't make assumptions that he did it out of malice, to make a fool of me.'

'Let's start by looking at the facts and consider positive reasons why Leon may not have told you the whole truth.' She holds up her right hand. 'He came to you when he was mourning his lover. His current job was never discussed in therapy. As time went on, your friendship started to develop and there never seemed to be the right moment. Then, when he started to care for you, he had more to lose by admitting he hadn't been completely honest. He's only just recovered from losing one woman he loved and didn't want to risk losing another. Maybe it's true that he never found the *right* time to raise it?'

'You could be right.' I rub my forehead. 'He was distraught yesterday. He begged me not to leave him.'

'Before we run off with that assumption, there are other possibilities.' Clare holds up her other hand, marking an alternative option. 'For example, maybe he *is* married and *is* a serial adulterer, as you seemed to assume last night. Yes, he was mourning Michelle when he came for therapy but you helped him through that and have now replaced her in his affections, swapping one lover for the next, while he has a wife – maybe children – at home.'

Hearing Clare voice my fears out loud, it doesn't sound right. 'I don't think it was a casual affair: he idolised Michelle – the way he talks about her ... He still has photos on his phone. I think he genuinely loved her – they planned to retire to Spain together.'

162

'*Idolised* – an interesting term. Do you believe he has constructed this perfect image of her since she died, or that he always put her on a pedestal?'

The description of their first meeting flashes into my mind, him bidding for the expensive painting so he could get to meet her. I swallow hard. 'I think he was quite obsessed with her from the start.'

'Has he shown any idolisation or obsessive behaviour towards you?' Clare sits up straight, alert. 'Has he kept phoning you or checking where you are? Other than that time when we were in the café, has he turned up unexpectedly at places you go?'

I hold my breath. *Not him, me. I've been the obsessed one. Going to the college, buying his book, constantly wanting to call him. Desperate for us to move on to a sexual relationship.* I shake my head and rub away a tear that wells in my eye.

As if reading my thoughts, she asks, 'Has there been anything sexual between you? Or is it merely a friendship?' She's seeking confirmation. She is trying to confirm how many boundaries I've knocked down; whether there are grounds for a professional complaint. Damage limitation.

'Nothing sexual,' I say, looking down at my lap. 'But he has been very affectionate.'

'So, whilst an inappropriate relationship, you've not crossed that particular boundary?'

'No.' My face reddens as I think of my feelings towards him. Whilst Clare and I have discussed sex in all its guises over the years in relation to client cases, this is the first time I've felt embarrassed. It's reminiscent of when Dad tried to have his 'birds and bees' Talk. He ended up giving me a book and asking Aunty Brenda to do the explaining.

When Clare eventually suggests that she takes over my client list, my relief is palpable. And I acknowledge how hard it's been carrying the responsibility for others' wellbeing when I'm barely coping myself.

'I think it would be good for you to see a therapist for a few sessions. You've not yet got over the loss of your dad and need to process your grief. I can recommend someone if that would be helpful.' She pauses, checking I'm in agreement. She's right of course. She was right all along, I wasn't ready to see clients again. Too much triggered by Dad's death – too many flashbacks to being eight years old and abandoned. Too much fear of being alone driving my desperate need to have someone special who loves and needs me.

I can see now how hard I've been trying to fill a Dad-shaped void. Maybe it's been the same for Leon – both of us searching for the lost part and landing on each other.

Clare leaves me alone for a while, giving me space to think. The sound of the tap running and the clunk of cupboard doors tells me she is making us coffee. When she comes back with two mugs she sits in the chair opposite me.

'May I give you some advice?' she asks. It is not her style to tell me what to do or what to think. She mentors, coaches and guides with a gentle hand on the tiller; knowing that I take everything she says to heart, she is cautious about advising. This is different.

I nod, hoping for an answer, anything to help me move on.

'Firstly, it's my belief that this won't be the end of it. He will try to make amends and not want to be seen as the bad guy. He may make excuses, play on your emotions by drawing parallels with your family history – likening himself to your father and how devastated he must've felt after your mother left. So desperate that it leads to out-of-character behaviour.'

'I can see that, yes.'

'So, I believe he will try to apologise and make things right. Knowing you, I also believe you will want to see the best in him and not want to reject him outright if he makes any overtures.'

She pauses, studying me and I bite my lip. She knows me so well.

'Listen to his explanations and excuses, forgive him by all means, but I don't think it wise for you to take this relationship any further. If it stops now, no real harm has been done. In a month or so we can assess whether you are ready to resume practising therapy or should extend your sabbatical.' She leans forward, earnest. 'But if you take this relationship further, I think it will be a grave mistake. Aside from having to give up your therapy practice, I don't think it would end well for you, Cristina.'

Cristina. Not Cris. I've disappointed her. Tears prick in my eyes and I swallow hard, but they keep coming and I rub my eyes with the back of my hand as I speak.

'You're right...' I sniff hard. 'How could I have been so unprofessional? It's against everything I value ... everything you've ever taught me. I've been a fool and I've really let you down. I'm sorry. I am so, so sorry.'

She shakes her head and reaches across the space between us to take my hand. 'You don't need my forgiveness. You need to forgive yourself.'

Back at home I pace as I think, figure of eights from the lounge through the hall to the kitchen and back again. Carpet, tile, wood, tile, carpet, tile, wood ... processing events, juggling the things he told me, how much of what he's said was true.

There's no cause to doubt anything he told me in therapy. And if he's left the college then some things begin to makes sense. It explains why he hasn't been able to introduce me to his work colleagues. That fat man at the Globe, talking about the German contract; the woman at the art gallery waving across the room – one 'Hallo, Leon, how are you enjoying your early retirement?' would be all it took.

If he'd wanted to keep it secret, it was a huge risk for him to take me to so many places where he might know people; it's almost like he wanted me to ask questions, so he could tell me the truth.

Maybe it's my fault – I should have made fewer assumptions and asked more questions.

But what about the ring? What if he is really married and I've been a complete fool? Despite Clare's warning ringing in my ears, I need to see him once more. I still need to know the truth.

At seven-thirty in the morning, the doorbell forces me to unravel myself from the sheets and get up.

My hand on the front door latch, I find, of course, it's locked. Still in my pyjamas I grab a coat from the hook, shouting, 'Hang on a minute.' As usual, the keys aren't in their assigned place and, with no memory of where I put them last night, I curse under my breath as I search. It's a good few minutes before I open the door with a cheery, 'Sorry about that.' But there's no one there. Just a cardboard box, printed with my name and address.

I take it inside, turning it this way and that, but there's no Amazon smile, no DHL stripes. No branding at all and no return address, just mine. Opening the front door again to check for a delivery vehicle, I see there's nothing but a young lad strolling up the Crescent.

'Hey, excuse me.'

When he doesn't respond, I jog after him in my

unfit-middle-aged-woman-run usually saved for buses. I catch up as he turns the corner and stops by a blue car.

'Excuse me,' I pant at him.

He looks me up and down, taking in my summer mac now flapping open exposing my floral cropped pjs, the look set off by bright pink Crocs. With my wild hair and breathless wheezing, he probably assumes there's some medical emergency.

'Nothing's wrong,' I say.

'That's good.' He must be about twenty, well spoken, confident in that way of gorgeous young people.

'Did you just deliver a parcel to Oakwood Crescent?'

'Yes. Number forty-six.'

'Do you know who sent it?'

The lad frowns like it's a particularly challenging question. 'No. Kiara asked me to drop it off.'

My turn for the quizzical look. I raise my eyebrows, encouraging him to say more.

'Kiara?'

'She does the admin.' He holds out a lanyard hanging round his neck; his name is Lakbir Singh but it's the company logo he is showing me. Intertwined letters, a monogram combining two Ms and a C. 'I'm just an intern. Do what I'm told.'

Watching him drive away, I ponder Kiara. Who is this woman and why is she sending me a parcel? Then it strikes me: I've seen that monogram before – on the pen Leon had lent me all those months ago.

Back in the house I kick the box under my desk with the toe of my Croc, my anger rising again, furious that he lied. Furious that he thinks he can win me over by sending one of his interns with an expensive gift; a gift no doubt selected by the delightful Kiara. Make a fool of me again.

So if he doesn't work at the college, where does he work? I grab my mobile and type in the letters MCM, then CMM, then MMC in the search but there are way too many options: motorcycles, classic cars; 'electrical solutions'; a clothing company. I try adding 'photography' To the search and get more relevant hits but nothing obvious or with Leon's name. I'm about to add Leon Jacobs to the search bar when I catch myself, finger poised over the enter key. This is not *me*. *I do not do this*. This is the type of obsessive behaviour I warn my clients against. I've seen it happen: a desire to find out more moves from a simple Google search to waking in the small hours, fixated, then leaping in the car to drive round the streets searching for clues. That way madness lies.

He will not make me his Ophelia.

I close the search engine. Count to ten, breathing deeply.

But I am still furious. I imagine him with a team of ex-student acolytes around him, all ooh-ing and ah-ing about his latest work of art, typing his lectures for him, organising his plane tickets and hotel rooms. I can see him leaning over the beautiful Kiara, standing that bit too close. 'You remember that woman I was with at the Private View we went to?' Kiara stifles a giggle, recalling my ill-chosen outfit. He snorts a laugh in response, their shared private joke. 'Yes, *her*. When you've finished the presentation for my lecture in Germany, can you find a gift to send her? Something suitably romantic that says "sorry". Get one of the lads to drop it off.'

Well, it won't work. I am not a soft touch. I will give the box to the charity shop unopened.

Chapter Fifteen

'Hi, Cris, it's me, Nisha.' She's worried about me. I can tell from her tone on the mobile. 'I was in the High Street and I thought maybe I could pop round for a coffee? Or we could go out if you like?'

I answer the unspoken question. 'I'm fine. Come over. It would be good to see you.'

'That's a relief because I've bought us doughnuts and otherwise I'd have to eat them on my own.' The doorbell rings before we've said our goodbyes and I open it with one hand, the other clasping the phone. And Nisha's standing there on the step with her mobile still to her ear.

'Bye,' she says into it, before hanging up, then: 'Hi. I want the salted caramel one.' She thrusts the bag of doughnuts at me.

'What if I'd been dyeing my hair or waxing my top lip?'

She shrugs. 'Seen it all before.'

She follows me to the kitchen, where she fetches plates and tears off kitchen roll as I make tea, each performing our tasks without need for communication.

As we sit down at the breakfast bar she says, 'I've missed you. But I understand how it is when you first meet someone.'

'I'm sorry, Nisha. I didn't mean to shut you out.' The last time I got all loved up over an unsuitable man, I promised myself that I'd never forget my friends again.

'Angie told us they met you at the pond. She says he seems really nice. Well, to be honest she was a bit cruder than that. "Sex on a stick" were her exact words.'

'I wouldn't know about that. We've only been on a few dates. Anyway I've called it off.'

'Why? I thought you sounded quite keen when you told me and Jen.'

'I am. I was. But I found out he lied to me from the start.'

'Oh. Married?'

'No, well maybe. He …' I'm so used to chatting about anything and everything with Nisha and Jen but this time I can't. He was my client and there are details I can't share. 'I went to where he said he worked and he hasn't worked there for a year.'

'Oh. But it's not so odd. A lot of people fib about their jobs on dating sites these days. The last guy I dated claimed he was a pilot; turns out he works for the same haulage firm as Davy.'

'I didn't meet him on an app. I can't tell you more than that, sorry.'

She reads between the lines, her eyes flicking through the window to my therapy room and back to me. 'Ah. Complicated.'

'I've told Clare, my supervisor. I'm taking a break from therapy for a while.'

She nods. 'So, is that it then, with the bloke? It's over? When did you last see him?'

'The night before last. We argued and I walked out on him.'

She picks the hundreds and thousands off her second doughnut, placing them round the edge of her plate. 'People lie for all sorts of reasons. Remember when Ali lied to Dan about her parents?'

170

'Yes, but he kept this lie up for months.'

'So did Ali. Dan only found out when he dropped her home one night. Gave him a shock when it turned out she was still living with Mum and Dad. Sometimes it's just easier to carry on with the story once you've started.' She takes a bite of doughnut, covers her mouth as she says, 'Has he called you?'

'No, but he got me a present. It arrived this morning.'

She looks round searching for the evidence. 'Where? Show me.'

'I've not opened it. I don't want it.' I'm petulant, a sulky child. 'You can have it.'

'In that case I hope it's a diamond necklace.'

I fetch the box and place it on the kitchen counter. 'It's all yours.'

'Ooh, exciting,' she says, her enthusiasm raising the flicker of curiosity I've been trying to dampen down. She tears at the cardboard. 'Sadly it's not diamonds unless it's wrapped like pass-the-parcel.'

I feign disinterest, taking our mugs to the dishwasher.

'Oh,' she says. 'Not at all what I'd expected.' She holds up three paperback books. 'They're not even new ...' She tries to pass me one. 'It's poetry. Look there's a Post-it note. See what's on that page.'

I shake my head. 'No. You look.' A teenager again.

She turns to the tabbed page. 'Brian Patten?' she says, checking if I know the poet. " 'Probably it is too early in the morning'." She laughs. 'He's got you sussed. He knows you're no lark!'

She opens the next book.

'Leonard Cohen. "*You Do Not Have To Love Me*".'

'A bit on the nose,' I say, trying to laugh it off, but he's used the L-word and I am touched.

171

Her lips move as she reads the poem to herself. 'It's a bit weird. He says he wants you to love him and he doesn't! Makes no sense at all.'

I reach for the third book to see for myself. *Modern Haiku And Other Poems.* Opening it at the Post-it note, I read through the highlighted words:

'The first step I took towards you was the point of no return.'

Tears prick my eyes and I have to swallow hard. Nisha is studying my face for a reaction. 'He knows you, Cris. It may have been only a few dates but he really gets you.'

I shrug.

'Do you think it might be worth hearing his explanation?'

My newfound resolve crumbles. 'I suppose I owe him that.'

Planning a short email, I can't think what to say.

I accept your apology. Is it an apology? If it is, do I accept it? And if I do, what comes next?

Thank you for the gift ... I was touched by your thoughtful gift ... I was touched by the poems. No. I'm showing my hand.

Third attempt. *If the poems express how you really feel about me, we need to talk. I would like to hear your side of the story to help me understand.* No sign-off and certainly no kisses. I hit send before I can change my mind.

I sit staring at the screen as if a response will pop up immediately, but no. When I check my phone in case there's a text from him, I recognise my obsessive behaviour and decide I should do something else. Like take a shower for the first time in two days and tidy up the evidence of my temper tantrums.

In the end he neither texts nor emails but turns up in person. It's early evening and I've already had a glass or two of wine. When the doorbell rings I know it can only be him and my guts churn with anxiety rather than excitement. This conversation could go either way and I can't face an argument.

He is standing back from the door on the pathway, as if ready to run should things turn nasty. Half turned from me, his posture slumped, head on one side, he looks defenceless as he rubs the back of his neck with one hand.

'Thank you,' he says quietly. 'Thank you for agreeing to talk.'

'Come in.'

He follows me as I lead the way to the kitchen. The half-empty bottle is on the side. 'Will you join me?' I ask.

'Thank you, yes.' He stands, watching me pour the wine and I'm conscious of how tightly controlled my movements are, how shallow my breathing, as if one false move could shatter everything.

I perch on the edge of one of the stools at the breakfast bar and he takes the other, opposite me.

'What can I say?' he asks. 'What do you want to know?'

'Can we start with the ring? Tell me the truth. Are you married?

'No. I told you the truth. Michelle gave it to me.' He takes out his wallet, removes the ring and holds it out towards me but I don't take it from him. 'Please look. There's an engraving inside.'

I hold it up to the light, turning it this way and that, squinting to read the tiny script, not wanting to admit I now need reading glasses. *'Til death do us part – M M',* The initials in a tiny heart. I swallow hard, the true meaning of that inscription so poignant now she is dead.

'*M M?*'

'Michelle Mitchell. Her maiden name. She gave it to me when we went to Spain to look at properties. When she said she'd leave her husband.' He looks down to the left, deep in his emotions. 'I keep it with me … It's a comfort when I need to feel her close. Seeing the photos in the book … it sparked things off again. I should've explained. I'm sorry.'

'No, I'm sorry for misjudging you. I'm sorry for being so quick to make assumptions.'

'What else do you want to know?'

Everything. But I say, 'Tell me about you leaving the college.'

'Well, you already know about the fight with her husband. He threatened a big exposé in the press. The college agreed to my leaving at the end of term and meanwhile she'd go back to her husband for a while. Let the dust settle while we finalised our plans. We already knew where we were going to live in Spain.'

'The golf resort. She sent me a card.'

'Ah, yes.'

'But you were both in England when she had the accident?'

'Yes. Still making plans … and then …' He shakes himself like a dog shaking out their wet coat; 'breaking state' as we therapists call it, shedding the emotions. 'But you helped me with that. Helped me move on and plan for a new future.' He puts his hand out towards me, resting it palm up on the counter halfway between us, waiting to see if I will respond. 'Is that still possible? A new future … For us?'

'No more lies,' I say.

'No more lies ever again.'

'Even if I ask, "Does my bum look big in this?"'

'Even then.'

I take his hand and he sighs deeply, closing his eyes.

★

174

My promise to myself to be careful, take it slowly, disappears in an instant when he kisses me, his passion matched by my own as he backs me against the fridge. Recipes, lists, thank you cards and magnets cascade to the floor around our feet and we both laugh. He spins me round towards the breakfast bar where, with my help, he hoists me onto the surface. I gasp as he lifts my hair and kisses my neck. He helps me to lie back and I'm momentarily aware of the brightness of the ceiling lights, the open curtains ... but only momentarily.

I don't know how much time passes but it's fair to say I didn't know foreplay could be like that. We're now sprawled half-naked on the kitchen floor, between the breakfast bar and the cooker and even though my breathing is still ragged, my skin still dancing from his touch, the worries leap back on my shoulders. Starting with: *Is this floor clean?* then quickly to: *When did I last shave my armpits? Did he notice my cellulite? Does he think I'm too fat?* I scan around for my clothing, stretching for my sweater, which is just out of reach.

'There's no need for coyness,' Leon says, flopping his arm across me and kissing me on the shoulder. 'You are wonderfully Rubenesque. My own Venus.'

Maybe I should give him some sort of compliment in return or make a joke but nothing comes to mind and all my brain offers up are critical self-comparisons to Michelle with her wrinkle-free skin, full firm breasts and model-girl poses. *Stop it!* 'Wow,' I say. 'That was ...'

'It was, wasn't it?' He laughs. He kisses me again then flips over on to his back beside me, both of us flat on the floor squished next to each other in the narrow gap. 'This is cosy. Although I think there might be a fridge magnet under my left buttock.'

'If you can't tell, you're clearly no prince.'

He snorts a laugh. 'I suppose I should go. I don't want to overstay my welcome.'

Now he's here I don't want him to leave, but I don't want to seem needy by asking him to stay, so I stall for time. 'Shall I make us a coffee?'

The next morning when I wake, the other half of the bed is empty. The sound of water running through the pipes tells me Leon is in the bathroom, clearly an early riser. I'm still shattered and could've done with a lie-in after a sleepless night. His presence next to me had proved very disturbing. Immediately after we'd made love again he turned on his back and closed his eyes. At first I thought he was catching his breath or needed a moment's calm. But no. There was no spooning or cuddles; straight off to sleep. It was quite sweet the first hour or so, studying his cheekbones, his lashes, the movement of his eyelids and lips as he dreamt. But after that it began to pall. He lay motionless on his back all night, so still that I was afraid to move. When his erratic breathing and occasional mumbling was added to the mix, it was far from an easy night. I rued the fact my sleeping tablets were in the bathroom cabinet and not in my bedside cupboard.

He comes through to my bedroom towelling his hair dry, my pink bath towel around his hips. 'I hope it's okay to use this? I didn't want to root around in your cupboards.'

It doesn't feel quite right but I don't know why. We have just spent an intimate night together and yet using my shower, my towels without asking first seems wrong, a step too far. I park it to think about later. 'That's fine.' I reach for my dressing gown, which is screwed up on the chair by my side of the bed where I left it yesterday morning. 'Do you fancy some breakfast? A coffee?'

176

'Thanks, but I ought to head off and leave you to get on with your day.'

I'm glad he's said that; I need some time to myself to take stock. But I want to ask when I'll see him again. *Is that reasonable?*

I leave him to dress, not feeling comfortable to stay in the room as I can't just sit there and watch. Although dressing myself without showering first wouldn't normally worry me if I wasn't going out somewhere, it could imply a slovenly approach. In the bathroom I clean my teeth, run a brush through my tangled curls, give my armpits a spray of deodorant so I smell a bit fresher and return still wearing my dressing gown.

As I see him out of the front door, he kisses me and the smell of mint makes me wonder if he used my toothbrush too and I'm so grossed out by this thought I don't respond with more than an 'okay' when he says, 'I'll call you.'

That afternoon I phone Nisha to update her.

'It's back on.'

'So, tell me!'

'Well … let's just say, we made up.'

She squeals, then in a sing-song voice recites the children's nursery rhyme: 'Cris and Leon sitting in a tree, K-I-S-S-I-N-G. First comes love, then comes marriage—'

'Enough!' I laugh.

'Well, how was it?'

'Nisha! To be honest pretty perfect… I'm really not sure what he sees in me. His ex was *really* pretty. A Botoxed blonde, big pert boobs, size ten. We're polar opposites.'

'I hate her! Anyway, he can't have liked her that much because they're not together now.'

I don't say that she's dead. Time to change the subject.

'Enough about me. I've hogged the air time. Any news I've missed?'

'Davy's birthday – I think Angie's planning something.'

Oh. That's my job. Our birthdays are coming up, a week apart. I usually organise a joint event with all the Wellies, although I haven't started thinking about it yet. I try to sound casual as I ask, 'What's she got in mind?'

'Don't know. She's "keeping her powder close to her chest" she says.'

I force a laugh in acknowledgement of Angie's mash-up. 'Let's hope it's not a surprise fancy dress party.' Davy's views on surprises and dressing up had been loudly voiced over the years. 'Do you remember Mick's fiftieth?'

The invite had said 'Come as your favourite pop star/ album'. At the party there was an Aladdin Sane, a couple of Madonnas – one with the coned breasts, the other more *Desperately Seeking Susan*; a Mick Jagger … Everyone had made an effort, bar Davy.

'God, yes. He just wore his normal clothes and that Sex Pistols badge.'

'Don't understate his effort! He'd used it to pin on a condom and some aspirins. *Sex and Drugs and Rock'n'Roll.*'

'Mind you, Mick's Alice Cooper was a bit of a mystery. He looked like some sad case roadie,' Nisha says. 'Talking of birthdays, we're still coming round as usual on the 31st. You're not planning to bump us for lover boy?'

'Would I dare?' It's become a ritual since we turned forty. A gathering at the birthday girl's house – me, Nisha, Jen and Ali – one chooses the theme for the evening, one does the food, one organises a jokey gift and the birthday queen supplies the booze. A sort of warm-up for the joint do with Davy a week later.

'Anyway, what's lover boy planning for your birthday?'

Nisha asks. 'If he really wants to win you over and say sorry it should be something really nice. Make up for those tatty poetry books.'

'I haven't told him. It's never come up in conversation.'

'Maybe you ought to drop some hints. Point at something expensive in a magazine.'

'Nisha! You're outrageous.'

'Gotta go, there's a call coming in – potential hot date on line two! See you Friday at the Lion.'

Chapter Sixteen

I don't hear from Leon for a couple of days and I work myself into a stew of worry – was it just a one-off? Was he using me? Is he laughing at me now? 'Can you believe that overweight/middle-aged/uneducated woman imagined we were going to be a couple!' Have I risked my whole therapy career for one night of sex? Why did I follow my gut when I should've listened to my head, listened to Clare?

Then in a more rational moment, I wonder if it's a commitment issue. Or a sense of guilt towards Michelle, a feeling he has betrayed her memory by moving on too quickly with me?

In my anxious state I fetch Michelle's file from my cabinet. Maybe I missed something when I looked through it before. Now that I know Leon better I might notice a hint I didn't pick up on, something subtle that would help me understand what they had together.

Tipping out the contents there is a faint smell of the coffee I spilt. The pages are stained and, even as I try to separate and order them, I suspect this is a fruitless task.

What is it I really want to know?

I want to know what was it about Michelle that made him want her so much. And is it possible for him to have the same depth of feeling about me? Whilst this relationship could be everything I want, if there's no future I don't want to waste my time.

Poring over the notes that I'd only skimmed before, I now work through them chronologically. The only new revelations are in the pages from her final session joining the dots that led up to the brawl at the college. Michelle had arrived promptly for the session for once – her husband had dropped her off. He had discovered she was coming for therapy and was *furious* that she hadn't told him. My notes suggest she was fearful, worried that he would insist on knowing her every move, suspicious of what she was up to. She wanted to leave him, said she couldn't bear to be with him and couldn't live without LJ – he was her *saviour*, had helped her realise that she could have a better life, a happy life …

The notes stop there.

Eventually Leon turns up unannounced some days later. There's a knock at the front door and I can't get it open as I've misplaced the key again and don't have time to search through trouser pockets and handbags. 'Come round the back,' I shout.

'Tradesmen's entrance, sorry. I've temporarily lost the key,' I say by way of explanation, lifting the gnome by the back door to retrieve the spare. Nisha had accused me of morphing into Charlie Dimmock and bought the gnome for me as a joke when I kept banging on about my plans for a herb garden and a fishpond. The gnome is called Titchmarsh and he has a jaunty red jacket and an orange plastic fish swings from his rod over a mirror pond. I wonder if I should explain the irony so Leon doesn't assume I just have bad taste, but instead I say, 'How are you?'

'Grand, thank you. And I have a day off and it's a gorgeous day and I thought it would be lovely to take my gorgeous girlfriend out for lunch.' He must notice something in my expression that accompanies the fleeting thought *you could have called me*, because he adds. 'Of course, you may have other plans. I know you're a busy woman.'

'I'm free until this evening. It would be lovely.'

I lead him to the kitchen, my cheeks reddening as he looks around and I recall the events of two nights ago, the flashbacks as I'd cleared up the morning after. Now I scan round to confirm there's nothing untoward on display and everything is back in place as it should be and it's all tidy and clean … and I should just stop fussing and try to relax … then as I'm juggling all these ridiculous thoughts, he catches my eye and smiles that way that takes in his whole face and I know everything is okay and for the first time smile back.

'You know where everything is. Make yourself a drink while I get changed.'

He takes us to a country pub. Not the one where we had the argument but a new one, further away. As the roads narrow and twist he tells me why they wind the way they do – following original footpaths round people's land or routes the cattle took. I relax as he chats about a car he's trying to import, a convertible – an MG RV8, apparently from Japan – and hopes it will arrive while it's still summer so 'we' can go for drives together and enjoy it. He names the wildflowers we pass and I tell him about my proposed wildflower garden, how I lost my motivation along with the poppy seeds after the break-in.

'We could stop at a garden centre and buy you replacements. Autumn's round the corner and September is the optimum time for planting,' he says, 'We could get tulips too. If we get them in soon they'll be beautiful next spring.' And I count the 'we's and get lost in a daydream of us together a year from now.

★

182

As we pull into the pub car park, I point out a repurposed phone box labelled *Defibrillator* and tell Leon about Jen's course. It's this evening and she's been rallying us all to attend, with bribes of cake for some and descriptions of the good-looking tutor for others. 'I need to be back by four, because I've promised I'll help her set up.'

'Didn't your father die of heart failure?' Leon says, turning off the engine, staring through the windscreen at the phone box.

'Yes, that's one of the reasons I want to get involved. I'm going to sign up as a first responder, one of the team that's trained to work the defib.' I've read up about it. 'It's quite well set up. You go and collect the equipment and do CPR until the ambulance arrives. I'll find out more about it this evening.'

He turns to face me, a slight frown of concern crinkling his brow. 'I don't think that's wise,' he says. 'I don't doubt you're physically capable, but I don't think you'd cope. You would be too emotionally vulnerable.'

'Why do you say that?'

'You've only just lost your father. Imagine if you were called to an elderly man whose heart had stopped. It's not like you see in these hospital dramas on TV. No dramatic shout of "Clear" and then a miracle occurs.'

He takes my hand, shaking his head as he continues to paint the scene. 'You would spend ten, fifteen minutes doing everything you could, trying to bring him back to life. All the while getting more and more exhausted and panicked. You could be on your own with no one to help you. Or if there was family, they would be scared and crying and making everything worse.'

My heartbeat quickens as he describes it. The stress of

being responsible for someone's life. 'The ambulance people would arrive and take over though…'

'And how long would they take to arrive? You may not be aware, Cristina, but defibrillators are only effective within the first couple of minutes after the heart stops. You would be under time pressure from the second the phone rang. Just imagine how you would feel if you failed.'

There's a flashback of Dad's pale face on the hospital pillow, his hair more white than grey, a ghost of himself; fading away, leaving me. His last moments, the difficulty catching his breath, his eyes rolling back in his head. Me calling for *help, please, anyone help me*. And what seems like hours, but must be minutes at most, before doctors come running. Shooing me away, pulling the screens round as I sit offering prayers to the universe. *Don't let him die.*

Imagine if I'd been on my own, responsible. Tears come to my eyes and I lower my head, hoping Leon won't see.

'Oh Cristina, don't cry. I'm sorry.' He reaches across and gently strokes my back. 'You are so vulnerable and I want to wrap you in cotton wool and protect you. I just don't want you doing anything that might upset you.'

Leon has me back at my house by four o'clock, ensuring I have plenty of time to get ready for Jen's training session. He's offered to drive me there, accepting that I can't possibly let her down by not going. But he's also made me promise that I won't sign up as a volunteer. *Scouts' honour, cross my heart.*

On the journey there he decides to come in with me. The hall is full, parents and staff from Jen's school I guess. She's busy pouring teas and coffees and settling people in so I don't introduce her to Leon. At the end of the talk, when she asks for people to come and sign the volunteer list, I look at Leon sitting next to me and he takes my hand and squeezes it gently. We slip out quietly and he puts his arm around my shoulders as he leads me back to the car.

Angie's invitation arrives a few days before my birthday. A photocopied sheet of A4 with handwritten bubble writing: *'Bangers & Booze BBQ,'* it says. Around the text, Angie's collaged images of barbecues, fireworks and beer cans. Whilst it's easy to be cynical about the invitation design, she's hit on exactly the thing that Davy will enjoy: a relaxed afternoon with his mates. She's signed off *'Ange & Dave xx'* and I feel that pang again. We've both been in relationships with other people before, but this time feels different. Like we're both heading off in different directions and will never be able to find our way back.

She's chosen the fourth of August for the party, the Sunday between our birthdays. I mark it on the calendar, attach the invite to the fridge with a smile on my face, unable to see the fridge magnets without recalling my evening with Leon. Angie has circled *'plus-one'* several times in green felt pen. Leon and all the Wellies in full-on party mode? Not so sure. Yes, he'd be polite, try to join in, but in reality undercooked sausages and lukewarm lager are unlikely to be his thing.

Something to ponder ...

I'm just dashing out to do a food shop when the landline phone rings. I let the answerphone pick it up, not wanting to be waylaid if it's someone informing me I recently had an accident and can make a claim.

'Hi, it's Clare. Just checking you're okay and you got my last message. Dereck is expecting your call. Let me know how you get on.' There's a click as she hangs up.

Dereck? I put down my bag-for-life and check the answer

machine. The flashing message indicator says *1*. I replay Clare's new message then delete it. Odd. I seem to be getting scattier – I searched everywhere for my journal yesterday and eventually found it on my bedside cabinet rather than in my desk drawer. I must've been distracted and gone to fetch something from upstairs with it still in my hand. And the keys to my filing cabinet have disappeared since I last used them a week ago.

But I'd definitely have written down a phone number if Clare had left me a message.

I'll email her later for the therapist's details rather than call her, just in case she asks any awkward questions. I'm not ready to confess my recent sins with Leon just yet.

On the day of my birthday the girls arrive together in a cab, correctly anticipating they may not wish to drive home later. They're all giggles and excitement already, like we're sixteen again. Nisha takes control, chivvying me out of the front room, to the kitchen where Ali is unpacking her cocktail kit. She surveys the ingredients I bought with a critical eye: 'I can't believe you got a tin of black cherries! I said maraschino cherries – Jen, you heard me didn't you? Back me up here.'

By the time we return bearing a tray of one of Ali's alcoholic experiments, Nisha has converted the front room into a flashback to our childhood.

'Retro games night,' she declares. 'Hope you can all manage Twister later without doing a warm-up.'

'Without putting our backs out more like.'

'Better get the hula hooping and the Ride-a-Roo race done before we eat, all that swirling and bouncing up and down.' Jen picks up the huge orange Ride-a-Roo ball by the ear-shaped handles. It was her tenth birthday present; half its smiley face has been rubbed off over the years and it's had a puncture or two as her own kids loved it as well. 'Outside?'

'It will give the neighbours something to talk about.'

'Knowing Susan she might want to join in.'

Nisha paces out twenty steps as the distance we must cover, marking the ends of the invisible finish line with two empty bottles from my recycling bin. 'Fastest time,' she declares and starts her timer for Ali's go. When it's my turn I fall off into the lavender bush after five 'hops' and lie sprawled on my back laughing, wedged between the water butt and the side of my therapy room. A shadow looms over me and I can't make out who it is as they're silhouetted by the early evening sun. 'Don't just stand there, get me up!'

The arm that grips me is stronger than I'd expected, the aftershave so familiar that I know it is Leon. He says nothing as he lifts me to my feet.

'Thanks,' I say. I smooth down my dress, brush dry dirt from my backside, uncertain how Leon will react to such frivolousness. 'I wasn't expecting you.'

'No,' he says. 'Quite a party.' He kisses me on the lips and I'm aware that the girls are watching and I see him through their eyes and feel a surge of pride that he is mine. But I'm also aware that the kiss is perfunctory, a passionless gesture. *Is he cross?*

'Girls, this is Leon.'

He is charming, cupping their hands in his as he is introduced to each in turn. 'Ah, let me see if I can remember what I've been told. Jen, of course, we didn't get a chance to talk but I sat in on your defibrillator training. A very worthy venture … Hmm, you've known Cristina since you were so high.' He holds his hand at mid-thigh level. 'But now you've two strapping lads of your own.' He beams his attention on Nisha: 'Nisha, you're the friend that's quite hard to get hold of at the moment. I gather you're very popular on the dating apps.' She grins and shrugs, all the while her eyes busy scanning him, assessing his suitability for me with her own snog-marry-avoid scale. 'And Ali, the go-to person for local market knowledge when I wish to sell my house.'

He's hit on the key things that each of them would want to be known for; and I wonder if that's my unconscious bias in what I tell him, or his analytical ability to sift my stories for the nuggets worth recalling.

He puts one arm around my waist and hugs me to his side. 'You look like you're having fun. Good to meet you all but I won't stay and interrupt you.' He makes no move to go.

'Oh, you must stay,' Nisha says. 'Ali, get Leon a drink. Not that ghastly cocktail you gave us. What will you have? A G'n'T?'

'That would be nice, yes. Thank you.'

Jen's retrieved the Ride-a-Roo from the lavender and glances at me to read my reaction. An unspoken 'no' flashes between us and she holds it out towards Nisha. 'Cris is disqualified for falling off in such an ungainly way.'

'My go! Watch and learn,' Nisha says. She hitches her skirt up and straddles the Ride-a-Roo, exposing her long slim legs, then sets off bounding down the garden, her breasts bouncing as she goes. She's completely unaware of how she looks and it's hardly a flirtatious thing to do, but I'm conscious of how striking she is. And that Leon is watching her.

She waves her arms victorious when Jen tells her she has achieved the quickest time. 'Best score! We should have taken bets. D'you want a go before I declare myself the winner?' she asks Leon.

He smiles politely, shakes his head. 'I'll leave it to the professionals.'

Ali comes out with the tray of drinks and passes them round. 'Happy birthday,' she says as she clinks glasses with me.

'To the birthday girl!'

Leon's expression tightens but he doesn't let on that he had no idea it was my birthday. Even if he'd seen it on my calendar in the kitchen, it only said 'Girls' Night'. He joins in with the toast, takes a sip of his drink and kisses me on the cheek. 'I think I'd best leave you ladies to it.'

'Won't you stay while we cut the cake?' Ali says. 'We could do it now rather than later.'

Jen adds, 'Or we can save you a slice and Cris can give you it when she next sees you.' She's read the situation, sees there's some tension, although she wouldn't know why.

'Thank you,' Leon says. 'And I'll have a balloon and a party bag too if one's going.' His smile is fake and it is clear how unhappy he is to be wrong-footed like this. 'Lovely to meet you all.'

'I'll see you out,' I say, hoping to clear the air and make things right.

'I think I know the way.' His tone is jovial for the benefit of the girls but when he turns to face me his expression is flat. Like he's disappointed in me but trying not to show it. 'What time will the party finish? Maybe I'll call round then for my goody bag.'

'Wow! Who? When? How?' Ali says after Leon has gone. 'Spill the beans.' She is the only one who doesn't know the backstory.

Nisha frowns, playing a petulant child. 'It's not fair. I want one like that!'

Only Jen senses my mood correctly, her reaction more muted. 'He seems nice. You look good together.'

I grab a pink and purple hula hoop and twirl it around

on my arm, feigning good humour that I don't feel. 'Enough about him.' I toss the hoop towards Ali who leaps sideways, hopeless at catching, then chases it as it bounces along the patio. 'A little less conversation, a little more action. On with the games.'

'Ooh, I love that song,' Nisha says, taking her phone from her pocket. 'It's on my playlist.' A few seconds later the Elvis/ JXL remix is blasting out and the hula hooping is underway.

Leon arrives at the back door less than five minutes after the girls leave in their cab.

'I'm sorry,' I say, opening the door wide to let him in.

'You'd better get me a drink,' is all he says.

I lead him to the lounge where an open Prosecco bottle stands in an ice bucket and I pour us both a glass. The chaos of the evening still clutters the room: Pin the Tail on the Donkey stapled to the curtains (Boris Johnson's face on the ass); the coffee table pushed back to make room for the Twister board; pick-up sticks scattered on the polished wood around the used glasses.

He is staring at the orchid positioned on the windowsill out of harm's way from our games. 'This is new. A jaguar orchid,' he says.

Maybe I'm mistaken and he isn't in such a bad mood. 'I definitely want you on my side in the pub quiz. It was a gift from my friend Clare. She loves orchids.'

'You've never mentioned a Clare before,' he says.

'I've known her years. She's my supervisor. But I'm not doing any therapy at the moment – she thought I should take a break … when I told her about us.'

'Ah. Yes. Boundaries were no doubt deemed to be broken.' He strokes a leaf, running his finger from stem to tip. 'Should she be sending you flowers? Isn't that blurring the bounds of the relationship?'

'She's a really close friend too. My surrogate mum. We've known each other years.'

The leaf is off the plant, pinched between his fingertips, an accident maybe or an attempt to prune it. 'Why didn't you tell me it was your birthday?' He sounds calm but his shoulders are rigid, his movements tight.

'I'm sorry.'

'For what? Not telling me it's your birthday? Or preferring to celebrate with your girlfriends rather than with me?'

I bite my lip. 'I—'

'Or did it slip your mind? Couldn't find a way to raise the subject? Honestly, Cristina, what is going on?' He pauses, runs both hands through his hair, shaking his head in disbelief. 'Don't tell me this is to pay me back for not telling you I'd left the college?'

'No. No. I wouldn't do that. I just... I was going to tell you tomorrow. I just always see the girls on my birthday.'

He studies me, saying nothing, takes another sip of Prosecco then picks up one of my birthday cards on the bookshelf, a view of a sunset over a lake. 'Who's Sam?' he asks. 'And why does he write his name in inverted commas?' His back is turned so I can't read his expression but his tone is cold.

'He's one of my acting group. You saw him in the play. Sam was his character's name. He was the doctor.'

'The one you flirted with.' He picks up another. It's the one Jake sent.

Sensing trouble brewing, I leap in with an explanation before he can ask. 'He's Davy's oldest friend. We've all known each other since school.'

He places the card back, straightening them so they are

aligned. 'Sam, Jake, Davy. If I didn't trust you I might think you were up to something with all these men friends.'

This feels like an echo of the night in the pub, but our roles are reversed. I'm the one who appears to have lied; he's the one with possessive jealousy. 'You can meet them all if you want. We've been invited to Davy's birthday party on Sunday. It's a barbecue.'

As if I'd not spoken, he says, 'We agreed no more lies … or does lying by evasion not count?'

'I am so sorry. I would've told you tomorrow. It's just I couldn't have let the girls down …'

'I thought – hoped – this was serious, Cristina, our relationship. That I was important to you. If not, I need to know. Now. Before I get even more emotionally involved with you. I don't think I can bear any more heartbreak.'

'It is serious. I am serious about you, about us.'

'I want to believe you.'

I now know how he felt in the pub, the night we argued. Wanting to make things good and prove my sincerity. 'What can I do to prove it to you?'

'Promise me you'll put us first. I can't take second place in your life if our relationship matters.' His eyes are sad, hopeful. 'I need to know that you care as much as I do. Don't keep me at a distance. Tell me what is going on and don't lie to me any more. I want us to share everything.'

'Of course, yes.' I lean into his chest and he wraps his arms around me.

He twines a length of my hair around his hand, pulling gently so my head is tipped to one side, my throat exposed. I hold my breath, waiting, anticipating a kiss, the start of a seduction. After a couple of seconds he lets go.

'Shall we go upstairs?' he asks.

★

He doesn't stay the night this time but he phones me at nine the next morning. 'I've made some arrangements for your belated birthday gift. You're seeing Stefano at two o'clock. He's giving you a make-over. I'll send a car to take you. Then you'll meet me at my club for dinner.'

'A make-over? Gosh. Thank you. I don't know what to say.'

'Thank you is more than enough. Now, let's not allow your little secret to spoil our belated celebration. It is all forgiven and forgotten.'

Chapter Seventeen

I'm dropped off outside a West End salon. The driver gives me an embossed card and tells me to call when I want to be picked up. A few shoves against the huge black door achieves nothing, but after a couple of jabs at one of those silent bells they buzz me in. Inside it's really posh, all fig-perfumed diffusers, white leather, chrome and mirrors. My reflection looks like a startled deer. *Relax*. Thank goodness I made a bit of an effort to dress up. When he appears, Stefano the head make-over man outdoes me for colour, make-up and general va-va-voom in his tangerine suit and waistcoat. After a quick gush of welcoming comments, he sizes me up, turning me this way and that, with various sighs, hmms and oh yeses. I don't think he's that impressed by my bodycon dress.

Eventually he says, 'You will be the belle of the ball when we're finished with you.'

As Stefano leads me down a corridor we only pass one other person, a tanned woman who looks like one of the cast of *TOWIE*. She blanks me as I try not to stare. Stefano takes me to a separate set of rooms, labelled Suite D. He pushes a button that lights an 'Occupied' sign, rings a bell, then ushers me to a seat in front of a full-length mirror. All this privacy must be for their famous clients and I wonder who else could be in Suites A to C.

Stefano leaves with an 'Enjoy.'

The door has hardly closed behind him before an immaculate young woman slips in like a ninja and offers a menu of drinks. Although sadly no alcohol to calm my nerves. Then a young man appears and hands me an iPad 'for my entertainment' or a choice of magazines just in case I'm old-school. Before I know it, I'm gowned and someone is putting foils in my hair, as a manicurist deals with my nails. The staff are uniform in style: quietly professional, responding to my attempts at conversation just enough to be polite but to discourage chat.

It is only when Stefano returns and sets to with the scissors that I realise: other than the choice of drink and magazine, no one has asked what I want done. My usually rounded nails have been covered with squared-off acrylics and painted with a matt French manicure. The natural curls of my hair have been tamed by Stefano, who is busy cutting layers.

'Uncross your legs, please,' he says. 'We do not want the cut lopsided.'

He starts on the blow-dry and the light gleams on three or four different shades, from auburn to copper. I turn my head to the side to see the effect but he gently pulls me back. There is something familiar about the style, the way my hair lies as he dries it: the side parting, the curls now straightened to end in a gentle wave at my shoulders. Stefano sprays it with copious amounts of lacquer and I try not to cough as he studies my reflection in the mirror, patting down invisible stray hairs.

A thought strikes me: how does Leon know of a place like this? Is it a standard gift he buys all his girlfriends ... something he arranges for his arty acolytes as a reward for good work, written off against his expenses? I feel guilty at the meanness of the thought but I have to ask. Assuming an accent suited to the class of the surroundings I say, 'I was just wondering, do you know any of my friends – Michelle? Or Sophie? Or Kiara?'

The reflection of Stefano in the mirror raises an eyebrow. 'You knew Michelle?'

My hair barely moves as I nod.

'Yes, of course,' he says. 'She came here for years.' He looks like he was about to say more but stops himself, fetching a mirror to show me the back of the cut.

From Hair they shunt me to Make-up, another room in Suite D. As they darken my eyebrows it strikes me: this is how Michelle wore her make-up and hair in those photos on Leon's phone. Is he trying to make me more like her? Or is it just a style he prefers? As I contemplate the transformation in the mirror, I ponder whether I actually mind … What's the problem if it makes him happy and I look this good?

Make-up finished, I'm ushered through to yet another room, this one without a door but hidden behind heavy velvet curtains. The seat of the cream couch is too deep for me to sit comfortably and I fuss with the cushions to support my back. These colours are desperately impractical, they must show every mark. And the matching curtains trail along the floor. A dust trap, but saves on hemming – could I get away with it on those IKEA curtains I bought? *This has been 'interesting' but how much longer?* I've no idea what comes next and take my phone out to check the time, handling it with difficulty with my new painted talons. Two missed calls from Jen. No message so she'll probably call again or leave a text on her third attempt.

A tall woman parts the curtain, managing to slink across the room towards me as if on a catwalk, despite the fact she's wheeling a metal clothes rail that clatters as she tows it across the tiled floor. She frowns at the mobile in my hand, flicks her eyes to the ornately framed image on the wall which politely requests that phones aren't used. It's a collage of stylish images from the Nineties and the text, *'Just pretend we're still analogue'*. I click the switch from silent to ring and put it on top of my bag, keeping it in view. My get-out-of-jail-free card. *Come on, Jen.*

The woman holds out her hand in that dead fish way some women use when introduced. 'Lydia,' she says, not asking my name. 'I'm here to help create your ensemble.' She has a slight accent – French? I wonder if I could adopt it for a future acting role; it implies a degree of sophistication. That must be how Sophie speaks; I must sound so uncultured in comparison.

The outfits on the rail have been selected 'to complete the look' and are all my size – there's a slight twitch of her nose as she says this and I suspect I am towards the larger end of the clientele they usually deal with. Lydia holds up each garment in turn, draping them over an arm, turning them in the light, telling me the designer, as if I should know who she's talking about. I nod in the right places, add the odd 'yes, indeed' when she comments on the beauty of the fabric or the cut, but I have one eye on my phone.

When it rings I grab it quickly. 'Sorry, I have to take this call.' I can use Jen as an excuse to cut this short and get out of here. Maybe get a coffee somewhere more relaxing before I meet Leon.

Lydia steps out of the room but I can sense her presence just behind the curtain, the unspoken tut of disapproval.

'Jen, hi.'

'Hi. Look don't worry, everything's okay but Davy's been taken to hospital. I just thought you'd want to know.'

'Oh God. What's happened?'

'They were mucking about with Mick's trials bike in the forest. I don't know exactly, but Davy came off. They had to call an ambulance and they put him in a neck brace just in case. He's at A&E.'

'Which hospital? I'm going there now.'

The second I say goodbye to Jen, Lydia appears through the curtain confirming my suspicion of her eavesdropping.

'I have to go,' I say. 'I'm sorry.'

'Now? Before your fitting, madam?' The *madam* in inverted commas, added as an afterthought.

'Yes, now.'

'You should at least choose your dress, even if there is not time to accessorise. The items were specifically selected for you so you could choose the outfit you liked most.'

This woman lives in another world. I point to the last outfit she showed me, a crushed-strawberry wraparound. 'That one. That will do.' Realising I sound ungracious, I add, 'It's beautiful. And I'm so disappointed to have to leave like this.'

'I will wrap it for you while you wait in reception.'

Five minutes later Stefano hands me a branded bag, the new outfit neatly folded inside. He nods his head in a slight bow, but there is the hint of a sneer in his voice as he says, 'We look forward to welcoming you again. When you have more time to spend with us.'

And the door shuts firmly behind me.

The driver was happy to pick me up early and divert to the hospital, 'Makes no odds to me. I get paid anyway.'

At A&E the electronic sign says, 'Waiting time 2 hours', which flashes to 3 hours as I watch. Davy may have gone through already; I don't know when they brought him in, nor how serious it is. I scan the range of people sitting on the rows of plastic chairs, hoping to find Davy amongst the walking wounded whilst fearing he could be at the emergency end of the spectrum. He's not there. But Angie is. She's pacing backwards and forwards near the drinks machine, clenching and unclenching her hands as she strides, like she's getting ready to punch someone.

I dodge round a muscly tattooed chap in a wheelchair to reach her. 'How is he? Any news?' I say, forgetting the niceties of *hallo, how are you?* Her jeans and trainers are grimy and she has a leaf tangled in her hair.

'He's okay. The doctor bloke said it ain't serious but he's a bit battered. There was blood.' Her eyes widen as she says 'blood'. Her hands are shaking and she looks pale. 'I'm not very good at this – hopitals and that.' She leaves out the 's', like a child.

'Come and sit down. Where's Davy now?'

'X-ray.' She looks like she might be sick. 'I hoped you'd come. I ain't got your number so I rang Jen so she'd tell you.'

I fetch her some water and rub her back when she starts crying. 'I'm sorry. I ain't like you – you always know what to do and what to say. I just get a fluster on.'

'It's okay. You did well. You got him here to the hospital. That's good.'

She sniffs loudly and I think she's about to wipe her nose on the arm of her mud-spattered sweatshirt but she's ferreting about up the sleeve for a tissue. 'I was racing him. It's my fault. He's never done trials before but it weren't a rough course, just those slopes on the edge of the forest over the far side of the pond near the split oak. No trees or logs or stuff like that to get round. He should've been okay.' She assumes I know the forest as well as she does, but I've no idea where she means.

'It sounds like he'll live to tell the tale.'

'I hope he's all right.'

So do I. 'He's tough as old boots. He fell off the top of a ladder once and didn't have a scratch on him.'

She gives me a wan smile. 'Your hair looks nice,' she says. 'You look really pretty.'

It's an hour or so later before Davy limps into the casualty waiting area. He's still wearing the neck brace and holding his arm at an awkward angle. The lower left leg of his jeans is blood-stained and ripped at the knee, the white of a bandage visible underneath. Spotting him, Angie and I stand up, take a step forward, then both turn to look at each other, like a choreographed routine. Her eyes are wide with an unspoken question and I nod a silent *Yes, go to him. He is yours now.* And she almost runs across the room towards him.

They walk slowly back towards me, hand in hand, her babbling away, almost bouncing with excitement to have him back safely, Davy smiling broadly. And any doubts I had about them as a couple immediately disappear.

'What're you doing here?' Davy says when he sees me.

'I thought they might appreciate my first-aid skills. Bandaging was always my forte. How are you feeling?'

'Like I've done ten rounds with her at her boxing class.' There's affection in his tone. 'Got to wait for the results of the scan so they can tell me what's what and if I need this neck thing. Could be another hour they reckon.'

I fetch hot drinks from the machine and the three of us sit down in a row, but I feel a bit redundant.

'Gnats,' I say, tasting the tea.

'At least it's wet,' Davy says. That's what Dad used to say. Is it mean of us to share a private joke like this?

Angie interrupts my train of thought. 'Dave, doesn't Cristy look lovely?'

200

'You going somewhere this evening?' he asks.

'Oh God. Yes.' I look round for a clock. 'What time is it?'

'Coming up to seven.'

'Oh no. I'll be late. I really ought to go. Are you sure you're okay?'

'Buzz off,' is all Davy says.

I'm going to be late. After yesterday I wanted to do everything right, to prove he comes first. And now I'm late, something Leon abhors, and I didn't even complete the make-over he arranged for me.

In the hospital toilets I grab five minutes to change into the wraparound dress, shoving my bodycon one into the bag. It's only when I bend to climb into the back of the cab I realise how much it gapes at the neckline. There's not just a sexy glimpse of bra strap or a flash of cleavage, but full-on exposure. At least I'm wearing my new black bra, not one of the off-white ones that I never get round to throwing away, but this dress calls for one of those push-up, push-together ones. Emptying out my handbag on the back seat, I conduct a fruitless search for something to hold the dress together.

I'm mumbling to myself as I sift through. 'Nothing in there ... hair clip? No. Damnation. Back in the Girl Guides I'd have had a safety pin ... and a sixpence.'

'Sorry?' The driver says.

'Have you got one? A safety pin?' I ask. I'm clutching at straws here.

'Want me to stop at a chemist's so you can buy some?'

'No time.'

Is it better to have my bra showing or to take it off completely. What would Nisha do? Definitely lose the bra, but she's a couple of sizes smaller than me ... Should I try to change back into my old dress here in the back of the car? Get the driver to avert his eyes?

I am going to the poshest venue I've been to in my life – probably the only time I'll get to go in my life – and I've completely messed up.

At Leon's club, I'm greeted by the staff with a 'Your dining partner is waiting for you, madam,' and I'm whisked through to a private dining area. The large oak doors creak and complain as they open onto a wood-panelled room. Candles flicker in the draught and old portraits of bearded men glare down at me, clutching one hand to my chest, trying to ensure a modicum of decency.

Leon is already seated at a large oval table, the two settings of glinting cutlery on a stiff white tablecloth. He stands as I enter. 'Good evening,' he says, forcing a smile, but his eyes show his displeasure.

'Oh, Leon, I'm so sorry I'm late. I was having a lovely day but I got a phone call and—' At that point I burst into tears, surprising us both.

He switches immediately from crossness to caring. 'Darling,' he says with concern. 'What's happened to upset you? Sit here and tell me.'

He settles me in his chair, pulls another over next to mine, offers me his hanky, places a hand on my arm. And a mean thought flashes through my mind, one that I push aside to explore later: he enjoys this saviour role.

He listens without interrupting until I finish my jumbled explanation, encompassing hair and make-up, Davy and Angie and A&E, dresses and safety pins.

When I stop, he says: 'So. Firstly you need to put your mind at rest. You make a call to find out the results of Davy's scan, while I step out and have a word with the maître d'.'

He returns smiling a few minutes later and, reading relief on my face, says, 'Good news, I hope?'

I nod. 'No neck fracture. They're on their way home.'

'Excellent. And look what I purloined for you.' He holds up a tiepin. 'No safety pins in the building but I thought this might work.'

He is helping me pin the fabric, when there's a knock at the door and a waiter enters bearing two glasses of champagne on a tray. Leon shows no embarrassment at our unusual stance – his hand buried down the front of my dress wrestling with the fabric – nor my tear-stained face. The waiter reacts as if it is nothing out of the ordinary: a polite 'madam' as he places the glass beside me and a 'Will that be all, sir?' before he leaves.

Leon waits until the door clicks shut then says, 'I suspect that you aren't in the mood for formal dining this evening, so I've arranged for them to prepare us a meal we can take away with us. Not their usual thing, but they'll rise to the challenge I'm sure. I thought a glass of champagne while we wait might be nice.'

My eyes well up at his thoughtfulness. How did I ever misjudge him?

I cuddle up to him in the back of the cab home, over-whelmed with love at his thoughtfulness.

He takes my key to unlock the door for me and, as we enter, the house smells different – a combination of his aftershave and a fresh floral smell that isn't air freshener. He leads me into the lounge, where the room is taken over by an arrangement of exotic flowers on the coffee table. The size and drama of the display wouldn't be out of place in a hotel reception: spirals of bamboo, lilies, ferns and a plant reminiscent of a bird's beak. There's an envelope leaning against the vase. *Cristina,* it says in small neat print.

'How did you ...' I catch myself. 'They're lovely. Thank you. But how did you get in?'

He flicks his fingers. 'As if by magic.' He stands behind me and his arms twine round my waist, pulling me towards him. 'Remember you showed me where the spare key is kept? I hope you don't mind that I borrowed it for my surprise.'

I do, but now is not the time to say so. 'They're lovely. Can I open the card?'

He sits and watches me as I open it.

The picture is a classic image: a couple, the man kissing the woman passionately, her neck exposed – *'Gustav Klimt,'* it says on the back, *'The Kiss 1907.'* Staring at the picture under his gaze, there's a surge of warmth, that familiar melting. I open the card, heading off a blush. He has handwritten a quote: *'Doubt truth to be a liar, But never doubt I love.'* It's from Hamlet's letter to Ophelia. There is no sign-off, no 'love Leon' or xxx, but I'm moved. He knew I would recognise these lines. This is the most personal message he could write.

'Thank you,' I say. 'You've been so lovely.'

'Your birthday gift is not complete yet.' He reaches to take my hand. My moisturised hand with its manicured beautifully varnished fingernails. 'I was thinking we could take a short holiday. A long weekend in Europe. Maybe next month?'

'Gosh, that would be lovely.'

'I'll arrange it then.'

I want to ask when he has in mind, where we're going, but it seems rude when he is being so generous. I'm sure he'll check with me before booking it.

★

Later, after we've eaten the food, drunk the champagne that he'd put to chill in my fridge earlier in the day, he says, 'So, today didn't end up being quite as either of us envisaged. But moments to enjoy. Yes?'

'Oh yes. Thank you so much. But I mustn't get too used to being spoilt like this!'

'And why not?'

He removes his tie, undoes the top button of his shirt, then he kisses me as he unclips the tiepin tethering my dress.

Chapter Eighteen

The next morning Leon prepares our breakfast – a salt-free omelette with tomatoes, the eggs being all he can find in my fridge. I start to make the tea but he soon takes over; apparently I should've warmed the pot. It's on the tip of my tongue to point out that the pot is stainless steel and heats in seconds, but I just laugh it off. Even easy-going Davy has his little foibles. We're learning each other's ways and in time I can help him chill out and become less pedantic.

As we eat Leon says, 'What do you have planned the next couple of days?'

'Today I'm taking my car in for MOT, which will no doubt cost a fortune. It's fifteen years old.'

'Yes, I've seen it. You're not working at the moment are you. Can you afford it?'

'Oh, gosh, I wasn't hinting for a loan!' I realise how it might have sounded. 'I've got some savings I can use.'

He smiles, shaking his head. 'No, you're not that type of woman. And next week?'

I pause – I've planned to see Jen but I'm not sure whether Leon approves of my friends, having seen us all mucking about at my party. But no more lies. 'Jen's only working a half-day on Monday so we thought we'd go round the summer sales.'

'Oh. That's a shame.' He looks disappointed rather than disapproving as he stands to take my plate. 'If you were free there was something I wanted some help with. Paid of course. It's not that exciting but it's a day's work and would give you some cash to cover that MOT.'

'That sounds interesting. It was only an idea, to see Jen, not a plan. We'll see her at the party this weekend and I can meet her any time really.' I'm burbling, wanting to underline that he comes first now.

And that's it, wrapped up. I'm to do this project for him on Monday. One of Leon's team.

When I get home from running chores later that day there's a message on the answerphone. I hope it's Davy or an update from Angie on how he is. But it's Clare, checking I'm okay and that I had a nice birthday. I realise I've not thanked her for the orchid but I can't face phoning her. I can't lie and I'm not ready to tell the truth, not until after our holiday when I know Leon and I are one hundred per cent committed to each other for the longer term. So I send her an email of thanks, say I'm thinking of going away for a few days' break to make some decisions, that I'll be in touch when I get back. Oh, and can she please resend the details of the psychotherapist she recommends as I seem to have misplaced them.

Which is all true.

I feel I'm at a turning point, committed to a new direction; not just a new relationship but a completely different way of life. It feels like it's all happened so quickly. Maybe too quickly. But why waste time?

The Saturday evening before Davy's party, Leon turns up with a coffee machine and a brand-new cafetiere. 'I can't tolerate that ersatz coffee a moment longer,' he says after kissing me. 'From now on we can have the real thing.'

He unpacks it on the kitchen island. 'I thought this would get more use here rather than at my place,' he says, passing me the empty box for the recycling. He manoeuvres the machine to the side unit. 'Do you think we can lose this clutter? It's just gathering dust.' He's talking about the pint beer mug standing harmlessly where it's lived for as long as I recall. It's a souvenir of Brighton – the first holiday I had with Davy. We had one each branded with our names: *Cris's beer – hands off!*

He doesn't wait for an answer, just places the cafetiere in its place, moving my recipe books along the countertop to make more space for the coffee machine. 'There,' he says. 'I'll show you how it works.'

I only half listen as he shows me what to do, trying to process my feelings. It's clear he intends to spend more time here with me but this feels … wrong. Like a decision's already been made and I've not been asked what I want.

He's mid-explanation – something about the need to turn the drip tray over if I'm using a large mug – when I interrupt him. 'I've not been to your house yet.'

'No. That's true.' He replaces the tray in its slot and clicks it into place. 'I'm having rebuilding work done. A huge extension.'

'Sounds exciting. Can I come and see it?'

'It's a building site at the moment, but as soon as the work's finished, definitely. I need your advice. Decor, furniture, everything – you can pick the lot.' He turns to me smiling, his eyes crinkling with pleasure. 'It's really important to me that you feel at home there.' He hugs me to him and when I raise my head to speak, he kisses me with such passion I forget what I wanted to say.

★

The next morning when we wake up at my house I find myself singing, still buzzing from the evening before. Leon goes out for a jog and to buy himself a newspaper. I've bought eggs so he can make the usual omelette when he gets back and it all feels homely and *right*. At my dressing table, I darken my eyebrows and add some mascara. I start to pull my hair back into a ponytail but decide to leave it down, as Leon prefers, and use straighteners and tongs to turn curls into waves. A bit fancy for sausages in the back garden but it does look nicer.

Davy's birthday barbecue.

A fluttering in my stomach reminds me that this could prove a challenging day. Leon's offered to teach me the basics of chess after breakfast and then we'll head off to Angie's for the party. Whilst I'm really looking forward to seeing everyone, I'm also nervous about how it will pan out. My plan is to get to Angie's as soon as it starts, when fewer people are there and everyone is sober. Whilst Leon will be charming, I'm not sure the chemistry works with the Wellies in full party mode – like that science experiment with potassium and water, something could explode and I'm not sure I can deal with the fallout. No, we'll stay an hour or so and then leave discreetly once Leon has met a few people. And I've lined up Jen and Nisha to sweep in and save us if Jake corners us before that.

I get all the breakfast things ready while I wait for Leon to return: digging out the frying pan that hasn't lost half its Teflon, opening the new bottle of olive oil, checking the cutlery for dishwasher marks. Making sure everything's perfect.

Half an hour later there's a banging on the front door. Leon's taken a key with him so I'm surprised to find him bent forward leaning against the doorjamb, his face pale and sweaty.

I assume he has cramp from jogging but as he stands up he grasps his head, not his stomach.

'What's happened? Are you hurt?'

'Migraine,' he says. 'Can you help me? My vision's not too good.'

I lead him to the front room and help him lie on the sofa, draw the curtains so the room is dark, fetch water. 'What else can I get you?'

'Nothing.' He has his eyes closed and frowns slightly as he speaks. 'I don't have my tablets with me. I just have to wait for it to pass.'

I place a damp flannel on his forehead and he opens his eyes a fraction, the light still troubling him in this darkened room. 'The party,' he says. 'You must go.'

'I don't want to leave you like this.'

'You've been looking forward to it.' His voice is weak and he screws up his forehead as if the words pain him. 'You don't want to let your friends down.'

'And I don't want to leave you like this. Maybe I'll pop in and see them later. You might feel a bit better in another hour or so.'

He asks me to leave him alone for a while, says he might be able to sleep it off.

Upstairs I put sun cream, a hat and sunglasses into an open shoulder bag, along with a card for Davy. I text Jen to update her, tell her I'm hoping to pop in for an hour or so, even if Leon can't join me. Setting my alarm for twenty minutes to remind me to check in on Leon – one thing I mustn't forget – I settle down with *Chess for Dummies*. A secret purchase to give me a head start.

Before the alarm rings I hear the bang of the toilet door, followed by the sounds of retching then a long period of groaning. He's in there a good five minutes and eventually I tap on the door gently.

'Leon, are you okay?'

'Not so good.'

And so it goes on all afternoon. He rests for a while then heads to the toilet to retch, refusing to use the bucket I place beside the couch; flushing and cleaning the toilet after him so it smells of bleach rather than vomit. So considerate, even when he's so ill.

Around six that evening he is calmer and allows me to bring a blanket when he starts to shiver.

'Lie with me,' he says, and I lie down next to him and he pulls my arm round him, clasping my wrist.

It isn't until much later he is able to sit up. He takes the cup of tea I bring him and smiles at me wanly.

'I was so looking forward to showing you the two-move checkmate,' he says. 'But, *in sickness and in health.*'

It seems I have passed a test.

Early on Monday morning I put on one of my two suits, the ones I used to wear for the corporate videos, psyching myself up for this new role as part of Leon's team. At least I know how to dress the part for this one. I have first-day jitters but I'm excited to meet his colleagues at last: a couple of students who work part-time as technicians for his artwork; Kiara, the woman who manages his diary; the young work experience chap who delivered the parcel.

I pack my biggest handbag with mobile, pens and a note-pad and anything else that might prove useful. For luck I've Dad's ring on a chain round my neck and the tiepin Leon acquired from the restaurant in my purse. I don't want to let him down.

Leon arrives promptly at eight-thirty, but instead of leaving immediately for the office he strides straight in. 'I'm so sorry, darling. There's a change of plan.' He takes my hand, steps back to look at my outfit. 'Such a shame. You look amazing. I'd be so proud to introduce you to everyone.'

'What's wrong? Aren't I coming to your office to help out?'

'I still need your help – it's all hands on deck. But I'm afraid you'll be working from home. A client's asked for some work to be done urgently. You do know how to do data entry?'

'Oh.' That *definitely* wasn't what I'd imagined. 'I've never done that sort of work.'

'You'll soon grasp it. Where's your laptop? I've got the spreadsheet on this memory stick.'

As he sets up my computer he explains. 'I'm sorry, darling, I'd hoped to spend time with you, show you off. But this is urgent work and they are my main client. They're in the import/export business. Antiques and collectibles. Very profitable apparently.'

'What do you do for them?'

'Lots of different things over the years. I value the artwork they sell. Write articles for trade magazines on the heritage of their antiques. Photograph the stock. That's where you come in. They've a huge backlog of images and articles they need catalogued.'

He sends me to make coffee while he finishes setting up and I leave him transferring files and clicking buttons.

When I come back he's fiddling about with the cables. 'I've plugged you in,' he says, clicking the switch on the socket. 'Safer than having it on battery. This is quite painstaking work and you don't want to risk losing any of your data. I suggest you work here all day rather than move the laptop around.'

'Okay, show me what I'm to do.'

There's a huge datafile of images – brown dining tables, brown side tables, brown wardrobes, the occasional flash of colour on an ornament or vase – each with a six-digit reference code. I'm to cross-reference these numbers with those on the spreadsheet and enter a short text description of the item, which I take from a hard-copy folder Leon provides. A folder with section headings like: GW1 – *Glassware* and FF3 – *French Furniture*. It looks desperately dull. To think I gave up shopping with Jen for this.

He kisses me on the forehead, preparing to leave. 'I'm sorry it's such an arduous task but I swear I'll make it up to you.'

A wink and he is gone.

The work is truly tedious and mid-morning I take a break to phone Jen for a chat and to find out about Davy's party. I've barely finished my apology for not turning up yesterday and cancelling our shopping trip this week when another call comes through and I can see it's Leon.

'Sorry, Jen. I have to go. There's another call.' For some reason I don't tell her who it is. 'I've got to pop into town tomorrow to go to the dentist's. Can we meet up after that for coffee? … I'll text you and Nisha to sort out the time. Gotta go, byeeee.'

I close the call, transfer to Leon.

'How's the work going?' he asks. I immediately feel guilty that he's caught me slacking.

'Fine, fine. I was just getting a glass of water.' Why have I lied? It's like being caught reading *Jackie* magazine when I'd promised I was doing my school homework.

' *"We never know the worth of water until the well is dry."* ' He's quoting someone, his tone slightly theatrical. 'A thought worth pondering.' He pauses a beat and I wait for him to speak, uncertain what to say. 'Who was on the phone?' he asks.

'The dentist confirming my appointment tomorrow.' *What am I doing?*

'Not Jennifer, then?'

'Why do you say that?' I try not to sound defensive.

'It would be only natural for the two of you to speak, since you didn't make it to the barbecue yesterday.'

'I might call her later. But I really need to crack on with this work. You know there's a lot to do.'

'Thank you, darling. I'm depending on you.'

The moment he hangs up I pick up my laptop, turning it from side to side, inspecting every surface, ashamed even as I continue my search for a bug or a camera that could be recording my every move. There's nothing obvious but I don't even know what I'm looking for. As I replace it on the desk I'm struck by the paranoid thought that if there is a camera somewhere in the room, Leon will have seen my weird behaviour and now I need to have a cover story. I start lifting other objects – the folder, my notepad – push the chair aside and scrabble about for a moment on the floor, pretending to search for something.

'Ah!' I look at an imaginary object in my hand as I stand. 'Found you!' Fiddle with my earlobe as if replacing a lost earring, tuck my hair behind my ear to underline the point. Pull my chair in tight to the desk as I resume work, feeling extremely foolish. This is all my imagination; it is no more than a coincidence that he called when I was on the phone. Why am I being so mistrusting when Leon has done nothing to deserve it? And why on earth would he want to track me anyway?

He checks in several times that day to make sure I'm all

right, constantly thanking me for all I'm doing, emphasising the importance of getting all the work completed for his client's deadline, showering me with compliments each time: 'You are a perfect angel, my dear sweet girl. Where would I be without you?'

I'm still at my desk when I hear his key in the door at six that evening. I've been beavering away all day, like that makes up for lying to him earlier and for my stupid paranoid thoughts.

He bounds up the stairs, leans over my shoulder and clicks 'save' before pulling me to standing and hugging me tightly. 'Come. Let's take a well-earned break.'

As I'm waiting for the kettle to boil he hands me a box of expensive truffles. 'They're yours but I sincerely hope you plan to share them.' He is boyish, charming, with that glint in his eye, and I feel a surge of guilt mingled with love.

We're taking our drinks through to the lounge when my mobile rings; it's Bernard Jones's number on my screen. The therapist Clare wants me to liaise with.

'I have to take this. Sorry. It's work.' I hit the button to answer, step out to the hallway for privacy. 'Hi, Bernard.' This is a complicated conversation as Clare is still seeing my clients and we haven't yet agreed that I'm ready to resume therapy let alone take on new referred clients. 'Yes, of course. I'm very interested ... Yes, meeting up would be great ...'

Absorbed in the call, I've not heard Leon come up behind me and I jump as a hand weaves through the hair on the back of my head. I know where this move leads, his trademark seduction, but this time there's no melting feeling – just a tinge of annoyance. *I'm trying to concentrate.* I shake my head, pulling forward, try to step away from him, but he doesn't let go and his other hand sneaks round my waist. His touch is gentle but persistent. I have no choice but to end the call. 'I'm sorry, Bernard. There's someone at the door. Can we arrange something by email?'

The moment I hang up Leon lets go of me, folding his arms. 'Who is this Bernard? Shall I add him to the list of your men friends?'

I straighten my blouse. I've never had to deal with possessive jealousy of this nature, but I understand where it comes from in Leon's case. When he was my client, Clare and I identified an ambivalent attachment style, fear of rejection, lack of trust. Michelle's return to her husband while they waited for a chance to leave for Spain, the horror of her sudden death ... all this would have made him worse.

'Bernard is a psychotherapist. I told you it's work. He's going to refer some clients to me.'

'You also told me your supervisor has taken over your clients.'

'Yes, that's right. She thought I should take a break from therapy for a while when I told her I was seeing you.'

'Then why is he contacting you?'

'So he can refer people to me in future.' Hearing myself say this I realise I'm still assuming I'll go back to therapy one day, not yet able to accept I've probably burnt that bridge already – the moment I slept with Leon. 'He needs to find out the type of clients I work with. Hear about my experience.'

'He can read about your experience on your website. And why would you want to go back to psychotherapy when I'll pay you more to work on projects for me?'

As we talk, he moves from jealous anger to hurt: 'I'm sure you don't consciously mean to upset me but I find it so painful when you're not open and honest with me.' Of course I could retaliate on that point, given his own lies, but I go to listening mode, recognising his need to feel in control. It's still early days for him learning to understand and manage his emotions and I need to be patient and work with him so he doesn't get overwhelmed.

But just as I think we've moved on, he loops back and the conversation goes round in circles for some time. In the end I'm too tired to maintain my calm and irritation comes through. 'Look, Leon. Bernard is a potential work colleague – no more. If you can't accept that and don't believe me, I don't know what more I can say.'

There's a silence, both of us taut with tension. I'm waiting for the barbed retort but instead I'm taken aback when he slumps in the chair as if winded. He puts his head in his hands and, while I can't see his expression, I can hear him breathing deeply.

'I'm sorry,' he mumbles, through his hands. 'You don't deserve this. I understand, of course you should get back to your professional work …'

My shoulders are tight, unable to relax despite the apology. But then he looks up at me and there are tears in his eyes. 'I'm trying to change. To be the man you deserve. Be patient with me … I can't tell you how much you've helped me already.'

He ends up staying the night and to be honest I sleep better knowing all is well between us.

Chapter Nineteen

'You look different. You've changed your hair,' Jen says. She takes her bag off a chair she's been reserving, shoves an iced coffee towards me. 'I didn't expect you to be on time.'

'New leaf.'

'How was the dentist? Was it that guy with the tattoos?' Nisha asks.

'All good.' I bare my teeth in a mad Jack Nicholson grin to show them, eyes rolling. The leaflet on teeth whitening is deep in my bag. Jen would not approve.

'Fancy nails,' says Nisha reaching for my hand to inspect them. 'Since when did you get acrylics?'

'Birthday treat. I'll tell you all about it when you've told me how Davy is. And I want to hear all about the party.'

They exchange a look and Jen says, 'Well...'

'Okay, look there's some news,' Nisha interjects.

I swallow hard. 'Davy's okay isn't he? They've not found something on the X-ray after all?'

'God, no, nothing like that.'

'Don't be daft. We'd have called you straight away,' Jen says. 'Davy would've called you. Anyway, Angie made an announcement at the barbecue—'

Nisha interrupts, excited to share the news. 'They've only known each other five minutes but they're getting engaged. They are so loved up!'

I hold my breath. *This shouldn't matter. I should be pleased for him. I am pleased for him.*

'Cris?' Jen says.

'She's turning puce. Do you think she needs a thump on the back?' Nisha asks. 'You haven't heard the worst of it.'

Jen frowns at her. 'Don't be mean.'

It turns out Angie wants the dog to deliver the ring when they get married.

It takes me a while to relax enough to join in the chat and ask more questions about the party. Jen says Davy embellished the story of his accident every time someone asked about his gammy leg. Nisha describes the usual Wellie stupidity – Jake falling asleep in the hammock and Teena putting make-up on him; Ali dancing so wildly she ended up in the kids' paddling pool soaked through – and whilst I really am sorry to have missed it, I'm so glad I didn't take Leon along.

'So, tell us about lover boy. What did you get for your birthday?'

I tell them about the make-over and the 'takeaway' dinner, create an anecdote out of the issues with the dress, not wanting the whole thing to sound too grand. When I say he's taking me away for a short holiday next month, they are full of questions.

'How romantic! Where are you going?'

'It's a surprise. I guess I find out at the airport.'

'Can you go to the Caribbean for a weekend? That would be my dream.'

'Duh!'

'He said Europe.'

'Maybe Paris?' Jen says. She looks serious. 'I don't mean to be funny but is this actually allowed?'

'What do you mean?' Nisha uses a spoon to get the last

of the froth out of her coffee cup. 'We're still in Europe you know.'

'Well, you know, what with you being his therapist. There was an article in the paper this week about a doctor who's been struck off for having an affair with a patient.'

Nisha taps her spoon on my cup. 'Imagine an exposé – you in the *Daily Mail*! Doorstepped by reporters, photos of you in your dressing gown collecting your post. You could be our new claim to fame.'

'I'm being serious, Nisha.' Jen's using her stern mother voice. 'Couldn't you get in trouble? You know how hard you worked for this – how proud your dad was. You don't want to risk throwing it all away for a fling.'

'It's okay. It's not a fling – I think he's serious about me. And he's not my client any more. It's almost six months now since he finished therapy.' Almost four really, but near enough. 'And anyway, apart from you two and my supervisor, nobody knows. And Leon would never bring a formal complaint against me so there's nothing to worry about.'

Why would he?

When I get home I'm surprised to find Leon there, sitting in my armchair.

'You're home early.' I bend down to kiss him and he holds my wrist, pulling me closer. But instead of kissing me he sniffs at my clothing before letting go of me.

'Where have you been? You shouldn't have been this long at the dentist.'

My good mood changes instantly. The flash of anger spills over, something he's not seen since our almost-break-up argument. 'For God's sake, Leon. It's only six o'clock, not midnight.'

'That doesn't stop me worrying. Accidents can happen in the daytime as well as at night.'

'Is that what you thought? That I'd had an accident?' The sarcasm is clear in my tone. I know what he suspected: that I was with another man.

'Don't do this, Cristina, make an argument out of a simple question. It's only polite to say where you are going and when you will be back.'

I raise my eyebrows and snort a laugh. 'Like you do? What is it, one rule for me, another for you?'

He looks like a disappointed parent. 'I'll ask you again. It's a simple question if you've nothing to hide. Where were you all this time?'

'Having a coffee with Jen and Nisha. Satisfied? Or do you want to phone them and check?' I start digging in the depths of my work bag, trying to locate my mobile so I can thrust it at him. 'Jesus, Leon, you've got to lighten up a bit. I'm not Michelle.' As soon as the words escape me I wish I could take them back, realising that he lost her in an accident.

He stands from the armchair and takes a step towards me and the cold look on his face makes me flinch even though he has never shown any aggression towards me.

'No,' he says. 'You are not.' He brushes past me towards the door. 'She would never dare be so ungracious.'

'I'm sorry,' I say. 'Please don't walk out. I shouldn't have said that.'

He stops, his hand on the doorknob, his back to me. 'You're right; you shouldn't have.'

'I was with Jen and Nisha – they wanted to tell me about the party on Sunday.'

'You seem to spend a lot of time with them.'

'Angie and Davy have got engaged.' I don't know why I tell him this. Several seconds pass and I can't stand the tension. 'Okay, I understand that you like to know where I'm going but I'm a grown woman and I'm not used to having to account for my every move. But I know you worry.'

'You *make* me worry. Sometimes I think you do it deliberately. You know how much I care about you and yet you seem to go out of your way to test me.'

'Leon, come on. Why would I do that?'

'I don't know.' He shakes his head as if to clear his thoughts, staring at the floor rather than at me. 'I had a nice surprise lined up for tonight ... but it seems I've rather wrecked the atmosphere.'

I stop myself from saying *'Again!'* out loud and decide to take that as an apology. 'Look, let's open a bottle of wine and forget about it. We can still have a nice evening.'

He looks at me, his head on one side as if weighing up this option, then he sighs deeply. 'It's tempting but I think it's best we both sleep on it. I'll phone you tomorrow. Sleep tight, Ophelia.'

I'm in bed, although not asleep when my mobile rings. Leon.

'I'm sorry. Forgive me. I am trying to change, I really am,' he says.

'I know.'

'I'd like to come round.'

'Now?' It's just after midnight.

'Yes. Are you in bed?'

'Yes.'

'Good,' he says. 'Stay there.' And he hangs up.

It's an hour later when I hear his key in the door, his tread on the stairs, my pulse quickening at each step.

He clicks on the sidelights. 'I want to show you something.'

It's a necklace. A proper necklace. Not like the cheap tat I bought with Jen at that Almost New sale.

'Emeralds. It's antique, worth a fortune,' he says turning it so the light plays on the seven green stones. 'Sadly I've only borrowed it – from a photoshoot.'

He asks me to stand in front of the wardrobe mirror, lifts my hair gently and places the necklace around my neck. There's a slight smell of perfume, I guess from the woman who modelled it for the photo, and I wonder what she looked like wearing it. Is he making comparisons as he looks at me now, naked but for these jewels?

He bends towards me to kiss my neck and I gasp at the touch of his tongue, his lips, the heat of his breath. I arch my back, pushing my body towards him.

'Is this what you want?' he asks softly, his fingers tracing the outline of my lips as he watches me in the mirror.

I nod.

'Tell me,' he says.

'It's what I want.' My voice is quiet, breathy, and doesn't sound quite like me.

Then he twines his hand through my hair and kisses me…

The next morning he acts as if nothing out of the ordinary happened the night before. Over breakfast he asks me who I think will be the next prime minister and I turn the question back to him to hide my ignorance of politics. He kisses me as usual before he leaves, tells me he's looking forward to our holiday next month and I smile in response.

I ponder the holiday as I clear up the breakfast things. When I think about it there's a combination of excitement and concern. It will be a real test of whether our relationship can work. He can be so generous, so passionate, charming and adorable, but swings to jealousy so quickly. I need him to trust me, to learn to discuss his concerns openly before his imagination turns it into a crisis. He says he is trying to change and if anyone can help him manage his emotions, I can.

The letter box jangles and the post lands on the doormat with a thud, which can only mean my monthly therapy magazine or something from my accountant – nothing interesting. It's not until I put the kettle on for a coffee that I bother to retrieve it. There are four items. I'm right about the therapy journal. They've started to package it in a biodegradable wrapping and I'm idly wondering if it's suitable for my new compost bin as I rip it open and scan the cover. The topics are obscure: 'Radical Candour in Therapy', Somatic Therapy for PTSD, and a thought piece on 'Who Holds the Power?' Ordinarily this would have triggered my feelings of inadequacy and I'd have studied each article until I understood. But now I'm no longer working, I admit the magazine won't get read any time soon and – with a small twinge of guilt – I throw it straight in the recycling.

When I've made my coffee I grab the stack of bills stuffed in the toast rack and the rest of the post, with some vague resolution of making this the day I Sort Out My Life. Sandwiched between the gas bill and a renewal notice for my resident's parking, there's a hand-addressed envelope. The writing looks vaguely familiar, but when I see the Spanish stamp I'm mystified, my brain running through friends who could possibly be on holiday and bored enough to write to me. Aunty Brenda and Uncle Fred are the only likely suspects. I tear it open anticipating one of Brenda's letters, full of rhetorical questions and 'ha-ha's: *'How are you dear? Keeping well I hope and no doubt as busy as ever? Not like us oldies! Ha-ha. Lazing on the beach here in Spain!'* Blah, blah stuff, Dad used to call it.

But inside there is an A5 photo of a small child, less than a year old. Very blond hair, blue eyes, his eyebrows so fair they're almost white. He's sitting on a sandy beach and laughing at something that's happening behind the photographer. The image is so perfectly natural it reminds me of the ones you see in the Sunday mags; like the photos the Duchess of Cambridge takes of the young royals. I turn the photo over and on the back is written *'Seb'* in large scrawly looping writing.

I do not know this child.

Tucked deep inside the envelope my fingers locate a folded piece of paper. It's a compliments slip, branded with a logo and a scribbled message that says: *Thanks for everything. Couldn't be happier! S x.* The signature S is large and looping, the dot above the i a tiny doodle of a heart.

Ah, that's nice; a client has sent me a photo of their child, wanting to thank me. I'm always pleased to receive the occasional postcard or Christmas card from ex-clients, the email updates that pop up every so often. It reassures me – I've made a difference and helped them move on.

But who is 'S'?

And why do I feel an underlying discomfort: that unsettled feeling that accompanies an unexpected knock on the door in the middle of the night?

I read the note again, my eyes flitting from the logo back to the looping S of the signature. The writing is so familiar... but, no – it cannot be. I must be mistaken.

I check the logo of the hotel: palm trees and sea, text which reads *La Isla Golf Resort ~ Residents Club.*

Where Shelly and Leon went.

I rush to unlock my filing cabinet. Shelly's records are at the front and I almost tear the cover in my haste. The postcard. I need to check the postcard she sent me last year.

I hold the two documents side by side: the compliments slip and the postcard.

The large looping S. The slope of the writing. The doodles. The writing is the same. And both have been sent from La Isla, Spain.

How can this be from Shelly? What does this mean?

This letter must have been lost in the post all this time. Sent by Shelly when she and Leon were making their plans for their future together. Then her accident, soon after she sent the postcard.

Picking up the envelope I check the stamp for a date. It's hard to make out even with my reading glasses and I rummage in my desk drawer for Dad's old magnifying glass.

A close study proves my initial impression correct. The envelope is dated this month.

That cannot be right. Is it some sort of joke?

I pick up the picture of the child again. Two tiny teeth showing in his broad grin. A quick search of *'When do babies teethe?'* on my phone tells me he is probably around eight to ten months.

The age Shelly's baby would have been if she was pregnant when she had the car accident.

Chapter Twenty

I'm still not sure what this all means but there is one thing I can check. I can compare the photos of the baby with Shelly's picture, to see if there's a likeness.

I stand on a chair to search for the copy of Leon's photography book, *Fresh Focus.* It's hidden behind the unused cookbooks on the top shelf of the kitchen cupboard, safely out of sight to prevent more upset.

The torn cover reminds me of our quarrel when he found I'd bought his book; the first argument of many, as it turns out. Setting that thought to one side, I climb down.

Perched on the kitchen stool I check the index, find the page number of Leon's section and flick through – but the first page of his chapter is missing.

It must've been damaged when Leon pushed the book off his lap and it hit the coffee table. But looking closer I see the page has been torn out near the binding, deliberately removed; just jagged edges of paper left behind. He must have torn it out when I wasn't in the room, while I was still getting ready to go out. But why?

Looking back through the rest of the book, I can see the introductory page to each section follows a standard layout. An image of the photographer, a short bio, and their personal favourite of their photos with a short explanation of why they chose it. Had he torn it out for sentimental reasons or because he thought it would upset me? Did he express something personal about Michelle as his model, 'his muse'? Something that was too emotional to share with me, so early in our relationship? I set that thought to one side for a moment.

Turning to the rest of the photos of Michelle, I'm once again struck by how stunning she looks. She is so relaxed and natural, her poses sensual but not forced, her eyes full of love. Pushing away the automatic negative thoughts, those self-critical comparisons women often make, I focus on my task. Finding a close-up of her face, I hold the picture of baby Seb next to it. With her hair chemically bleached, her eyebrows darkened, there is no way to know Michelle's natural colouring. But there is something in the shape of the nose. What Gran used to call a button nose. But it's hard to pick out anything else specific; I cannot judge similarities of eyes or face shape in such a happy, chubby baby face. There is one thing for certain though: this child bears no resemblance to Leon with his dark colouring.

What is going on?

I arrange all the evidence on my desk: Leon's book, the postcard, the baby photo and the short message from Shelly. *Think logically. Take it one step at a time.* I write notes to try to make sense of the muddle that is in my brain.

1) This is either some sort of twisted joke or Michelle is not dead.
2) If it is a joke – who would do such a thing and why?
3) The letter was definitely sent from Spain and the compliments slip is from La Isla.
4) Michelle is the only person who would know my address to send something from there.

I pause. My hands to my mouth: *No, it can't be true ...* My hand shakes as I write the next logical conclusion.

5) Michelle is alive!
6) But Leon believes she died in a car accident, having been told this by her family.

How can that be?

I suck on the end of the pen as I think. *Oh my God.* He didn't go to the hospital or the funeral. He didn't actually get to see her. He only ever had the family's word that she died in the accident ...

But why would they tell him she is dead if she isn't?

Because she – or someone else – wanted Leon to believe she was dead? Because they wanted Leon out of her life? But why? I stare at the photo of Seb, his face smiling back at me, a picture of happiness. *Stick to the facts.*

7) She is living in La Isla with a young baby.
8) The baby <u>doesn't</u> look like Leon.

Maybe it's her husband's baby? What if she never left Matthew? Maybe she is with him now, in La Isla, with their baby?

Or maybe her family encouraged her to leave them both – take the child and go ... divorce Matthew, move abroad so he didn't find out she was pregnant; break all ties with her lover and start again?

I have to talk to Leon. Between us maybe we can work out the truth. I need to know.

When Leon returns that evening I'm in the kitchen, nursing a small glass of wine to take the edge off my nerves. How do you tell your boyfriend that the lover they've been mourning is still alive? It's important that I keep the mood calm if I'm to have any chance that he will listen and not jump to conclusions. I've rehearsed what I want to say, but now the time's come I just want to hide behind small talk; pretend everything is the same as normal. I don't get up as he enters the room and he comes over to kiss me on the cheek, placing a bottle of wine on the kitchen counter in front of me.

'Great minds,' he says, nodding towards my glass. He hugs me to him and kisses me again, but steps back when I don't respond. His hands on my shoulders, he holds me at arm's length, scanning my face. 'What's wrong? Has something happened to upset you, darling?'

I sigh, then gesture to the seat opposite me across the breakfast bar. 'There's something we need to talk about.'

'That sounds a bit ominous. I'd better pour myself a drink first.'

He takes a while faffing about finding the corkscrew and getting the bottle open; humming under his breath all the while, making out nothing is wrong when he can tell there is.

'I popped round to my place today. The builders are making good progress and the scaffolding should be down soon. Once it's no longer a hard hat zone, I'll take you round. We can have fun choosing the decor together.' His back is to me and he can't see the way my shoulders slump as he tries to sound upbeat. Only yesterday I would probably have leapt with excitement to hear this news, our life moving on to the next stage. Now I'm not so sure what is going on, what the future holds for us.

I mumble a response, 'Sounds good.'

Eventually he comes to sit down, reaches across the breakfast bar to take my hand. 'What is it, darling? What's wrong?'

I swallow hard before I begin. 'I had a strange message today. Something I don't understand and I wondered if you might be able to explain it or help me make sense of it.'

He frowns, takes a swig of his wine, then smiles. 'Well, that's not much for me to go on.'

'It's a message from Michelle. At least I believe that's who it's from.'

'You're not making sense. Michelle is dead, so unless you've been to a medium you must be very confused.'

'She's alive, Leon.' I speak slowly, pause, to give him time to take it in. 'She wrote to me to thank me for working with her. I recognise her writing.'

He shakes his head, withdraws his hand from mine. 'Is this your idea of a joke?'

'Leon. Listen to me. I understand this must be a shock to you. But it's true. I received a letter today from Spain.'

He stands and turns his head away from me, staring at the floor. He is clenching and unclenching his hands and breathing so deeply his chest rises and falls as if he's been jogging. Several minutes pass while I wait for him to take in this news.

Eventually, without looking at me, he says, 'You're telling me Michelle isn't dead? She's been alive all this time?'

'Yes. It's only a short note but it says she's happy.' As soon as I've said it, I wish I hadn't.

'Happy?' He bangs his fist on the countertop and I jump. 'Happy having broken my heart and ruined my life! Show me this letter.'

'I don't think that's a good idea.' I don't feel comfortable confirming she is in La Isla.

'What are you hiding from me, Cristina? What else do you know?'

His face is very red and although he has never been

aggressive to me, his angry reaction is unexpected and I'm suddenly very uncomfortable being around him.

'Cristina! Tell me what you know.'

'I've told you. She said she is happy. The letter was sent this week. She is alive, Leon.'

'Which part of Spain?'

'I don't know,' I lie, but I'm not sure whether he believes me.

'Did she mention the child?'

My face must give me away.

'I knew it.' He shoves the stool out of his way, pacing back and forth, running his hands through his hair. 'I knew it.'

'Knew what? Tell me what you knew.'

He takes a few seconds to regain self-control and I wait for him to speak, conscious of my racing heartbeat.

'Her family are to blame. They turned her against me. They knew she wanted a baby … They must have encouraged her to run away like this … It's the only explanation.'

'Are you saying they lied to you? About the accident? About her death?'

'Yes. Yes.' His tone is impatient, as if I'm slow to catch on. Like I'm distracting him from his thoughts. 'I have to find her. I need all the information you have. Get me the letter. Get me her therapy notes. I can work out where she is.'

'No, Leon. You know I can't do that.' I am resolute even though my hands are shaking.

He looks at me with contempt. 'I'll find it myself then.' He strides out of the kitchen towards the front room, to my desk and filing cabinet. 'Don't worry, you get to maintain the moral high ground!'

I follow him, unsure what to say, or do, to bring him back from this rage. 'Please just take a breath. Sit down for a moment and let's talk this through and try to make sense of it together. It's a shock to us both.'

He ignores me and starts rifling through the papers on my desk, throwing things on the floor once he has checked for signs of the letter. He pulls out the top drawer and empties it on the desktop.

'This is insane. Will you please stop! There is nothing to find.' I decide to lie to him. 'I destroyed the letter. I was so jealous and angry when I saw it, I burnt it ... I can't bear the thought that she is alive and you might go back to her.'

He stops what he is doing and stares at me, unsure whether to believe me or not. 'Give me her file,' he says. 'I need to know everything she said about me. All her lies.'

I shake my head, no.

And he picks up the drawer he has just emptied and throws it at the wall, smashing the glass on the picture above my desk. A shard lands on top of my laptop, splinters of glass scattered across the surface and my memory leaps back to the break-in all those months ago. Leon pulls out my stationery drawer and tips everything out, a reel of Sellotape rolling across the floor to rest on the carpet by my old therapy chair. He frantically sifts through staplers, pens and Post-its, finally grabbing Dad's old letter opener. I take a step back towards the door, feeling for my mobile in the pocket of my jeans, but he doesn't come towards me. Instead he tries to jimmy the filing cabinet open, but the blade on the letter opener snaps.

In a rage he pushes the filing cabinet over and it crashes to the floor. He starts pulling things off the shelves – books, ornaments, photos – whether in temper or searching for something he can use to open the lock, I can't tell. He is dangerously out of control.

'I want you to leave. I will not stand for this.' My voice

has an authority I'm not feeling. 'You need to go now or else I will call the police.' I hold the mobile up, my finger already tapping on the screen.

He stops what he is doing and turns to me. One hand on the back of his neck he rotates his head, left then right, then back again. A familiar gesture when he is tense, something I've always found charming and vulnerable before today. I say nothing, waiting for his next move.

He takes a step towards me and I will myself to hold my ground. His jaw tenses as he looks me up and down, his expression disparaging. 'I *will* find her with or without your help. She will regret this. I will make her pay for what she's done. She will not make a fool out of *me*.'

And then he storms out, leaving me standing in the wreckage of my home, my life. I wait until I hear the front door slam, his car engine start, then immediately rush to bolt all the doors and windows, draw the curtains closed so no one can see in. Only then do I allow myself to let out the emotions I've been holding inside, tears pouring down my face as I rock back and forth. Wanting my dad here to hug me and make it all better.

But I can't waste time on self-pity. I wipe my cheeks with the back of my hand and take a deep breath. I don't understand what is going on, but he threatened Michelle. *'I will find her ... She will regret this ...'* I have to warn her. Tell her that Leon knows she is alive, knows she's in Spain. Tell her that he may put two and two together and realise she's at one of the Spanish resorts they used to go to, work out it's La Isla.

The keys to the filing cabinet are under the edge of the carpet, in the gap between the wall and the television, where I hid them earlier. I squat on the floor to unlock the toppled filing cabinet, then lift out all the files. Flicking through, I quickly find what I'm looking for – a folder labelled TAX RETURNS, where I concealed Shelly's therapy paperwork, along with the photo and the note, earlier today. I need her contact details from her therapy notes. Obviously her address in the UK will be useless – it's where she lived with Matthew before all this – but I'm hoping her mobile number and email might work.

I try the mobile number first but it's been reissued and I get through to a very confused elderly man with a strong Scottish accent. Of course, if she was trying to hide from everyone she would have changed her SIM card as soon as she could. No doubt her email too, but I try it anyway and I'm not surprised when it bounces back within a minute. I experiment with a few other combinations mirroring the structure of her original email address – full name and year of birth – trying initials only, Hotmail and Gmail accounts, to no avail. I even try *Seb2018*.

Running out of options, I do a quick name search on Twitter and Facebook, knowing in my heart that anyone in hiding will not be posting their daily news for the world to see, even under an assumed name.

I look up the details of La Isla and find a contact number that's available to call until midnight. It takes me through to a general reception/concierge type office. They are polite and professional when I say I'm trying to find the address of my friend who lives there. They advise me that I would probably be best to call the Resident Members Club tomorrow morning. They open at 9 a.m.

However, the man adds, before wishing me a good evening, they are not allowed to give out residents' personal details. He says I might be able to leave a message that they can pass on.

But how can I explain all this in a message? And even

if I ask her to phone me, there could be a delay in them getting the message to her, a delay in her calling me. How on earth am I going to warn her that Leon is trying to find her and get her to take it seriously? Get her to understand how angry he is?

And, how can I tell her that Leon knows where she is? Now I've stupidly confirmed she's in Spain, he only has to work his way through the golf resorts they looked at to narrow it down and identify where she is. And what if Leon gets there first — before I can warn her?

It's my fault that she is in danger. My professional negligence has led to this.

I juggle with this thought for an hour or so, but in the end conclude there is only one way to resolve this problem. I made this mess and it's my responsibility to help sort it out.

I have to find her myself and warn her.

And part of me needs to find out what exactly has been going on. I need to know the truth about her relationship with Leon.

I book a cheap flight ticket from Stansted to the airport nearest La Isla. The first flight out in the morning. I need to be at Stansted by 4 a.m. for check-in. I book a car to pick me up at three.

Chapter Twenty-One

Once on the flight, all the energy that has been driving me disappears and, slumped in my seat, I realise I've hit an emotional low. Focused on the practicalities of passport and transport and packing, I'd been able to push aside the thought that is now forcing its way to the fore. I have thrown away everything for Leon – lost my career, risked my friendships – for an imagined future with a man, it seems, I know nothing about.

How can I have got everything so wrong?

My brain cycles through the events of the past six months. His stories of Michelle in those early therapy sessions, the way he idolised her from their first meeting. Did I realise how obsessional he was and just chose to ignore it, so wrapped up in my own fantasies about him ... imagining our future together?

But I'm sure he cared – cares – about me too. His gifts always so thoughtful, the poetry books, the quote in my birthday card. The first man who *really* understood me. When he looks at me sometimes, it's like being in the spotlight on stage, feeling the undivided attention of the audience, everything focused on you. Even his jealousy makes sense – he'd lost Michelle and didn't want to risk losing me. It's the passionate jealousy of a passionate man.

But then I think of the places we went: the museum, the restaurant ... recall my early concerns that he was reliving his life with Michelle through me. Concerns I pushed aside, so intent on making this relationship work. Grabbing at an opportunity to change my life.

How could I not have seen the depth of his obsession with Michelle? That I was a second-rate substitute, filling a gap in his life.

The woman in the seat next to me offers a pack of tissues and I realise the tears are dripping from my chin.

'Thank you,' I mumble.

'Are you okay?'

I nod, blow my nose.

'We've still got two hours if you want to talk about it.'

'Thank you. It's all right. I'll be okay.'

Where on earth would I start? The only person I could discuss this mess with is Clare. Clare, the woman I've always trusted with everything, no matter how dark my thoughts or how needy my behaviour; knowing she will not judge, merely listen and help me make sense of everything. The woman I've now lied to again and again. Who I've pushed out of my life. Replacing her with Leon, like a lovestruck adolescent.

What have I done?

As we descend the steps from the plane, the heat hits me. There's no need to wait for the baggage to be unloaded; I only have my carry-on wheelie case, plastered with the dumb stickers bought on trips with Nisha. For a moment I wish one of the girls was with me, that we were starting a holiday adventure together. I take a deep breath, pull myself together – now is the time to focus on finding Shelly.

The taxi driver knows La Isla and doesn't need my crumpled piece of paper with the address. His English is perfect and I'm ashamed at my inability to say more than *Hola* and

Dos cervezas, por favor in Spanish. He asks me how long I'm staying and I tell him I'm visiting a friend. When he hears that I've not been to the resort before, he asks:

'You play golf? Your friend, does he play golf?'

I don't correct him on his assumption. I ask about the resort, trying to glean as much information as possible to help my search for Michelle. Misinterpreting my interest, he tells me about the beaches near the complex – the best one to avoid the tourists – then segues into chat about the shopping complex in the next town where there is a factory outlet. There's an advert for the latter on the back of his seat and I wonder how much they pay him to promote it.

'We're five minutes from La Isla,' he says eventually. 'What is your friend's address?'

'I'm meeting her at the Resident Members Club. She thought we could have a coffee there first.' I try to project confidence in this invented scenario, heading off any further questions.

He pulls up outside a wide archway that spans a set of steps leading to a white-painted building, the La Isla logo of palm trees and sea promising a holiday vibe I do not feel. The sun glares off the walls and I rue not packing my sunglasses last night. The arch is festooned with bougainvillea, the peachy orange and raspberry pink reminding me of the Fruit Salad chews Jen and I used to love as kids.

I wish one of the gang was here with me. But I *can* do this alone.

At the reception desk they are apologetic as they tell me they can't allow me into the club unless I'm accompanied by a member. Which is just as I'd hoped.

'I'm meeting my friend here but I took an earlier flight.' I point to my luggage, supporting evidence of the truth of my recent arrival. Looking at my watch I add, 'She won't be coming to meet me for a couple of hours and I stupidly forgot to bring her address with me. If I give you her name, could you tell me where her apartment is?'

'I'm sorry, madam. We're not allowed to give out personal information. Would you like me to check whether she is already in the clubhouse? What is her name?'

'Shelly ...' I pause. She is unlikely to be using her married name. What was the maiden name that Leon had told me when he'd shown me his ring? 'She recently got married ...' I offer, in an attempt to cover my ignorance. It began with M ...

'She was Harrison ... she's now ... Mitchell. Yes, Shelly Mitchell.'

He looks at me as if he knows I'm lying. 'There is no one of that name signed in on the register today.' He turns the landline phone towards me and I feel he is calling my bluff. 'You may use our phone if you wish to call her.'

'I think she might be playing golf this morning.'

'Ah. Then maybe I can direct you to the golf course? You could wait for her at the coffee house there ... while she finishes her game.' He produces a map and points out the colour coding for key locations: green for the golf areas, orange for shops and restaurants, blue for the pool areas and holiday lets, pink for residents' apartments. His tanned forefinger traces a route through the complex to the larger of the golfing greens.

'This is the main course, the one the residents prefer. It is open all year.' He hands me the map. 'Of course if you don't want to walk that far you could visit the shops, maybe get a coffee, and return here to meet your friend later?'

'Thank you. I might do that.'

My wheelie suitcase bumps down each step in my rush

to get away and when I look back to the clubhouse he is watching me, unsmiling, through the window. Belying how I am feeling, I give him a cheery wave.

I turn the map to try to orientate myself and set off towards the residents' areas. But my sense of direction is terrible and by the time I realise that the plan only shows the main roads, I have taken several wrong turns. I find myself in a small shopping arcade that leads to one of the public pools. But which one? They are scattered all over the complex.

Weaving my way through the deckchairs I pass a young family and decide to ask for help with the map. The woman is jiggling a small child on her knee and looks up, shading her eyes, as I stop beside her sun lounger.

'Excuse me. Do you speak English? I'm a bit lost. Can you help me find where I am on this map?'

'Yeah. Hang on a mo.' A thick Birmingham accent. She hails her husband then passes him the baby to hold so she can take the map from me. Watching him as he paces up and down, soothing the little girl, a thought strikes me.

'I'm visiting my friend for a few days. Her name's Shelly and she has a baby about your daughter's age. Do you know her?'

The woman frowns, thinking, and it reminds me of Leon. *Focus.*

The woman starts speaking. 'I might know the child rather than the mum. What's her daughter's name?'

'It's a boy actually. Sebastian, but she calls him Seb. Seb Mitchell.'

A discussion ensues between her and her husband. It seems they met a couple called Mitchell at a golf club dinner. My hopes rise.

'What was his first name? You remember the chap – he was an accountant back in England.'

'Simon wasn't it?'

'No. No, I remember now. He was Mitchell Simon. That was it, Mitch Simon. Nice wife – Caroline? Carolyn?'

'Carol Anne.'

Luckily they are more helpful with the directions.

From what they've told me, there is another fifteen-minute walk up a steep hill to reach the main residential area. Perspiration runs down my forehead and I wipe it away with the sleeve of my sweatshirt, now tied round my waist. It seems occasional Pilates doesn't make me fit enough for this amount of activity in the heat of the day. The wheels of my case seem to catch in every crack in the uneven paving, its weight increasing with every step. After a while I have to slow my pace. At a bend in the road I'm worn out and slump against a wall in the shade, fanning myself with the map.

A golf buggy pulls alongside me and stops.

'You look knackered.' He's a plump chap with rounded cheeks and this likeness to Davy gives me a pang for my old life and makes me want to cry. But his arms are covered with blond hairs, not dark, and when he opens his mouth his teeth are perfect: very straight and alarmingly white.

'I just walked up the hill. It's pretty steep.'

'You need one of these if you're staying long.' He pats the side of the golf cart. 'Ideal for getting around here.'

'Do you live here?' I ask, hoping against hope.

'All year round. Wouldn't be anywhere else.'

'I don't suppose you know my friend, Shelly Mitchell?' I trot out the story I told the man at the Resident Members Club.

'I don't know her but there's a Shelly who does photo-graphy lives here. Kiddies' portraits and beach scenes. She advertises in the *Members' Magazine* sometimes.'

I want to hug him. 'Yes, that's her! Do you know where she lives?'

'No, but there's a restaurant she goes to and they have her photography on the walls. They'll know how you can reach her.'

I thrust the map towards him.

'Can you show me where it is?'

He screws up his nose, turning the map to get his bearings. His stubby finger jabs at an orange area. 'There you go. Casa Camara. Renowned for their fish.'

Hope gives me a new surge of energy and I head off in the direction he's identified, yanking the case behind me.

At the fish restaurant I trot out my story for the third time. I must look as overheated as I feel, because they make me drink a bottle of water while someone finds her business card. I glug it down in one, thanking them as if it was the finest wine. Shelly's pictures are displayed on the walls of the bar area. She's captured children playing on the beach, some sunsets, a few portraits of people going about their daily lives. There's a muscly young man half turned from the camera, preparing a lobster pot on a wall at the harbour; an older bald chap, his eyes hidden behind sunglasses. He's carrying paper bags of shopping in his arm, his other hand holding the hand of a toddler off camera. I don't know anything about art, but the way she's captured the shots is interesting; she seems to have a natural talent for catching people unguarded. The love of photography, probably what drew Leon to her in the first place …

This leads me deep into a chain of critical comparisons between me and Shelly. I've just got to *'How did I ever imagine he could love me in the way he'd loved her?'* when my thoughts are interrupted by the production of her business card. Sadly it is a disappointment: her logo is an ornate S and there's a website address with an info@ email, but no other contact details.

'Do you know where she lives?' I ask.

'Miguel might know.'

Miguel is called from the kitchen. Apparently he is a woodworker in his spare time and has made frames for her photographs. He takes me to the front of the restaurant and points to a flower-strewn alleyway, tells me to go up a set of steps at the end, turn left and walk for five minutes, then I will see villas on my right. That's where she lives. He doesn't know the name of the property but says it has a wooden door, painted blue.

I am nearly there!

Chapter Twenty-Two

There are two villas with bright blue doors.

I stand looking between them, breathing heavily. There's nothing obvious that suggests it's one rather than the other. Festooned with flowers and vines, both have ornate metal gates across side alleys that, I assume, lead to back gardens or pools. No kiddies' playthings, or arty constructions shout 'Shelly's House!' but it is one or the other, so I have a fifty-fifty chance.

Okay, I've as good as found her. I can take a moment to catch my breath and run through what I plan to say.

I perch on the edge of a low stone wall. Hair awry, flushed and sweating, I must look as bad as I feel. Far from the poised therapist Shelly first met two years ago. That seems so long ago now – I was a different person. Before Dad died. Before Leon came into my life and turned everything upside down with promises of such a new and exciting future together.

I need to know exactly what happened between him and Shelly: if she really faked her death and went into hiding. I need to warn her that his obsession with her has turned into something dark. That he is bent on revenge. Maybe when I have the full picture and can understand, it will help me to see the part I played in their drama, how I got drawn into it all. Maybe confirm whether he really loved me, or if I was a merely a poor Michelle substitute, as I'm beginning to fear.

My thoughts are broken by the movement of a shadow on

the ground beside me. I look up to see who it is. Hopeful they may know Shelly.

But – to my horror – it's Leon.

'What…?'

How did he get here?

'Leon?' I move to stand up but he places his hand on my shoulder, gentle but firm. 'I … I don't understand. How did—'

'Cristina, my darling. Come now.' He places a neat black backpack on the ground and sits down beside me on the wall, smoothing his cream chinos, his dark glasses hiding his eyes. 'You left a trail of breadcrumbs. You weren't that hard to track.'

'Did you go to my house?' He still has a key. Did he see my scribbled notes as I checked flight options, the printout of the receipt confirmation?

'Ha. That's so "old-school", as I think you would say.' He smiles, turning his neck from side to side – that familiar gesture. 'There's really no need for all that tiresome breaking and entry in this day and age. Remember I did some installations on your laptop earlier this week?'

He's been tracking me.

'You booked your EasyJet flight online just after midnight, the first flight out from Stansted. So I booked on the Spanish airlines flight, leaving fifteen minutes earlier, from Luton.' He smiles, pats my hand. 'I waited for your flight to land. I've figuratively been one step behind you since you left the airport.'

I snatch my hand away, furious at him, furious with myself for, literally, leading him to Shelly's door.

'How could you do this? What is wrong with you, Leon? What is it you think you'll achieve?'

He shrugs. 'Closure?'

246

He is taking the mickey out of me. Baiting me. I stand up and turn to face him.

'Don't be so arrogant. It's not normal to be so obsessed. It's not normal to bug someone's laptop. You are ill, seriously mentally ill, and you need help.'

'But that's why I came to see you all those months ago. Does it upset you that you failed so badly?' He pretends to study his nails. 'Remember that it was *you* who broke all professional boundaries pursuing *me*. Is that what galls you? A tragic end to a treasured career. Is that what this temper tantrum is about?'

My pulse is pounding and I'm on the edge of losing my self-control, sinking to his level. But right now, I mustn't get trapped in an argument about what's happened between us. I need to focus on what he is doing here.

Deep breath. I must try to ground him in reality.

'You came to see me because you were in mourning for Michelle. It's a shock to us both to find out she's alive.'

'A shock to you maybe.'

'What do you mean by that?'

'I knew all along. I just didn't know where she was hiding out. I came to you for information, Cristina, information. But that proved more challenging than I'd imagined, what with all your professional ethics.' He pauses, takes off his sunglasses and locks eyes with me. 'To think of the trouble I went to, breaking into your shed! Sorry I messed it up so much, but not finding what I wanted made me a tad frustrated, as you can no doubt imagine, *Kiddo*. I'll admit I got a bit... theatrical. What's that American expression? I went a bit postal.'

It was him. Why hadn't I realised before? 'You were after Michelle's therapy notes. You wanted to see if she'd told me where she was going.'

247

He gives me a slow hand-clap. 'Strategy and tactics, Cristina. But then you wouldn't know about that. A tactical migraine meant I never got to teach you how to play the game of chess. Ah yes. Strategy and tactics. In fact my seduction strategy was so much fun I stretched it out for more moves that I'd initially imagined, just to be one hundred per cent sure that I'd get round all your professional morals. It was fun though, you have to admit.'

I've been such a fool.

'How could you be so cruel? You've deceived me all this time.'

'Manipulated,' he corrects me. 'You've been a worthy opponent in the game, my love, more challenging than I expected. But remember I'm always several moves ahead of you. You gave so much away; it was so easy to see your plans, that calendar in your kitchen – such a creature of habit! And your journal was a source of inspiration to me, gave me so many ideas. Although if you don't mind me saying, a tad schoolgirl. All those insecurities. You ought to see a therapist yourself.'

Oh my God. He has been in my house when I'm not there, gone through my personal things. I must keep calm, not rise to his provocation. I need to understand what he plans now.

'And what do you want with Michelle? Why are you here?'

'Revenge. I want to destroy the happy little life she's built – just like she destroyed mine.'

There's a noise behind me and I turn just as Leon stands and steps forward.

'Well, well,' he says quietly. 'Right on cue. You could learn from that, Cristina.'

I wouldn't have recognised this woman as Shelly had I passed her on the street, she's changed so much. But from

Leon's reaction it can only be her. Her mousy hair is cropped and she's wearing a baggy T-shirt and cut-offs. There's a young child in her arms, his head on her shoulder, nuzzling into her neck. The sun is glaring in her eyes and she shields the child's face with her free hand as she speaks, walking towards us where we stand in the shadow of the trees.

'Hi, I heard voices and came out to see if you were lost. We don't get many—' She stops in her tracks, staring at Leon.

'You knew I'd find you in the end,' Leon says.

There's a flurry of movement as Shelly takes a step back towards the house and Leon runs towards her. She realises he is coming for her and tries to get to the door, but he is too quick and grabs her wrist. I'm momentarily frozen in shock as she wrestles to get free and the baby starts crying. Shelly is gripping the child so tightly with her free arm, trying to keep him safe, holding him away from Leon.

'Leon!' she shouts, then. 'Help us.' I spring into action and try to pull Leon off of Shelly tugging on his arm. But he pushes me to one side and I lose my balance and fall to my knees on the ground. Her voice gets louder, shriller: 'Leon!'

She's shouting his name but the intonation and pitch are as if she is hailing someone.

'Leon, help us!'

The sound of running, the clang of the metal gate and an older bald-headed man appears.

'Let go of her!' His voice is loud, firm, authoritative and Leon turns to face him, still holding Shelly's wrist.

'So here we are again! Round two.'

I look from Leon to the older man. His face is familiar – it's the avuncular man in the photo in the fish restaurant, the final traces of grey-blond hair fringing his bald head. And I now know where else I've seen him, before that. There's a photo of him in Shelly's folder, in my office at home – one of the examples she gave me two years ago, when she offered to take my professional headshot.

The older man moves closer to help Shelly, but Leon holds up a warning hand.

'Stay where you are.'

Shelly speaks, her voice imploring, 'Matthew, please. No.' But she is looking at Leon as she says it, tears rolling down her cheeks. 'Matthew, I'm begging you. Just leave us be. He's not yours. He's not your child.'

'And you think that makes it better?'

Shelly is calling Leon *Matthew*.

But Matthew was her husband's name.

'Matthew. Please … Just let me go.'

Matthew was her husband. She called the bald man Leon.

And suddenly things slot into place. The man I've known as Leon is Shelly's husband, Matthew. The man who is seeking revenge – who has hold of her now – is her husband.

And the older man trying to save her and the child is her lover, Leon.

Oh my God. How did I not see it? It was there in front of me all along. He's made such a fool of me.

I am fuelled by anger and guilt. I know what I have to do – save Shelly and the baby from harm. No one is paying attention to me and, from my position where I've fallen on the ground, I have an advantage. As the bald man takes another step forward, I use the distraction to leap up and hit Matthew's arm as hard as I can to break his hold – a move Nisha taught us after her self-defence class. The second he lets go, I shout 'Run' To Shelly. I push her forward towards the house and we both stumble into the hallway and I slam the door behind us, pushing the bolt across.

'Is there a back entrance?' Shelly points and I head in

that direction, calling to her over my shoulder, 'Shut all the windows while I secure the back.'

When I return, she's sitting on the sofa rocking Seb to and fro, both of them crying.

'Cristina?' she says, frowning, trying to make sense of me being here.

'Yes, I'm Cristina. Look, I'll explain everything later. But now we have to call the police. You have to phone them. Tell them we need help.'

She nods and reaches for her mobile and I listen to her urgent Spanish.

'Will you be okay on your own? I'm going outside to try to stop them fighting. Lock the door after me and call the La Isla security people. They may get here quicker.'

There's no time to plan what I will do but I have to try to stop a brawl before anyone gets hurt. Matthew is dangerously unpredictable. I experienced a taste of his anger last night when he trashed my front room and he could do much worse now he is fired up and set on revenge.

They are in the alleyway at the side of the house. The older man – the real Leon – has a cut lip, which is bleeding, and the skin over his cheekbone is reddened. Matthew is pushing and prodding him, trying to goad him to fight, but Leon just keeps stepping back out of reach as Matthew pursues him.

'Not man enough now are you? You thought you were a hero stealing her away from me, but look at you! You're nothing but an old man. How long do you think it will be before she loses interest in you and goes off with a sexy young Spaniard? She's nothing but a whore.'

The slandering of Shelly causes the real Leon to attempt a retaliatory blow but the punch misses, catching the side of Matthew's head. Matthew laughs before launching forward and toppling his opponent to the ground. He drops on top of Leon, pinning him down, continuing to taunt with slurs against Shelly. He raises his left fist, kneels up to put more weight behind the blow, and I realise I have to stop him.

I grab the nearest thing to hand – a garden statue of Venus – and swing it with all my might at Matthew's left shoulder. And time seems to go into slow motion – the statue breaks as Matthew is knocked to one side. He bangs his head hard on the side of the house, then topples backwards to fall, dazed, at my feet. Blood runs from a gash in his head where he collided with the wall and his eyes flicker as he looks up. Registering it's me who hit him, the bottom half of the statue still in my hands, a twisted smile forms on his lips.

'*Et tu, Brute?*' he says.

Leon is soon on his feet but the fight seems to have gone out of Matthew. He doesn't resist as we use a length of garden twine to tie his wrists together in case he tries to launch another assault. Leon then secures him to the ornate metal gate to wait for the police.

Leon checks I'm okay then heads into the villa to reassure Shelly that it is safe and he's not hurt. I ask him to bring me a bowl of warm water and a cloth, so I can clean up the gash on Matthew's head and check he doesn't need stitches. He looks vulnerable lying there and, now my anger has dissipated, I feel strangely calm.

'I'm sorry,' I say as I wipe the blood from his face. 'I didn't mean to hurt you like this but I had to stop you.'

He snorts a laugh. 'Your concern for my wellbeing is very touching. Your problem is you care too much.'

I stop what I'm doing and sit back on my haunches to look at him. 'You might be right. I cared a lot for you. And now I discover it was all built on lies.'

'Ah, not all of it. Primarily the name I gave you … and

the job ... and a few other inconsequential details.' Unable to use his hands, he lifts his shoulder, turning his chin to wipe off some sweat trickling down his face.

'They're not inconsequential when you think you're building a future with someone. Did you feel anything for me, or was this always about Michelle?'

He tips his head on one side and searches my face. 'You want honesty? You started out no more than a pawn in my quest for information, but I've actually become strangely attached to you. I find you a curiosity – your concern for others and all your doubts and worries.'

'I may have lots of doubts and I'm certainly not as educated as you, but I think I understand you – probably more than anyone ever has.'

'Hmm, maybe so. But, even now, I'm sure you think you could've *fixed* me if only you'd tried hard enough. But that way madness lies, my Ophelia. So damned exhausting.'

As the security guards appear in the courtyard, he smiles at me. 'What an adventure we're having. This will give you something to tell the Wellies!'

And that is the last I see of him.

Leon declines the offer to go to the hospital for a check-up, wanting to stay with Shelly. When Matthew has been taken away by the security guards to wait for the police, I explain to Leon who I am, how I know Shelly. He invites me into the villa, but while I'm keen to know the full story, I'm nervous of intruding, of causing yet more upset.

'No, no. It's fine. Shelly wants to talk to you.' He is quietly spoken, a calming air about him. 'There is no blame for any of this. But we would like to know what's going on – how you came to turn up here with Matthew.'

Matthew, not Leon. I can't get used to calling him that.

The real Leon leads me into the lounge where Shelly sits with Seb asleep on her lap. She is singing to him softly, fingertips stroking his forehead and his white-blond curls. Leon offers to fetch us all a drink and as he passes Shelly, he gently touches her head and she reaches up to hold his hand. The gesture so intimate, carrying so much love, I have to look away.

I nearly destroyed all this.

'I'm so sorry,' I mumble.

Shelly shakes her head, 'No. It's not your fault. He was bound to find us at some stage. It's weird ... but, in some ways, it's almost a relief. I guess you can understand that, as a therapist? We don't need to keep looking over our shoulders any more.'

Leon places the cold drinks on the table.

'Tell us how you met him,' he says.

I explain how he first came for therapy. How he pretended to be Leon, told me he had lost his lover Michelle in a car crash. I explain how he used me to try to get information about Michelle.

'I truly believed you had died in an accident, because that's what Leon – Matthew – had told me. So when I got your letter and the photo this week, it made no sense. But he was so convincing that the only possible explanation was that you had faked your own death. But I didn't know why you would be in hiding.'

I tell them of Matthew's rage last night when I wouldn't disclose where she was. 'I needed to get hold of you, to warn you. But I didn't have any means of contacting you. I only knew you were here at La Isla. Matthew must've bugged my house or my laptop and seen what I was planning. He followed me here.'

They ask lots of questions as they piece it together. And I

confess that I fell in love with him, only recently beginning to question the extremes of his behaviour.

Shelly rubs her forehead. 'I know his pattern. Let me guess. He love-bombed you with gifts and exciting trips. Seemed to idolise you, gave you hundreds of compliments. And then things started to change? He became more possessive … more obsessive?'

'Yes, that's it. Is that how he was with you?'

'Yes. It started off well – it was flattering to be adored. I thought he loved me …'

As Shelly describes her relationship with Matthew, her story feels so familiar. Soon the compliments became double-edged: 'You look lovely in that *but*…'; 'It was a lovely evening *but you spoilt it* when …'

Leon takes up the story: 'He treated Shelly like a dress-up doll, telling her what to wear, how to do her hair. How to behave. What to say and when. She lost all confidence. All sense of who she was.'

'Then he proposed …' Shelly says. 'He gave me an antique emerald necklace. He told me it was his grandmother's … He banged on about how thrilled she'd have been to have see how happy I made him.' She sighs deeply. 'I felt there was no way out. I hoped he might change once we were married. You know, if I made him feel more secure and less worried about losing me?'

'We all make that mistake, believe we can change others. People can change, but they have to want to.'

After the marriage Matthew bought a house for the two of them, far away from her family. Always wanting to know where she was going, who she was with. He was so suspicious of any friends she made that she stopped going out.

'Eventually it got too much. I was in the house all day with nothing to do and no one to see. I was so miserable.

I was on antidepressants and just didn't care any more. We argued and I told him I was leaving and wanted a divorce. That was when he said he'd pay for me to go back to college, to give me something to do.'

And that was where she met Leon, one of her tutors on the photography diploma.

'Why didn't you tell me about your husband's behaviour when you came for therapy?'

'I didn't know if I could trust you. Matthew was paying for it – I'd never had therapy before and I didn't know if he could ask you for a report or something.'

She thought I might break confidences. 'If I'd understood the whole situation – everything you were going through – I could've helped you think through what you wanted to do. Think about options and how to make a decision.'

'You did help me. I just couldn't discuss it with you openly. I couldn't risk the fact that you might divulge something to Matthew. He's very clever at getting round people.'

I bracket the feelings of guilt, how he manipulated me, the memories of my lack of professionalism. These thoughts aren't helpful now.

She explains that Matthew started getting more suspicious when she was on the photography course. He followed her one day and saw her with Leon, tracked them to the college and confronted Leon in reception. 'After that I had to give up the course. And he insisted on driving me everywhere or getting one of his employees to do it.'

It's only then it strikes me: I know very little about the real Matthew. Of course, he wasn't a photographer! 'What's Matthew's profession? He runs his own company, doesn't he?'

'Yes, MMC. Importing and exporting antiques. It's very profitable. He was planning to sell the company, "so we could spend more time together"… He went away to Germany for a week for some negotiations ... But, before he left, he had someone install cameras and monitors in the house to keep track of my movements. That was the final straw. I left everything behind – including the jewellery he bought me and that damn necklace that guilt-tripped me into marrying him.'

Leon chips in, 'We'd already planned to escape to Spain – it just brought things forward by a month or two. We travelled around looking for somewhere very public and very anonymous. And here we are – La Isla!'

'What will happen to him?'

'He'll probably get a sentence for assault. The three of us will be asked to give statements but it's clear it was self-defence and our security camera will have video footage that backs us up.'

'Do you think he'll bother the two of you again?'

'I honestly don't know,' Leon says. 'But I'll contact our solicitor to get a restraining order in place.'

'He's made his point,' Shelly says. 'He'll probably move on to his next obsession.'

'But we won't hang around to find out. We were thinking of moving somewhere less touristy, weren't we, darling? Somewhere Seb can grow up knowing the real Spain.'

Chapter Twenty-Three

Back at home in England, I can't face seeing anyone.

Jen and Nisha deserve to know what's happened so I send a brief email, trying to make the experience sound less stressful than it was; heading off the inevitable visit offering support through the medium of chocolate and alcohol. My cover story for the Wellies is a boiled-down version of the truth: a bad break-up after a trip abroad. Jen and Nisha will know to keep them at bay until I'm ready to put my face on and join the world again.

Everything in my life has been changed by these past months, just not in the way I anticipated.

My therapy work is over. Even if I wanted to, I couldn't go back to it, not after all this. During my training with Clare, she once told the story of the monkey trap, a way that poachers catch monkeys unharmed. A simple contraption, it consists of tempting fruit hidden in a container with a hole just big enough for the animal to insert its paw. Having grasped the bait the monkey can no longer get its hand out, but it refuses to let go, even at the risk of being caught. It is trapped by its own desires.

That's me, unable to let go of my desire to save people. Believing I can make them whole, make them happy – if I just try hard enough. That has always been my trap.

So, I've learnt that much.

★

After mulling things over, I decide there are two key conversations I need to have.

I've been putting it off but I need to see Clare. She's first on my list.

I write a long letter explaining events in Spain, apologising for all my deceit, owning up but not making excuses. I tell her everything I've learnt over the past months. That I can see why I was so enamoured by Matthew. He is so different to anyone I've ever known – while his dark moods were so low, his passionate moments were so high, so intense, I got carried along, giddy with the excitement of it all. I can see it now for what it is: *intermittent reinforcement*, the unpredictable random rewards of being with him. And they were so addictive.

I tell her what I've learnt about myself, my monkey trap, and how I want to change.

She will understand – that's her training – but she may not be willing to forgive. My heart is in my mouth as I post the letter, hoping I can rebuild her trust in me but knowing our friendship may not survive the depth of my lies.

She replies several days later, sharing a personal story about one of her own deceits. Clare had never told her mother she was gay; she even dated a male friend of the family to help keep her cover. Both her parents had died before she came out. 'Many decisions that we live to regret were once a solution to a problem,' she writes.

She agrees to see me.

We meet in the local forest.

After a hug hallo, we walk in silence for several minutes. Yesterday's rain has left its traces on the grasses and our trousers are dampened as we pass through the undergrowth, drops landing on our hair as we duck under low-hanging branches. The slight breeze joins forces with the sun to make the shadows of the leaves dance on the forest floor. I breathe deeply, taking this calm into my body, feeling the sense of wellbeing spread.

We will come through this. I can make it right.

We reach a wider track and as we fall into step with each other, she asks, 'Do you want to talk about what's happened?'

'Yes, I'd rather talk to you than anyone, if you can bear to listen.'

'What are friends for?' She shrugs. 'But no more apologies, no berating yourself.'

I hold back an overly ambitious bramble blocking the path, so Clare can pass through.

'I thought it was love …' I say. 'But that's not the right word. It was more like an overpowering hormonal teenage crush.'

'An obsession?'

'Yes. It became an obsession. And he knew what he was doing – exactly how to make me fall in love with him … He's so different from anyone I've ever known.'

'And how do you feel now?

'A bit lost really. Like I've been through a nasty break-up and I'm going cold turkey … I miss him. Or at least, I miss the good version of him. And the excitement of it all.'

'It will be tough. He promised you a different way of life, away from familiar routine. But you know that underneath that polished surface he was a dangerous man. He used his charm to manipulate you from the start. He is an ill man.'

'I know, I know.'

'I can hear the "but",' she says.

I push my hands deep in the pockets of my jacket, feeling for the tiepin he gave me to hold my dress together. I've taken to carrying it with me, I don't know why. 'But what should I do now? How do I get over him?'

We come to a clearing in the forest, a well-trampled pathway leading round a large expanse of water. The mallards swim towards us hoping for food.

'What would you advise an obsessional client?' Clare sits down on a huge log, a fallen branch from the oak above. I sit next to her, the surface rough through my jeans.

I know exactly what I would say. 'Separate out the ideal version of the person you're carrying in your head and look at how they are in reality. Look at the facts. Think about the real person warts and all.'

'And in Matthew's case you have to admit the real person has a number of sociopathic characteristics.' She snorts a rueful laugh. 'Hiding his real self by pretending to be someone else. Charismatic manipulation and control of others.'

I continue the list: 'A sense of superiority. Compulsive lying. Risk-taking behaviour.' I've researched it since I got back, trying to make sense of Matthew's behaviour. 'He pretty much has the whole hand.'

'Learn from the experience, but don't fixate on the "what ifs", or taunt yourself that you could have changed him if you'd only tried harder or had more time.'

It's like she can read my mind. I scuff the dirt with the toe of my boot. I'm so lucky to have her in my life.

'Print out that description of antisocial personality disorder and pin it on your fridge to remind you. You were not to blame.' She takes off her glasses and wipes them on a tissue. 'What do you think you might do over the coming months now you've stopped therapy work?'

'Firstly, I'm going to phone Dereck, make that therapy appointment like you suggested. Get some help making sense of … everything … Matthew, Mum leaving, losing Dad.' I sit up straight, look up to the sky, the blue on the horizon. 'I've been toying with the idea of tracking her down, my mother. I'd been thinking about it since Dad died … And then all the events in Spain, realising Michelle had a good reason for the affair … It made me realise I've only ever heard Dad's version … Maybe Mum wasn't entirely to blame.'

'It's possible.'

'I'm not sure what to think. I wish we'd talked about it, me and Dad.'

The clouds are parting and a beam of sunlight falls across the pond. A female mallard dips her head under water, diving for food beneath the surface.

'I've made my decision though. I want to learn more about my mum. I've arranged to meet up with their old friends, Brenda and Fred, to see if there's anything they can tell me. I might even try to find her if I can, if she's still alive.' The mallard's still down there, searching, small ripples spreading round her. 'Maybe I can get some answers, find out "why?"'

'There may not be a simple answer.'

'I'm learning that there never is.'

'Jen told me what happened. I was worried about you,' Davy says, when I phone him. My second mission. 'You never come down the Lion no more.'

'I will, but I just needed some time to think. I'm sorry, I should've called you before today.'

'So it's finished then, with that bloke? Are you upset?'

'No. It's fine. I'm happy to spend some time on my own.' For the first time in my adult life there is no man to turn to for company or cuddles. 'How's Angie?'

'Yeah. She's good. You'll like her when you get to know her better.'

That's how we end up sharing a ploughman's and some beers in my garden on a sunny afternoon; the three of us and Churchill, the dog. And Davy is right. The more time I spend with Angie, the more I like her. I don't even mind that she calls him Dave and me Chrissy. Like Davy, she has no pretence or agenda. 'One size fits Paul,' as she would probably say.

I start to clear the plates. 'Are you ready for dessert? I made summer pudding.' One of Davy's favourites.

'I'm off pud. Trying to lose some weight,' Davy says. 'Before the big day.'

Their wedding. It turns out the story about Churchill and the ring was a joke. They've planned a quiet registry office event with a handful of close friends. Apparently they fought over me − chief bridesmaid for Angie or best girl for Davy. I tell them I'm honoured and happy to combine the roles, but I'm not dressing up in any kind of fancy frock. We agree on a cocktail jacket and trousers.

'But not black!' Angie says.

Churchill wanders off to sniff around in the bushes, rejects the lavender bush and cocks his leg to pee up the side of my old therapy room, which makes me laugh.

'If you ain't doing therapy no more, what you going to do with that shed?' Davy asks.

I'm about to correct him with 'summerhouse' but he's right. It's a shed. 'I thought I'd knock it down, put up a greenhouse. Grow some veg.'

'You should keep the wood,' Angie says, collecting the empty bottles. 'You might want to build something.'

'Want some help getting rid of it?' Davy wanders over

to the shed, gives it a shove. 'It's leaning on that tree. A few blows with a sledgehammer and that'd be down, I reckon.'

That would be quite cathartic.

'Have you got one? When can I borrow it?'

'Let's do it now. This afternoon.' Angie claps her hands, excited. 'The three of us. It'd be fun.'

A 'coo-ee' from next door's garden distracts us from our planning. Susan, my neighbour, has to raise her voice to be heard above Churchill's low growl, defending us and his territory even though he's only been here a few hours.

'That new postman's done it again. Your post was mixed in with mine.' Susan waves the letters at me.

'Thanks.' I reach over the fence to take them.

'A couple of bills by the looks of it. And there's a postcard. You don't see them often these days.'

It's on the top of the pile.

La Isla Golf Resort.

An image of the golfing green, the sea in the distance, blue skies overhead.

Not a cloud to be seen.

My pulse quickening, I turn it over to read the message.

It's the quote from my therapy card: *'There is nothing either good or bad but thinking makes it so.'*

It is signed *'M'*.

The writing is even tinier than I remember, so straight it's as if he's ruled pencil lines and then erased them. My heart beats fast as I read the PS written just above the photographer's credit at the bottom of the card. So neat it could have been printed.

'Your move,' it says.

Acknowledgements

Just as the African proverb says 'it takes a village to raise a child', so it takes an amazing team to grow a novel from an initial idea. I'd like to thank a whole herd of Unicorns for their constant support, constructive challenges, shared wisdom, and for being there through all the ups and downs (not to mention all the cake, champagne and chips) – Shivanthi Sathanandan, Diane Wilson, Anna Davidson, Elizabeth Price, Stella Barnes, Tamara Henriques, David Grievson, David Haywood and Lucy Watkins.

Huge gratitude also to the following people:
- Blue Pencil's Emma Haynes and Fiona Barton for kick-starting my journey.
- The team at Madeleine Milburn Literary, TV and Film Agency, especially Maddy Milburn, Liv Maidment, Georgia McVeigh and Rachel Yeo for their support, insight and ideas.
- Rhea Kurien, my editor at Orion, for her enthusiasm in championing the book and for her inspiring editorial advice.
- Clare C and John E for being the inspiration behind Clare's calm wisdom.
- My friends Ken Hummerstone and Carolyn Simon for their unwavering backing and encouragement.
- And, of course, my partner Martin for helping me to focus on the things that matter.